THE KING
AND
THE CORPSE

By the same author
★

The Voice of the Corpse
The Right Honourable Corpse
The Doctor and the Corpse
The Sunshine Corpse
Wait for a Corpse
Royal Bed for a Corpse
Good Luck to the Corpse

THE KING
AND
THE CORPSE

Max Murray

GALILEO PUBLISHERS, CAMBRIDGE

Galileo Publishers
16 Woodlands Road, Great Shelford,
Cambridge
CB22 5LW UK

www.galileopublishing.co.uk

Distributed in the USA by SCB Distributors
15608 S. New Century Drive
Gardena, CA 90248-2129, USA

Australia: Peribo Pty Limited
58 Beaumont Road
Mount Kuring-Gai NSW 2080
Australia

ISBN 978-1-915530158

First published in 1949
This edition © 2023 The Estate of Max Murray

Series Editor: Richard Reynolds

All rights reserved.

This book is sold subject to the
condition that it shall not, by way of trade or otherwise, be lent,
resold, hired out or otherwise circulated in any form of binding or
cover other than that in which it is published and without a similar
condition including this condition being imposed
on the subsequent purchaser.

Printed in the EU

CONTENTS

Chapter 1 1
Chapter 2 15
Chapter 3 24
Chapter 4 31
Chapter 5 44
Chapter 6 64
Chapter 7 77
Chapter 8 87
Chapter 9 105
Chapter 10 122
Chapter 11 140
Chapter 12 151
Chapter 13 165
Chapter 14 173
Chapter 15 184
Chapter 16 194
Chapter 17 201
Chapter 18 208
Chapter 19 215
Chapter 20 220

CHAPTER 1

LEONARDO MANETTI, lying in the warm sun on the beach at Beaumont-sur-Mer, looked no less dead than the dozens of others, equally prostrate on the sand. But Leonardo not only looked dead; he was dead.

No one noticed. Polite children walked round him, nimble ones jumped over him. The evening sun began to slant over the sea. The cocktail hour band began to play on the terrace of the Casino. One by one the almost naked sun-drunk idlers climbed to their feet and staggered off to dress. Leonardo stayed behind. The attendants let down the umbrellas and put away the deck chairs, counted their money and went off home.

When the King's speed boat put Anthony Tolworth ashore at the bathing jetty it was nearly seven o'clock. He walked idly along the beach and paused to look down at the gross figure of Leonardo and he thought in words: 'Dear me, how very untidy.' Then he noticed that a fly had alighted on the flabby expanse of brown back. The fly walked round in an exploratory circle. It ran up the neck to the ear, hesitated, and then scuttled inside the drum. It was a little incident that set Anthony's teeth on edge. He looked more closely at the body. There was no rhythm to denote the intake and outlet of breath. Leonardo was completely inanimate . . . dead.

'Dear me, even more untidy than I thought.'

He turned away and strolled on up the beach thinking of Leonardo Manetti, blatantly unsavoury to the last.

The manager came forward to meet him as he climbed to the terrace.

'Mr. Tolworth . . . how charming . . . how delightful to see you. And His Majesty, is His Majesty enjoying his stay?'

Anthony answered vaguely. 'I expect so. It seems a safe enough place, the weather's fine, what more can a King want? Some of the poor chaps have to live in England.'

'Ah, England. How I sometimes long to be back there, the people, the . . .' he finished peevishly, 'Ministry of Labour won't give me a permit.'

Anthony smiled. 'Too bad. I imagine they look on you as a luxury. They're probably right. May I have a dry Martini, please?'

The little manager went off as fussily as if Anthony had ordered dressed duck. He supervised the making of the dry Martini and brought it back himself, a most flattering attention. But not only that, he held himself in a professional flutter till he was satisfied that his honoured guest approved of the drink. Anthony knew quite well that all this was one of the rewards of working for a King. He did not, however, care very much what caused it. It was the effect that mattered, and this was a good dry Martini.

The manager was following a line of thought inspired by his guest. 'His Majesty,' he added, 'we hardly dare hope that he will condescend to visit these humble premises, but if he should . . .' He paused.

'Yes?'

'Our gratitude to you personally would be enormous.'

'How enormous?'

'Of course, sir, we should ask you to be our guest as often as you cared to honour us.'

Anthony finished his drink and stood up. 'If His Majesty drops in casually and strolls curiously but unenthusiastically through your establishment the token of your gratitude to me will be one hundred pounds sterling. If, on the other hand, we notify you in advance, come to dinner and spend the evening and thoroughly enjoy ourselves, I shall expect five hundred pounds.'

The little man held up his hand in horrified protest, but Anthony could see that behind the hard little eyes there was some calculating going on.

'Mr. Tolworth, this has been our worst season for years. We are small . . . struggling.'

'All the more reason for having a King to rescue you. One royal visit and you'd be made.'

'But, Mr. Tolworth, we can't afford . . .'

'My dear chap, you know and I know what these things are worth.'

The little man looked desperate. 'But so much money. I would have to get the authority from my directors.'

Anthony shrugged. 'I'll be in the Casino for half an hour.' He was about to stroll away, but turned back again. 'Oh yes, and before we visit you I think it might be an idea to tidy up a bit.'

'Tidy up? But, Mr. Tolworth, before the season began we redecorated everything, fresh paint, fresh linen, fresh flowers to bloom on the terrace, everything.'

'What a pity you've spoiled it all by leaving a body on the beach.'

'A body?'

'A dead body, most unsightly. Right on your doorstep.'

'A dead body . . . a dead body.' The little man turned pale. 'But who could be dead on our beach, to leave himself there dead. Who could be so cruel?'

'Don't ask me, it's your body,' Anthony said. 'If I had any advice to give you it would be to get the body away while it's nice and quiet and dark.'

The manager at once became coldly efficient. 'I'll attend to it, sir.' He dropped his voice. 'Do you by any chance know whose body it is?'

Anthony said gently: 'I think in the interests of everyone concerned it would be better if you made this discovery yourself. The King might not be pleased if one of his household got his name mentioned in this business. It might turn your nasty corpse into a sensation.' He nodded toward the beach. 'If you stroll to the wall and look down you can see enough to make you wonder who could be lying out on the beach at this time in the evening. Take someone discreet and go down and investigate.'

He turned and strolled from the terrace into the Casino.

Anthony Tolworth was a natural gambler, but he was not the sort who can sit down and doggedly lose his money to enrich a municipality in France. If he played it was because he was bored, and in that case he generally remained bored. But tonight he had said he would stay half an hour. He paid five thousand francs for five rectangular chips.

'One,' he said to himself, 'for a dark deed.' He tossed a chip on the black diamond. Black came up. He gathered up his winnings and stake and put both on red. 'Now two for red blood.' Red won. Half smiling at himself he strolled over to the bar and had a drink.

With his drink at his elbow he leaned against the bar and looked down over the tables. They were fairly crowded, but only a few of the crowd were really gambling, most were playing the minimum stake of twenty francs. Most of them were obviously people taking their annual holiday, a week or two in the sun. Those at the end of the holiday were brown, those at the beginning were flaming red, and those half-way through had an oddly scaly look about them. Flakes of skin were coming off these, but they had got over the worst. They were dressed in every conceivable kind of costume, long, brief, colourful, drab, tailored, home-made. The smart idle crowd that could still afford to drift about in a kind of disdainful half world of their own were definitely not patronizing this place. Anthony did see several of them whom he recognized, but they managed to give the impression that they were slumming. Anthony's experienced eye told him that all the new paint and new linen and the flowers on the terrace had failed so far to make the season a success. It made him wonder all the more what had brought Leonardo Manetti to the place. Apart from the fact that he had come there to die, Leonardo must have had a special reason for being there, because he did nothing without one.

Most, but not all of Leonardo's special reasons had to do with money. When he gambled he liked to gamble with people who had a lot of money to lose, and not people taking a few weeks away from work.

'Can I say hello, or do you want to be alone?' He looked up with a start and saw Eve Raymond perched on the stool next to him.

'Oh hello,' he said. 'Did you get home safely?'

'Safely from where?'

'Eden Roc.'

'Darling, I could kick a pebble from Eden Roc to where I live.'

'I know, but last time I saw you was at Eden Roc. I like to know if people get home.'

'That was twelve months ago.'

'I know.'

'Well, thanks, I got home safely.'

'Oh, good. I had to leave you finishing a drink. Have another, won't you?'

'Do you think I should on top of the other?'

'Do, two can't possibly hurt you.'

'What about the one we had in forty-four?'

'Oh, the hell with it, why can't we be gay if we want to be?' Eve had that sophisticated, well-groomed look that some women wear as a habit and others die in the search of. She was twenty-five years old, five feet five inches tall, and beautifully made. Her skin was golden. Her hair was bronze. Her rather full lips rested very lightly together and her dark grey eyes had quiet depths in them.

Anthony produced the drinks, smiled at her vaguely and said, 'I love you more and more.'

'I know. I can recognize it in your trembling tones. We must be seeing too much of each other. . ... Luck.' She took an abrupt drink and set the glass aside.

'To continue the conversation of last year, you hate this place.'

'I shouldn't, I suppose, but I do.'

'But you've had twelve months in which to make a get-away.'

'It's father. He's writing a book on the psychology of the gambler, and feels that he must remain close to his material.'

'But he was writing a book on the psychology of the gambler last year and the year before that.'

'I know. He adds about a hundred thousand words a year to it.'

'It must be going to be quite a book.'

'Yes, the trouble is that the psychology of the gambler changes with the times, so he has to keep on rewriting the book.'

'Wouldn't it be an idea to write a book on the psychology of the gambler of 1947?'

'I suggested that, but he seems to think that it is the current gamblers who matter, and he is in a perpetual state of nerves trying to keep up with them.'

'It sounds an awkward sort of book to handle.'

'It is. It's like trying to catch up with the future.'

'Not profitable either.'

'No, we more or less live on my wits.'

Anthony said quickly, 'Sorry, I thought you had money.'

'Had is the word. Money, as you should know, has been doing a disappearing act in recent years.'

He nodded. 'It doesn't stay put like it did. How do you make ends meet, as granny used to say?'

'I don't, but I keep them within hailing distance as it were.'

'And the method?'

'Oh, a few of the less responsible newspapers look to me for some of their more frothy material. And also I act as a part-time secretary hostess to a man.'

'That sounds very squalid.'

'It is. He is a very squalid man. He's one of the gamblers who win. I found that part of my job was to introduce him to his victims. He doesn't know it, but I've quit. But as a last act, dear, I'm going to introduce him to you.'

'And why should you do this cruel thing to me?'

'Because, Anthony darling, you are a better gambler than he is.'

'Dear me. Perhaps I should go into training with your father's book, What is this squalid fellow's name?'

'Leonardo Manetti. He would be better dead.'

She saw the expression on his face change. All at once it was as still as a mask.

'Why, what's the matter? Have I said anything silly?'

He glanced slowly round the bar and then leaned casually towards her. 'Not silly, darling, out of date. Leonardo Manetti is dead.'

Her eyes dilated and with a violent motion she pressed her clenched hands to her lips. It seemed for a moment that she would fall from the chair.

Anthony laughed loudly. 'Marvellous, darling, marvellous, that's exactly how she did it in "The Trembling Veil".'

The barman who had been looking startled and inquisitive now smiled. Anthony diverted his attention further by ordering more drinks. Eve, he was glad to see, was pulling herself together. She even managed to laugh.

'Overacting,' she said. 'Purest ham.' Still trembling a little, she looked at him gratefully and slipped her hand over his.

'Come and sit at a table,' he said. 'Whenever I sit up on a bar stool like this I have a feeling that someone is going to shoot me in the back.'

She moved away. 'Maybe someone will one day.'

She had herself under control now and walked beside him steadily to a table in the corner. Then as if to indicate that the exhibition was over she opened her bag and inspected her face in the mirror. The waiter brought the drinks and went unsuspectingly away, convinced that what he had witnessed was not a scene, but a piece of nonsense.

'That was a disgusting performance, Anthony. You're a quick thinker.'

He sat a while without answering, and presently she asked him with a note of challenge in her voice:

'Well, darling, what's on your mind?'

'I was thinking of that performance of yours.'

'I admitted it stank, didn't I?'

'Yes, you did, and it did, but why the violence?'

'I was shocked. After all, he was my employer.'

'All employers die.'

'I imagine that I hadn't expected it of Leo.'

'Why not?'

'I don't know. I suppose I couldn't grasp that his capacity for evil-doing was so nearly expended . . . otherwise . . .' She stopped speaking and abruptly finished her drink.

'Otherwise,' he reminded her.

But she replied with a question, 'What did he die of?'

'I think one of his victims must have bitten the hand that fleeced him.' He said this quite conversationally, but he heard her quick intake of breath.

'You . . . mean he was killed . . . murdered?'

'There is blood on the sand . . . nothing to notice because Leonardo has been covering it discreetly with his flesh. But being of a curious nature, I lifted him up and peered underneath.'

'Where . . . where was he, Anthony?' He had an odd impression that although she asked, she knew what he was going to say.

'A stone's throw from where we sit, as they say in the guide books. That is to say he was ten minutes ago: I sent the servants to collect him.'

'But why wasn't he found before . . .' she quickly amended that. 'When did it happen?'

'God knows, darling. No one takes any notice of a body in bathing trunks, lying on a beach. He could have been there since yesterday . . . or say as long as he'd keep fresh.'

'But how . . . how could he be murdered on the beach?'

He shook his head. 'I merely said that he was dead on the beach, not that he was murdered there.'

There was a pause, and then Eve said: 'Anthony, do you know what it's like to be frightened . . . in a panic, I mean?'

'Yes, more or less. Why?'

She laughed unevenly. 'It's a phrase that more or less sums up me.'

'That's a pity. It's more a pity because I suspect you don't get in a panic without a reason.'

She shook her head. 'I've been waiting for something to happen, and it just has, that's all. I feel empty in the stomach. Perhaps I'm just not used to murders. Do you think I might have a drink?'

He signalled to the waiter. 'Don't talk if you don't want to,' he said.

'I don't want to, but it's just that some words of mine that I spoke with conviction keep coming back to me: "How delightful it would be, Mr. Manetti, to see you dead." That's what I said, loudly and publicly.'

'I see; a little ill-timed.' He looked at her and added: 'And have you availed yourself of the opportunity of seeing Mr. Manetti dead?'

Instead of answering she asked: 'How does my behaviour strike you? Does it seem a little odd?'

'Possibly. It would easily be the natural outcome of the shock. I don't believe you murdered Mr. Manetti.'

'Why don't you?'

He smiled at her in the engaging simple way he had.

'I can't bear to have my illusions shattered. In your case I definitely refuse. You shall go to the gallows with me declaring your innocence.'

'I may need all the faith and help I can get.'

'Dear me, an almost holy zeal is possessing me. I might even write out a confession and light out for foreign parts.'

'Yes, you might. The trouble is that you didn't ever know the man.'

He looked at her reproachfully. 'Eve, I am a respected if somewhat lowly member of what was once known as the International Set. As such I know all the Manettis in the world. I knew Leonardo Manetti. I know where he was born and where he got his money and what he did with it. If I do not know who Leonardo's father was, that is not my fault; neither did Leonardo.'

'But you had no motive for murdering him.'

'Eve dear,' he said gently, 'if ever I decide to confess to the murder of Leonardo Manetti, I assure you the world will feel that it has every reason for believing me.'

'But you didn't murder him.'

He raised his eyebrows. 'What makes you so certain? One would think you had some special knowledge.'

'You just don't look like a murderer.'

'If we all looked our real selves the world would be uninhabitable. Anyway, darling, I've made a lifelong practice of never looking anything but inane; not because I think the pose is a particularly good one, but it's the only one I feel capable of sustaining.'

She smiled for the first time since they had come to the table. 'How nice of you to confide in me. I thought it was all so natural.'

'Second nature only, my sweet. I can be quite ruthless.' He looked at her and amused crinkles puckered under his eyes. 'My appearance is really quite deceptive; just as your own brassy exterior hides a simple girlish heart.'

'Nuts.' She was serious again at once. 'Tony, there's going to be a fearful stink about this, isn't there?'

'Yes, if all Leonardo's past is to be made public there will be a monstrous stink. But one never knows with a man like Leonardo. Some great man may raise a warning finger and let it be known that he is a state secret. When you start investigations into the past of Mr. Manetti you can't be sure where they will end. The tentacles go low, but also high.'

'In that case I suppose they would welcome a nice ordinary little motive for his murder?'

'Such as?'

She shivered a little. 'Such as passion.'

He asked the question mildly, without looking at her: 'You didn't love him, did you?'

'I hated him.'

'Quite. But I shouldn't make public statements to that effect.'

'Why not; it's true.'

'Eve, I can see a French defending counsel with a bald head and a black beard. Tears are pouring down his cheeks as he appeals for the life of an innocent girl who fell into the clutches of a monster. He'll point to you dramatically in the dock, and all the time he'll be thinking to himself that the monster was a good picker. Everyone but you will be having the time of their lives, and of course you'll get off. But all the same I find the prospect distasteful, so don't please be so emphatic about your hatred of the late Mr. Manetti. If they question you try to keep your mind on good works and your first visit to the Louvre.'

'I've never been to the Louvre.'

'All right, think pensively of your neglected but happy childhood.'

'Do you think they'll question me, Tony?'

'I should say it depends on how discreet you've been.'

'I'm not awfully good at being discreet, I'm afraid.'

'Never mind; try to start now.'

She said bitterly: 'Why couldn't I have stuck to my snippets for my snippety little newspapers?'

'Speaking of what you regard now as your true rôle in life, I may be able to offer you a crumb or two.'

'Of course, that's what I came to see you about, wasn't it . . . that seems hours ago. No,' she added quickly, 'don't be disturbed, Anthony, I have now banished that other life from my thoughts.' Her voice was hard and bright.

'I'm planning a little evening out for the King. I thought you might come along.'

'Do you really think he could bear it?'

'Oh yes, he's been cooped up on the yacht waiting for a bidder for his patronage.'

She laughed. 'How interesting. Who won him?'

'Oh, they'll all have their turn. This place, I think, will be first. Then we will make our royal progress along the coast. Let's see, today's Monday, isn't it? Would Wednesday suit you, or would you rather His Majesty made it some other day?'

'No, no, I'll cram in Wednesday, even if it does mean putting off cribbage with father. Can I tell my gasping public what is afoot?'

'Oh, dear, yes. We welcome the publicity. In fact, darling, we live on it.'

He looked across and saw Jean Baretti, the manager, hovering discreetly. 'Ah, that will be news,' he said. 'Excuse me, and I'll come hurrying back.' He got up and strolled over to the manager.

'Mr. Tolworth,' he said, 'I have discussed the matter with my directors. Mr. Tolworth, they are horrified.'

'Indeed?' Anthony said. 'But to cut a long story short they decided to pay.'

The little man looked desperate. 'Mr. Tolworth, you are an English gentleman, a man of honour, you love our France.'

'And I want five hundred pounds.'

'Very well, Mr. Tolworth, we will say no more. Now about the arrangements.'

Tony listened patiently to the little man's plans for a sort of super-gala night. It was only when they were about to part that he asked about the body.

The manager shrugged. 'Oh yes, it has been removed. I have forgotten it.'

'Have you now? What did he die of?'

'Heart failure, certainly.'

Anthony smiled. 'Brought on no doubt by violently lying in the sun. No sign of a wound, I suppose?'

'A wound? Since you mention it the body has a small square of adhesive plaster on the chest . . . a scratch on the rocks perhaps, or an insect bite.'

'Well, well . . .' Tony parted from the manager and went back to join Eve.

'The party for Wednesday night is confirmed.'

'In other words, the Casino is prepared to come across.'

'Put with great vulgarity, yes. What shall I do, pick you up and bring you along? Or would you rather have the King pick you out from all the assembled beauty and ask you to join him?'

She shook her head. 'Too risky. He might pick the wrong girl.'

'No, no; he's quite agreeable about these things. Anyway, he's had enough experience of his own judgment not to trust it.'

'I see, but I wonder what makes him so confident in yours.'

'He knows I wouldn't recommend anything I had not thoroughly investigated myself.'

'Such as me, for instance?'

'No, darling, I'm taking you to the party, not His Majesty.' She looked at him. 'You are an odd creature, Tony. I wonder what you are really like.'

He smiled. 'If I knew that I'd be able to settle a lot of things.'

He made a move. 'I'd better go, or the royal soup will be getting cold.'

She picked up her bag and said thoughtfully: 'It must be fun to live with a King.'

'I find it has its compensations . . . but you weren't thinking of me, were you?'

She hesitated and then smiled at him. 'Of course.'

'Good. I say good because it's safer. Good night, Eve.'

He walked back along the beach toward the landing-stage. The moon was up and was shining on a white empty expanse of sand. The remains of Leonardo Manetti had been taken to a more discreet resting-place.

CHAPTER 2

THE more romantic columns of many newspapers were apt to refer to the yacht *Helena Maria* as a floating palace. That being so, she was certainly the only palace currently possessed by Rudolph the Third. A real palace is one of those items that you definitely cannot take about with you, and Rudolph during recent years had been an exceedingly mobile monarch.

Anthony handed over the speedboat to the sailor on the gangway and climbed on deck. Two people were sitting in wicker chairs. The smaller one was holding a skein of wool and the larger was winding it into a ball. The larger was the Queen Mother, and the smaller the Lord Chamberlain. Queen Charlotte was a regal woman with a regal bosom and bearing, but fate had altered her expression in recent years to one of uncomprehending forbearance.

The Lord Chamberlain, Count Otto Shavia, was a mincing little man with lovely white hair, white spats, white facings to his waistcoat and a white silk riband to his monocle. He flattered himself that he was a courtier of the old school, very subtle and cunning. So cunning and subtle had he become that in any conversation beyond everyday commonplaces no one had very much idea what he was talking about. The Count did not walk about, he darted, which may have been what kept him so thin. He never forgot a name and he never neglected a lady of rank. He never paid for a meal and he was never without an invitation to dinner.

'Well, Anthony,' Queen Charlotte said. 'Have you been slumming again?'

'Yes, ma'am,' Anthony smiled. 'And what is more if you stay on deck you'll get a chill. You may not have noticed, but it's turning cold.'

'My dear boy,' she answered in her deep resonant voice, 'there is such a smell of petrol on this floating workshop that a cold would be almost a protection.'

'Bad as that, is it?'

Count Otto raised his hand and the knitting-wool in a gesture of despair. 'His Majesty is so coated in petroleum by-products as to be almost unrecognizable.'

'In that case perhaps I'd better remind him about dressing for dinner.'

'Is it as late as that?' The Queen rose and handed the half-completed ball of wool to the Lord Chamberlain, who leapt up clasping it to his bosom. 'I suppose I must steel myself to face the odours of my stateroom.'

She led the little procession indoors.

Anthony followed an alleyway that led past the staff rooms to the crew's quarters, and then went down an iron companion-way to what looked like a big well-equipped garage that seemed to run almost the full length of the ship. A lathe was humming at the far end. Somebody hammering was making the iron bulkheads echo angrily. Almost all the available space was taken up with cars. There must have been fifty of them, all big, all brand new.

It was here that King Rudolph the Third came for happiness and peace. At this moment Anthony could see his royal posterior protruding from the bonnet of a Cadillac.

Anthony came to a pause beside him and called 'Hi.'

The King brought himself reluctantly to the upright. He was a tall young man, very blond and very good-looking, and about him there was a look of amiable simplicity. Only he was not simple.

'Oh, it's you.'

Anthony looked at him with distaste. 'You know, Ticker, if ever history takes any note of you at all it will be to record that you were the dirtiest monarch in Europe. The Royal overall has not been washed since we left the United States.'

The King divested himself of this garment and left it lying on the floor. 'Which merely underlines the remarkable inefficiency of my staff. You, for instance. I don't in the least mind you addressing me vulgarly, if affectionately, as Ticker, but to sneer at me on the matter of my wardrobe is to do so with regard to something over which I have no control.' He poured some petrol over his hands and removed the first layers of grease. Then he said with an odd note of formality: 'How is my dear mother?'

'Very well. I think she finds these garage smells something of a strain.'

'Yes. I seem to remember that our prevailing ancestral smell was one of stables. Do you think it would abate the nuisance,' he added hopefully, 'if we kept a horse?'

Anthony said quickly and emphatically: 'We have no place for a horse in this establishment, Ticker, none.'

'I will speak to my mother.' He led the way up the companionway, obviously preoccupied with the notion of finding the space for a horse.

Twenty minutes later he appeared in a Savile Row dinner jacket, formal and immaculate, ready to escort his mother to the dining saloon.

Otto Shavia, at his place by the door, bowed so deeply that he was not unlike a little ostrich putting his head in the sand. That function completed, he darted to the foot of the table where it was his function to say grace. He asked a blessing for the food, the royal household, and drew God's attention to the miserable tyrants who had usurped power in their country. The meal then proceeded as it would do in any other well-ordered establishment.

'Anthony has been telling me that you are unhappy about the smell of petrol, mother,' the King said.

'Don't worry, dear, it is only really noticeable when we are at anchor and there is very little wind.'

'I suggested to him that we might get you a horse.'

'But darling, whatever for? I couldn't possibly ride it round that deck.'

Anthony grinned. 'His Majesty's idea, ma'am, is that the more familiar odour of the stables might act as a counter-irritant to that of motor cars.'

'My dear Rudolph,' the Queen said, 'there were two consolations only for me when I left Althenia. One was that I had not been hanged to a lamp-post, and the other was that I was getting away from the stables at the Winter Palace.' She added apologetically: 'I'm afraid I must have a sensitive nose.'

'Oh.' The King reluctantly gave up the notion of keeping a horse. 'I'd like to promise to give up the cars, but the business is much too good.'

'Business.' Otto held up his hands in protest. 'Your Majesty, it pains me to hear you speak so.'

Rudolph eyed him with a kind of tolerant disfavour.

'Otto, you must surely be the damnedest little snob the world has ever known.'

'If I have learned to uphold the dignity of Kings,' said Otto with gravity, 'it is a lesson learned in the service of my royal masters.' He was so pleased with this speech that he looked positively smug.

'There, Otto,' the Queen said, 'His Majesty was teasing you. He knows you would die for him.' She added dryly: 'You have often said so yourself.'

'I would kill to defend the honour of this household,' said the little man fiercely. And all at once Anthony had the astonishing feeling that he meant it. His thoughts turned to the body of Leonardo Manetti, that he had seen lying so still on the beach and that had been so discreetly removed.

But the King remained preoccupied with his motor cars. 'We've done quite well out of motor cars,' he said, and added, 'I will say this for the car manufacturers, they never refuse priority to a king. So we have generosity from manufacturers and Royal immunity from customs authorities. Mother, do you know what we averaged for the last lot we sold in Persia?'

'No dear,' the Queen said, although of course she knew quite well, having got the figures from Otto.

'Seven thousand pounds each,' said the King. 'That means an average profit of six thousand on each car... twenty cars... one hundred and twenty thousand pounds from Persia alone.' He looked at her and grinned. 'It really is worth putting up with a few nasty smells for, isn't it, Mother?'

'Of course it is, dear. It is very clever of you.'

'The bottom is dropping out of the market now, of course. This will have to be our last cargo.'

'Yes dear.'

'The idea, of course, was Tony's.'

'I know it was,' she added a little grimly, 'that is what makes me think perhaps it is not quite honest.'

Rudolph the Third laughed. 'Even Tony thinks of something honest sometimes. It is certainly more honest than smuggling stockings like Otto does.'

'Your Majesty!' Otto almost shot out of his seat.

The King grinned at him. 'Thought I didn't know, didn't you? Last time we were in England he sold a hundred and fifty pairs to the Duchess of Dreen for two pounds a pair. God knows what that old vulture got for them when she retailed them to her friends.'

'Your Majesty, if I took stockings to the Duchess, it was merely to oblige an old and valued friend.'

'Rubbish, the pair of you were heard haggling over the price like a couple of Turks.'

Otto was flabbergasted. 'But . . . but Your Majesty, how could you possibly know?'

'That was simple. I heard the story from the Duchess's grand-daughter, Phyllis, who under threat of exposure blackmailed her granny to the tune of two pairs. She said it was like getting blood out of a stone.'

'That girl,' Otto said vindictively, 'is utterly depraved.'

'Nothing of the sort, she is quite charming. And what is more, she said you pinched her bottom, you old rake.'

The outraged little man leapt to his feet and stood facing the Queen.

'Your Majesty, Your Majesty . . . you must hear me . . .'

The Queen chuckled. 'I'm quite sure you meant well, Otto. Phyllis is quite a tall girl, otherwise I am sure you would have pinched her cheek instead. We will assume that that was your intention. Officially, I have forgotten the whole thing.'

'Your Majesty,' said Otto with desperate calm, 'is most kind.'

They were about to leave the table when the King asked casually: 'You were ashore, weren't you, Tony?'

'Yes, for an hour.'

'See anyone we knew?'

Anthony hesitated and then said: 'Yes, as a matter of fact I did.'

'Oh, who was that?'

'Leonardo Manetti.'

There was a moment of complete silence. The little group seemed somehow to draw together.

'That vile man!' It was the Queen who spoke. Her voice, as she went on, seemed like a challenge to the men. 'I wonder that he has lived so long.'

'He has not,' Anthony said. 'He is dead.'

'Ah . . .' Again the first sound came from the Queen. She stood up, then turned with gentle formality to her son.

'If Your Majesty will forgive me, I am a little tired.'

Rudolph kissed her cheek. 'Yes, mother dear. Run along now and see that you really go to bed and rest.'

'I promise, dear.'

The Queen, with little Otto trotting at her heels, walked sedately from the room. The door closed behind them.

'Well, Ticker?'

The King helped himself to a cigarette.

'The "well," of course, refers to the late Leonardo Manetti.'
'Did you kill him?'
'I'm much too modest to claim the credit for such a good deed.'
'Maybe, but you haven't answered my question.'
'My dear Tony, do I have to answer all your questions? After all, if I had killed him that would be quite a personal matter, wouldn't it?'
'Yes, from the atmosphere a minute ago I should have said the feelings between the Royal House of Badenburg and Leonardo Manetti were quite definitely personal ones.'
'Oh, my dear chap, I'd not have any compunction about killing the fellow, if that's what you mean. But even deposed Kings very seldom do their own killing. There are so many of their loyal subjects ready to do it for them.'
'You're a cold-blooded devil under that amiable exterior of yours, Ticker.'
'By the way,' the King said with sudden interest, 'I never could understand why the day after I arrived at Oxford they started to call me Ticker and they continued to call me Ticker. ... Silly name, isn't it?'
'What else could you call a freshman who arrived with twelve wrist-watches and proceeded to sell them?' Tony said impatiently. 'Now to get back to the subject, Leonardo Manetti.'
'Alive Leonardo was interesting. Dead, he bores me.'
'Yes, but did you kill him?'
'Really, Tony, your conversation is repetitive to a point of imbecility. What possible interest can it be to you whether I killed the abominable creature or not? He is better dead, he is dead, and so, as the proletariat say, what?'
'Only that a very dear friend of mine may be arrested for the murder.'
'A friend of yours?' Rudolph looked quite startled. 'We can't have that, you know.'

'Why can't we?'

'We must have somebody confess,' Rudolph said it naturally.

'If you can persuade whoever did it to confess, it might be a good idea.'

'My dear chap, what does it matter whether he did it or not?'

'Oh, it doesn't matter a bit.' Tony said with a kind of desperate airiness. 'Only the poor chap might not like the idea.'

'Sometimes, Tony,' the King said, 'you are quite stupid. You have no conception whatever of the idea of loyalty. If they thought it would earn my approbation there are a thousand people who would confess to the murder of the wretched Manetti.'

'You are a barbarian.'

The King looked at him coldly. 'You are being impertinent. There is nothing barbaric about the loyalty of the subject to the monarch.'

'That I should have thought depended on the Monarch's ideas of loyalty. But I'm not so interested in who confesses to the murder as I am in who did it.'

'Does it matter?'

'Yes, the French police, for instance, might want to know.'

'And so you think possibly they will settle on your friend?' He grinned. 'What odd company you do keep when my back is turned, Anthony. Do I know this friend, by the way?'

'Not yet. You are meeting her the day after tomorrow.'

'Am I, by Jove? What is the purpose? Do I present her with the usual gold and enamel clip with the Royal Arms on it, and thank her for disposing of Manetti?'

'I think the less we say about Manetti the better.'

'But that is exactly what I said some minutes ago.'

'We are going to drop in at the Casino.'

'We are going to be bored.'

'On the contrary, we are going to drop in, and find ourselves enjoying ourselves so much that we are going to spend the evening there.'
'How much?'
'Five hundred.'
'Dollars or pounds.'
'Pounds.'
'In that case I suppose we'll have to try not to be bored.'

CHAPTER 3

EVE RAYMOND walked up the winding path through the pine trees to the pink villa on the hillside. She climbed the steps to its small terrace and stood looking out over the bay. The lights were on, tracing the foreshore as far as she could see. The lights of the traffic on the mountain roads seemed to float down like drifting stars. A smell of the pines was in the warm wind. Distantly she could hear the music of the Casino orchestra. She remembered when it had all seemed so wonderful. Now it seemed to hold her perpetually in a warm cloying embrace.

Through the lighted windows she could see her father. He was pacing back and forth, seemingly deep in thought. His hands were clasped behind his back. His lean frame was stooped slightly and the light shone on his greying hair. He gave an impression of assurance and poise.

Eve felt a lump rising in her throat. Her father looked almost everything that he was not. He really should have looked like a bewildered child. The realities of the world were too harsh for him. He preferred to search for the crock of gold at the foot of the rainbow. She knew he would never find it, of course, but then she was a realist and a genuine enough realist to know that to seek the rainbow may easily be as satisfying as a disillusioned struggle with reality. What she had still to learn was why her father had retreated.

He stopped pacing as she came into the room and his face lighted with a welcoming smile.

'Eve, you're home early. That is nice. I was resigning myself to a quiet evening with a book.'

'You were doing nothing of the sort, you humbug,' she answered. 'You were waiting till you could feel justified in nipping off to the Café de la Poste to play chess.'

'Eve, dear,' his voice sank reproachfully, 'you shouldn't say things like that even jokingly.'

'I know.' She was properly contrite. 'Anyway, why shouldn't you play chess? After all, it's a branch of your studies. Chess players gamble, don't they?'

'Well,' he was doubtful, 'they hardly come under the heading of gamblers.' He added hopefully: 'Of course, they do take chances. A good chess player naturally gambles on his opponent's weaknesses.'

'Of course he does.' She added on a note of bitterness: 'Don't we all?'

He was very sensitive to her moods and said quietly: 'You sound tired, Eve.'

'Tired? Of course not. I've been talking to Anthony Tolworth.'

'Tolworth . . . I don't seem to remember.' Then his face lighted. 'Ah yes, Anthony. That's the nice boy who brought me the Georgian snuff-box. Has he been away?'

'About a year.'

'Dear dear; well now, since you mention it, I wondered where he'd been.'

'So did I, sometimes.'

He looked at her with a kind of childlike shrewdness. 'Seeing him has not upset you, has it, Eve?'

'Good heavens, daddy, why should it do that?'

'I don't know.'

That was the truth about her father, he did not know. She could see him watching her now, knowing with a kind of unspoiled instinct that there was something wrong; so sensitive and yet so uninformed.

He added ineffectually: 'I understood that you were fond of him.'

She laughed. 'So I am.'

He escaped gratefully. 'Splendid, then there's nothing to worry about.'

'Nothing whatever. We'll have our drink, shall we?'

'Excellent idea, I'll make it.'

He proceeded to make it. It was quite a ceremony. For five minutes Antoinette in the kitchen and Eve in the lounge were at his beck and call. . . the ice, the slices of lemon, the peel of lime, the icing of the cocktail shaker, the pouring away of the surplus water, the tiny additions of this and that. He stood like a general beside the cocktail cabinet while the womenfolk did his bidding. This Eve knew was her father's finest hour. Presently the time would come when with his own hands he would bear the frosted shaker and the two glasses out on to the balcony. He would switch on the light, draw up their chairs, pour out their drinks, stretch out his legs, look at his glass and say: 'Ha, it's good to be able to relax.' And nobody had ever been so ungracious as to say: 'Relax from what?'

They followed the usual ritual and, with a final flourish, he poured out the drinks. Eve knew before she tasted it that it wouldn't be a particularly good cocktail. This would be due to her father's habit of putting in little bits of this and that as the fancy moved him. Watching him was like watching a child playing at cooking, severe, intense, and not quite knowing what it was all about. However, it was generally quite drinkable and tonight was no exception.

'Do you like it, my dear?'

'Marvellous.'

He was delighted. 'One must have the subtle touch, what?'

'Absolutely.'

'Good, now tell me what you have been doing all day.'

'Oh, the usual things. I wrote a few bits of chatter for the English editions in Paris. I went into Monte Carlo and got the usual crumbs from the reception desk at the Hotel de Paris. I was able to write brightly that Mrs. Van Thal and her two clever daughters had arrived from Paris. I tried to write beautiful daughters and felt just like George Washington, and so I crossed out beautiful and substituted clever. Well, anyway,

I have no definite evidence that they are not clever. After several other such world-shaking discoveries the management of the Paris stood me lunch and I came home.'

'Did you go to the Casino?'

'Oh yes, I got the week's numbers for you from Lady Meaker.' She opened her bag and handed him a grubby sheaf of papers. They were covered with a series of spidery numbers.

He ran a professional hand down the columns. He might have been assessing a balance sheet. 'I should have had a good week,' he announced.

'Lady Meaker didn't. She practically accused Louis, that croupier with the walrus moustache, of cheating. She told me she was down a hundred francs on the week.'

'What does she expect? She consistently ignores my advice.'

'She ignores everything. Do you know she told me that she hasn't missed a day at that Casino for twenty years? Even when the Italians were occupying it she stayed on. She averages five hours a day, endlessly writing down the numbers as they come up.'

'She has been invaluable to me, I must say.'

'She's got old without even knowing it.' Eve added impatiently: 'And yet when she's away from the place she's an absolute darling. Father, what is it that makes so many people crazy down here?'

'Crazy?' His voice was quite shocked. 'My dear Eve, whatever makes you say such a thing?'

'But they are. The things they do have no relation whatever to reality. Whatever happens outside this little world of fifty miles along the coast they simply ignore. It only rains when it rains on the Cote d'Azur.'

'They are the most interesting, charming, cultivated people in the world.' He added snobbishly: 'I refer to the English and American *residents*, of course. And I must say that I find even some of the regular visitors agreeable.'

She was silent. It was no use telling him how she felt about things. She would cause him pain, add to his confusion, but she could never make him see things as she did.

'And you, dear, did you win?'

She laughed. 'Darling, it took me exactly six months to learn that I would never win so, naturally, I don't play.'

'But my dear, if you will play these games without a system how can you expect to win?'

'I don't know. I suppose that nothing will ever convince me that two and two make five, and that's more or less what the clients are hoping for, isn't it?'

'But don't you see, my dear, it's all a matter of psychology?'

'Yes, yes, Daddy, it's all in the book.' She sighed and added apologetically: 'Tonight I don't seem to be in the mood to appreciate it.'

'I'm sorry you've had a bad day, Eve.'

'The day was all right,' she hesitated. 'It was the end that spoiled it.'

'I hope it was nothing to upset you, child?'

She laughed shortly. 'A murder isn't exactly soothing.'

He seemed startled, shocked. 'A murder? Surely, Eve, not someone we know?'

'Leonardo Manetti.'

He was silent for a long time, sitting very still. Presently he roused himself and said: 'Oh yes, of course, Leonardo Manetti. His death will be a sensation. Unfortunate for a small resort like this.'

She was looking at him strangely. 'Had you heard about this before, father?'

'No dear, why?'

'You didn't seem, well, you didn't seem surprised.'

'No, I was not surprised. I knew he would be murdered.'

'You knew?' She reached out and put her glass unsteadily on the table.

'Of course.' The light was behind him, leaving his face in shadow, but his voice was quite calm, almost reflective.

'But why do you say that?'

'Because, Eve dear, a human being can endure much, some can endure more than others. It was Manetti's gift that he could drive his fellow creatures beyond endurance.'

'Yes . . . I know. People hated him.'

'Leo Manetti's pound of flesh was not enough for him.'

'But you let me go and work for him. As a matter of fact it was you who arranged it.' She hesitated: 'Father, what was there between you and Leonardo Manetti? Sometimes it seemed, well it seemed as if he had some sort of hold over you. I know you didn't like him.'

'Like him?' He laughed softly. 'Oh, dear no, I did not like him at all.'

'Then why . . .?'

'I told him that if he touched so much as a hair on your head I would kill him. He did not take me seriously. I, on the other hand, was quite serious.'

She gasped. 'But, father, he did nothing to me . . . nothing!'

'I'm glad.'

'You haven't told me, father, what was it between you.'

He stood up and put a hand on her shining hair, softly caressing it. 'Some day I may have to tell you, darling, but perhaps now at last I may be allowed to forget it. I pray so.' He sighed. 'The past is a sleepless thing.'

She gripped his slender hand in her own firm one. 'Listen, father, you let me take care of you, don't you?'

'You're wonderful, Eve.'

'Well, why don't you let me take care of the past as well?'

But he straightened his shoulders and turned away. 'I can see that Antoinette is bringing in the soup. We'll go in, shall we?' He stood waiting for her to go in ahead of him.

They tried to talk of other things, but it was an uneasy meal. She was glad when it was over.

'Good heavens,' her father said as if the memory startled him, 'I quite forgot. I have an appointment to play chess with M. Bloc.'

She was surprised. 'But I understood you were playing with him last night. You weren't home when I got in quite late.'

'No, dear. I rang up and told him I had a headache, but as a matter of fact I felt restless.' He added with wintry humour: 'Instead I went for a walk with my past.'

She said quickly: 'Where did you go?'

He smiled at her. 'I was too engrossed in my companion to notice, dear.'

He took up his hat and stick and made his way to the door.

'I shan't be late, but don't wait up for me.'

'I won't. Have a nice game.'

'I like chess. One realizes that even a pawn should not be overlooked. It makes me feel quite important, that. Good night, Eve.'

'Have you got enough money?'

'Oh yes, fifty francs. I shall have a cognac and buy myself an American cigarette.'

He hooked his stick over his arm and as he sauntered away there was about him an air of self-assurance and success and Eve, watching him, wanted to cry.

CHAPTER 4

IF it is necessary to be discreet there is no man in the world more discreet than an official in a French provincial town. And in a tourist town discretion is everything—or almost everything. The official of Beaumont-sur-Mer conspired in discretion. No one inquired of anyone else who it was who placed the adhesive plaster over the scratch on Leonardo Manetti's chest. These heavy men who attaining middle-age still live hard, drink, keep late hours, play hard; well, naturally the heart . . . Leonardo Manetti's way of life was well known, and the doctor had no difficulty in deciding his way of death.

No doubt it all would have passed off very nicely except for a man who arrived from Paris by 'plane. He went straight to the police and presented his card, which proclaimed him to be the first secretary of the Althenian Legation. He was a fat swarthy little man in a badly-cut, double-breasted grey suit and black patent leather shoes. He had no manners. He did not exchange pleasantries. He did not offer cigarettes, although with his diplomatic privileges he must have been able to get plenty of them cheap. He did not express a wish to see Manetti's body: he demanded it. And the maddening thing about it was that there was no good excuse for refusing him. He produced proof that the dead man was an Althenian citizen and showed his own authority from the Foreign Office in Paris. There was nothing one could do but treat him with dignified calm and do what one was told.

His examination of the body was as brutal as the rest of his behaviour. He looked at the body, ripped off the adhesive tape and stared at the now not so pleasant hole in Leonardo Manetti's chest. The escorting policeman felt not unlike a small boy who has been caught in the larder and the feeling made him very angry.

The Althenian first secretary tossed the useless piece of adhesive tape back on to the body, turned round and walked out of the room, out of the building and went back by 'plane to Paris, just like that. It was a bit shattering, no matter how you looked at it.

It had all happened so quickly, none of the usual formalities, no murmured confidences, no politesse whatever. The man had come, gone and left them to put the body away.

There was no doubt whatever that this was one of those times for second thoughts and they would have to be pretty brisk ones. The doctor, for instance, would have to throw discretion to the winds and make the startling discovery that Leonardo's heart failure was due to a stab.

This he did do. That with an assistant to hold his tools for him he cut Leonardo open was evidence that he was leaving no stone unturned. At the same time he confirmed his second impression that the dead man had been stabbed to death. By this time Leonardo was beginning to look rather the worse for wear. If he could have known what was going on he would not have liked it at all. Neither for that matter would several other people who had been lulling themselves into a sense of false security. It is one thing to be discreet when the unsullied reputation of a resort is at stake. It is quite another when one's Government might be accused of condoning an international crime.

The appropriate officials might be disturbed at the turn of events, but so far, the resort itself was pursuing its seasonal way. The palm trees and the flags were rustling and idling on the gentle breeze.

The Place President Wilson was solely possessed by the sun, a dog and a man who was indolently reconstructing a wall that the Germans had knocked down years ago.

A resident could have told you that the time was exactly twelve o'clock. The man, building the wall, galvanized suddenly into action, leaped on his bicycle and pedalled off to his lunch as if it were a matter of life and death. Madame Hect, the modiste, came out of her shop and raised the pink and white awning that had been protecting her window display from the morning sun. The American resident from the pink villa in the Rue de Fleurie walked by as always at precisely this time. The orchestra struck up in the Cafe des Bains. And three men in dark coats and striped trousers walked down the steps from the Casino on to the beach and picked their way delicately over the sand. They looked decidedly out of place. The sand was carpeted with sun-bathers, all shapes, all sizes, all ages, and nearly all wearing the minimum of clothing accepted currently as complying with the rules of decency. This season the minimum was minute.

One of the men was the manager of the Casino, one the doctor, and the third the Chief of Police himself. The manager was leading the way. He came to a halt and stood looking down at the figure of a plump, elderly woman, lying on the sand.

'So,' he said, 'the body was lying almost exactly so, face down in that exact spot.'

'Ah,' the police official pulled his large dark lower lip. He was a tall man, very thin, and he wore a black hat. 'The body could have been brought in from the sea.'

'But not washed up, so high on the sand.'

'I remind you that I said brought in: by boat, for instance.'

The subdued voice of the manager prompted: 'It could equally have been carried from the road. The passage you will note is exactly opposite. At night in the shadow of the Casino it is very dark. The beach also is unlighted.'

'But he was a heavy man.'

'That being the case, presumably the easiest way to get him here would be on his own feet.'

'Force him to come here to be killed, is that what you suggest?'

'He need not have known he was going to be killed. He may have thought his appointment had much more attractive possibilities.'

'But, Monsieur, he was in bathing trunks.'

'The suggestion may have been for a midnight bathe. No lunacy is beyond the scope of some. If you remember it was a very warm night.'

The other shrugged. 'It is possible. It is also possible that he was undressed here on the beach.'

'But why?'

'Why? For the simple reason that a man, say in evening clothes, if he were lying on the beach would be noticed immediately.' He looked down at the lady at his feet and at the naked limbs that sprawled over the sand. 'But a body half naked . . . Perhaps someone needed time, time to leave the town, to search his apartment at the Majestic, to establish an alibi. Doctor,' he turned to his companion, 'could he have been stabbed somewhere else and then made his way here?'

The doctor looked doubtful. 'It is possible, of course, but why should he? Presumably, if he went anywhere, it would be for help.'

'He might have expected to find it here. You think he could have done it?'

'He could not have walked very far.'

'Well, from the Casino, for example.'

The manager gasped. 'My God, you don't suggest . . .'

'No, I suggest nothing.' He gave a worried tug at his lip. 'I am asking questions; just as I predict that I myself will be asked a great many questions before many hours have passed.'

They stood looking down, a small semi-circle of gloom.

Suddenly the lady who had unknowingly acted as stand-in for Leonardo Manetti rose to a sitting posture and looked up at them. She had a broad homely face, but at the moment it showed evidence of undoubted peevishness.

'Gentlemen,' she said firmly, 'I am at a loss to know what you are staring at. If your attentions are lascivious I am sure you will find others on this beach far more suitable to your purpose, both as to nakedness and shape. If, on the other hand,

I interest you as a personality, let me tell you you are wasting your time. For twenty years in a suburb of London I have owned and conducted a school for small boys. I have come here for a few weeks to get away from their blank impersonal stares which have never failed to unnerve me. Now I find myself subjected to the same ordeal by three grown but inappropriately dressed men. I would be singularly obliged if you would go away.'

But they were already on their way, stumbling over mortified apologies as they fled. The elderly lady indulged in a singularly girlish grin and lowered herself back on to the sand. Etheldra Martha Truman was not as easily put out as she pretended.

Half an hour later the three men had gone, but Etheldra was still prone on the beach. Anthony Tolworth found her there when he came along from the jetty. He stood looking down at her speculatively.

'Aunt Ethel,' he said, 'you are a positive eyesore.'

She sat up and glared at him. 'I can well believe,' she answered, 'that respectable middle-age is a reproach and an offence to you, but I can assure you that there are places where it is held in respect and regard.' She sighed. 'Particularly in Sydenham.'

'I'll buy you a drink.'

She heaved herself up and staggered giddily with the effort. From the sand she picked up a flowered cretonne beachrobe which she donned with the maximum of satisfaction.

'I bought this in Dulwich,' she said.

'I shouldn't like to condemn Dulwich on one mistake, however glaring. Don't you think it would look smarter just carried over the arm?'

'It covers my not altogether prepossessing thighs,' she said. 'That is what I bought it for.'

Anthony sighed gently and took her arm. He placed her inconspicuously in a corner of the terrace, not, he told her, because he was not proud of her personality, but the Dulwich kimono might get the restaurant a bad name.

She grinned and unceremoniously took hold of one of her legs and heaved it over the other and then modestly tucked in her beach robe.

'I know, by experience, that no establishment frequented by any member of the Tolworth family could possibly have a worse name. I am thirsty. I'll have a beer.'

'Must you, Aunt Ethel? There are other long drinks, you know.'

'Beer.'

He called a waiter and ordered the beer and a dry Martini. 'Why is it,' she asked him, 'that immediately any of your wretched tribe get into a mess they send for me?'

'Habit, I suppose. I'm not in a mess.'

'Oh no, you've only got a murder on your hands. Did you do it?'

'No.'

'Well, why go to the trouble of telephoning to London and asking me to come here?'

'I thought you'd like a holiday.'

She looked appreciatively out over the shining bay.

'It's not bad, I must say. I was once in Deauville.'

'Born traveller, eh?'

'I fell in love with a romantic young man whom I later discovered to be the assistant of the old woman who hired out the donkeys. I fled home and your uncle caught me on the rebound.'

'What strength!'

'I was about half a ton lighter in those days and the belle of the hockey team.' She threw back her head and laughed at the memory. 'I was an energetic girl. In those days I wouldn't have been content to lie on the beach. I should have been far out at sea, alone and swimming doggedly.'

'What possessed you this morning to do your sunbathing in that particular spot?'

'You did.'

'I?'

'You showed me where you found the body, didn't you? I decided to lie there.'

'That was very morbid of you.'

'On the contrary. It is the scene of the crime, is it not? After all, the interested parties do come to the scene of the crime, don't they?'

'You are not suggesting that you are going to solve this mystery, Aunt Ethel?'

'Wasn't that what you brought me here for?'

'I brought you here for quite another reason.'

'Oh yes, you said something about a girl. Are you in love with her?'

'What do you expect me to say or do? Giggle and blush and say yes?' He added seriously: 'She might need your help.'

'Eve Raymond,' she paused thoughtfully and repeated the name. 'Raymond. I hope you didn't mind, Anthony, but I went to your London flat yesterday morning and looked at her photograph.'

He looked at her in surprise. 'Why on earth should you do that?'

'Because last time I visited you I remembered thinking there was something vaguely familiar about her face.'

'But you've never met Eve. She hasn't been in England since she was four years old.'

Still thoughtful she replied: 'No, but when you deal with children as much as I do, you learn in an odd way to see the adult in them.'

'I don't really think it would be very likely that you'd know her.'

'No, perhaps not, and then there was the name.' Again she repeated it, 'Raymond. Anyway, that's what decided me to come here so quickly.'

'But how could you have known Eve? What is the association?'

She shook her head. 'No, I can't tell you that. Anyway, it's all too vague. Just the same, Anthony, I think we had better clear this matter up with as little delay as possible.'

He said politely, but firmly: 'Aunt Ethel, it's awfully nice of you to have come. It is good to know that you will be here should the need arise. I think at the moment the police are satisfied that it was not murder at all. We'll let sleeping dogs lie, shall we?'

'But the dogs are not lying. They are snuffling. They came and inspected me this morning.'

'Inspected you?'

'Three of them, when I was conveniently taking the place of the corpse. They did not, of course, know that I knew. They were very self-important and seldom if ever raised their voices above a whisper. I would describe their demeanour as reluctantly eager, like little boys who have been kept back after school to do some bad work a second time. Does that suggest anything to you?'

Anthony answered reluctantly: 'It might mean a great deal. On the other hand, you might be imagining the whole thing.'

'I have no imagination whatever; none. But I have learned to interpret what I see. Don't forget that I have spent twenty years of my life interpreting the furtive actions of small boys.' She snorted: 'French officials... chicken feed!'

'Aunt Ethel,' he said firmly, 'all I ask you to do is to lie on the beach and enjoy yourself.'

She laughed. 'My dear boy, that is exactly what I am going to do.'

'And keep away from the scene of the crime.'

His aunt laughed, and as suddenly the laugh froze on her face and she stared down over the terrace railings.

'Roger Bassett and John Carpenter, what are *you* doing here?'

'Playing, ma'am.'

'*Playing*, and with the whole of Europe at your disposal you chose to play here!'

'My daddy drove us down in his car,' Roger said. 'At a hundred miles an hour all the way.'

'Quite untrue.'

'Well, anyway sixty. My daddy's the fastest driver in the world, and we have the fastest car in the world. You ask Carpenter.'

'I shall not ask Carpenter. It is not necessary, apart from which almost all of Carpenter's information is grossly inaccurate.'

'The people here speak French awfully well,' Carpenter said, and added in self-defence: 'Of course they practise all the time. They're French.'

They climbed on the rail and sat politely ready to be conversational.

'Aren't you going to bathe?' Etheldra asked them.

'We've bathed,' Roger said. 'I went in and in up to my chin, and then I went up to my mouth and nose and eyes.'

'No you didn't,' John Carpenter said, 'or you couldn't have breathed.'

'I didn't breathe till I came out again.'

'If you didn't breathe you'd be dead, like the man they found on the beach.'

Anthony took a deep breath. 'What man?'

John began picking the sand from between his toes.

'It was a fat man about as fat as you, ma'am.' Quite inoffensively he gauged Etheldra's weight with his eye. 'Anyway, nearly. He was dead on the beach all day.'

'Rubbish.' She said it mechanically.

'We sat and watched him,' Roger said. 'Once Carpenter jumped right over him; well, anyway, over the legs.'

'We could tell he was dead because he didn't breathe. We watched a lot of other people and they were all breathing. Roger touched him!'

'It would have served you damn well right if he'd got up and given you a whack on the behind to go on with! I wonder he didn't do it!'

'Yes, but we told you, he was dead.'

Etheldra said slowly: 'Having reached the astonishing conclusion that he was dead, did you pass on the information to anyone else?'

'We couldn't think of the French for dead.'

'Mort,' Roger said. 'I know.'

'Yes, you know because you asked your daddy.'

'I told my daddy,' Roger said, 'and he said everyone looked dead on a beach.'

'He didn't believe you, eh?'

'Oh, yes, he did,' Roger said. 'He promised he'd come and look at him in the morning. But in the morning he wasn't there. I suppose he went to Heaven.'

Anthony looked at them thoughtfully. 'If *you* noticed he was dead, why did no one else?'

'We were counting the ones asleep and the ones awake, and he was the only one asleep with his eyes open.'

'I suppose,' Roger said, 'he walked into the sea over his head and when he walked out again he was dead. Wasn't he silly? Do they sell ice-creams here, please ma'am?'

'They do,' Etheldra said.

'They don't put pockets in bathing trunks,' said Carpenter. 'They should, shouldn't they?'

Anthony put his hand in his own pocket. 'If I buy these ice-creams you are angling for, will you promise to go away?'

'Yes,' they said together.

He handed them the money. 'The service here is very slow, go to the kiosk at the other end of the beach. They don't care whom they serve there and they do it much more quickly.' They slid off the rail. 'He was really and truthfully mort,' Roger said and they walked sedately away, with their small blonde heads bent over the money.

'They were quite right, of course,' Anthony repeated. 'He was really and truthfully mort. I wonder who else knew that?'

'The murderer, presumably. Do you know who it was?'

'I know several people who found him a bit tiresome.'

'And so, naturally, being rugged individualists, they got rid of him. But why leave him on the beach?'

'Why indeed?'

'Those wretched men in black coats and striped trousers don't even know where he came from.'

'I thought you couldn't hear what they were saying.'

'No, but I could see the way they were looking; out to sea, up that little passage that leads down past the Casino, into the Casino itself; a most ridiculous performance. Why do people say that actors overact?'

'You probably imagined the whole thing.'

'You said that before. Even to say it once is quite unoriginal.' She scowled. 'Fatter than the dead man, indeed. . . . Those little fiends would say anything. Anthony, that remark identifies me with this murder. I shall solve it.'

'Aunt Ethel, you will do nothing of the kind. You are a homely, kindly lady in late middle age. As a chaperone and friend in need, you have, at least, the outward aspect of suitability, and that, my plump but awkward aunt, is what you are here for. And no matter how great a strain it imposes on you, you will mind your own business.'

Etheldra sat up straight and in a loud clear English voice, audible at a great range, said in English: 'Waiter, bring me a beer.'

All the waiters and probably all the waiters in the Café des Bains next door halted in their tracks. It seemed to require a series of hurried consultations to set them in motion again. The manager himself came bustling forward, eager, but not too eager when he saw who owned the voice.

Etheldra eyed him coldly. 'We have met before,' she said.

'Madam?'

'On the beach. In company with several others who should have been better occupied. You were inspecting me.'

'But I assure you, madam...'

'What I really disliked were your expressions: that respectful curiosity with which it is customary to inspect a corpse. Did you really think I was dead?'

The manager was horrified. 'Madam, such a thought would not have crossed my mind.' He gave a noble little laugh. 'Here we think only of life ... of gaiety.'

'In that case you have my sympathy, because from what I have heard you are going to have a tussle to keep your minds off the corpse.'

The manager started and looked reproachfully at Anthony, but Anthony was accepting no responsibility for his aunt.

'I think,' he said, 'if my aunt is ordering beer I'll struggle with another dry Martini.'

'Certainly, Mr. Tolworth.' He lowered his voice. 'Perhaps you might impress upon your aunt our eagerness to be discreet.'

'I'll try. But I can only warn you that it will be uphill work.' The manager bowed and withdrew, and, as he did so, the smile he bestowed on Etheldra was shadowy in the extreme.

'Ostrich,' said Etheldra.

'Professionally perhaps. It pays in places like this.' He grinned. 'You should try it yourself some time.'

'Thank you, Anthony, but I refuse to put my head in this or any other sand. My figure is unsuitable.'

The manager did not return... discreet again, no doubt, but he sent a waiter with their drinks.

'I think perhaps,' Anthony said, 'it might be better if you patronized some other beach.' He added half seriously: 'I don't want another murder on my hands.'

She looked at him sombrely. 'He was a rather awful man, wasn't he, Tony?'

'You mean Leonardo Manetti? Yes, he was pretty frightful.'

'And this girl Eve; is she a nice girl?'

'Very; I'm prejudiced, of course.'

'Odd that she should be mixed up with a ruffian like that.'

'Ruffian is not the exact word for him. He could be very charming.'

'Like a snake.'

He nodded. 'Yes.'

'But he seems to have been pretty well known, his reputation, I mean.'

'Very well indeed. It stank.'

'Then she should not have let herself get involved with him. In fact, you should have stopped it.'

'I didn't know. Anyway, on her own account she had decided to have nothing more to do with him.'

'Somebody implemented the decision pretty effectively. I only hope the decision holds good with regard to his remains.' She added irritably: 'Why an English girl can't make her home in England, I can't think.'

'That, I gather, has something to do with her father.'

'You mean he prefers to live here?'

Tony smiled. 'Some people do, you know. In his case I think the tie is a professional one.'

'What is his profession?'

'The study of gamblers. He's writing a book about them.'

'Well, why doesn't he finish it and be off home? How long has he been here?'

'Oh, years and years.'

'And he hasn't finished the book?'

'No.'

'The poor silly misguided fool. What is it that makes such cowards of some of us and turns some of the best of us into criminals? Francis Raymond. . .' she paused thoughtfully.

'Is his name Francis? I didn't know?'

'Perhaps not. You might ask.'

CHAPTER 5

THERE were plenty of signs if one knew where to look for them that the Casino Municipal was determined to do its best. The waiters had discarded their second-best uniforms and put on their precious best. The tails of Jean Baretti's coat almost swept the floor and he wore a large gardenia in his buttonhole. The tables shone with the best linen. There were fresh flowers everywhere. The commissionaire in front of the building had waxed his moustache to pin points and, being one of the most wealthy citizens of the town, he had instructed the maid to press his uniform before he got up. The white cover on his cap was being worn for the first time.

In one of the smaller pensions the three members of the acrobatic dancing act had been involved in something of a scene. The girl of the troupe had been discovered by the owner in the bathroom washing the green silk blouses of the two men. It was only after it was tearfully explained to her that King Rudolph the Third was going to pay a surprise visit to the Casino that the lady relented and loaned them the family iron. Even the croupiers had contrived to remove some of the dark marks that the table edges had left on their coats.

In the fashionable hotels in Nice, Cannes and Monte Carlo, they all knew that Beaumont-sur-Mer was having a surprise visit. They gossiped about it on the Boulevard des Anglais and mentioned it idly as they lay stretched out in the sun on the Eden Roc terraces of Cap d'Antibes. Other Casino managements agreed that something like this was just what was needed to put Beaumont back on the map again. Several of them began discreetly to check up on current prices for popular Royalty. Young good-looking Kings, reigning or not reigning, were becoming singularly rare. Rudolph was undoubtedly the best available to the purveyors of idleness along the Cote d'Azur.

In spite of his air of amiable indifference Rudolph the Third knew quite a deal about the art of creating an impression. If he had not, of course, the time of a large number of people would have been wasted; the fencing master, the dancing master, the tutors, the officers of the military academy, the Queen, and all the dozens who had conspired to make him aware that he was different from other human beings.

As the little party came into the Casino he looked about him, curious and at the same time detached. Half a dozen waiters, discreetly posted at various points, began to clap. This was taken up enthusiastically by the patrons. The band with a nice flurry of spontaneity struck up the Althenian National Anthem (the old one, of course), which they had been practising all the afternoon. Most of the audience grasped at once what it was and stood up. A political enemy began to protest and was shot out through the waiters' entrance before anyone realized what he was trying to do.

Jean Baretti, his managerial coat-tails flying, came forward to express his humble surprise and gratification.

The King shook his hand and graciously remembered his name, told him that on no account was the normal routine to be disturbed and they would like a cocktail on the terrace. The little manager, beckoning waiters with either hand, swept ahead of them. The King put his hand under Eve Raymond's elbow, smiled down at her and followed the manager as if they had the place entirely to themselves. She was glad, of course, that they hadn't because it was nice to see the green in the other women's eyes.

The manager took himself off and Anthony leaned over and said with a grin: 'Very nicely done, Your Majesty. I was afraid you might be getting a little stale.'

Rudolph replied without malice: 'As my great-grandmother's cousin once said, "We are not amused."' He added: 'the only worthwhile contribution that you have made to my happiness is that you have found me Miss Raymond.'

'It's odd that you should say that, because the fact is that I found Miss Raymond for myself.' Anthony was quite shocked at his own feeling of annoyance. It was worse because Eve for some reason of her own looked as if she were about to purr.

Rudolph smiled and said: 'Avril can have you.'

Avril Pares was not the slightest bit put out by this piece of generosity. She had known Rudolph since he was five and she was three, since her father had first gone as American Minister to Althenia. Her father, in fact, had arranged their loans, had shown them how to improve their railways, how to educate their children and look after their sick and had almost but not quite convinced them that there was no point in killing each other. And when, at last, the people had been convinced that Rudolph's father was too much of a luxury it was Avril's father who got them away in an American warship. And it was through no fault of his that Rudolph the Second got himself assassinated immediately the warship had landed him in Alexandria. The Althenians are a very passionate people. Avril herself had never been convinced that the house of Badenburg was any more important than the house of Pares; on the evidence she would have said less. She had always loved Rudolph, but she had got used to it; at least that was a statement that she was prepared to stick to. She was small and lovely, her dark hair waved and shone. Her skin was the colour of ivory. When she smiled she looked like a little girl, when she was serious she was intensely serious. At the moment she was not serious. She was looking at Anthony with a kind of amused challenge in her eyes.

'Do we accept the gentleman's kind offer, or don't we?'

'We might do worse.' He smiled at Avril, but he was thinking of Eve. Eve was the woman of the hour and she knew it, and she was loving it. About the whole thing there was a sort of lovely make-believe; that one-glorious-hour sort of idea.

'Are you interested in cars?' Rudolph asked, and suddenly she wanted to laugh because the remark was so incredibly blank.

'Fascinated!' She did laugh. 'Are you making conversation, or does it really matter?'

'I think,' he said with royal simplicity, 'I might give you one.'

Anthony said with commendable vigour: 'You will do nothing of the kind.'

Rudolph raised his eyes. 'You amaze me, Tolworth. I will not have you stifle my generous impulses.'

'Nothing of the sort. Your royal generosity is quite commendable, but in this case the usual platinum and enamel clip with the Royal coat of arms will be both adequate and appropriate.' He grinned. 'As a matter of fact, I saw you put two of them into your pocket before you left the yacht.'

'The lady would prefer a motor car.'

'And what will all the old harridans along this coast say when they see Eve driving about in a car they know perfectly well she couldn't have afforded to buy?'

'I presume they will know where it came from because I shall put my crest on it. That,' he said to Eve quite simply, 'will put a hundred pounds on to the value of it. I always sell them with a crest; unless of course I am dealing with another King, and then he generally prefers his own.'

This mixture of simplicity and guile left Eve looking at him in wonder. 'I didn't know you sold motor cars.'

'Oh dear yes, when they were very scarce we could get them when no one else could. A manufacturer will always cough up a few cars for a King, quite often as a gift. Of course in that case I send them an autographed photograph of myself sitting at the wheel. We've had some scenery painted so that we can take the pictures on the yacht. I am pictured entering the palace gates. It was Tony's idea actually. He's a useful chap. Would you like one by the way, I mean a picture?'

'Yes, I really would like that.'

'I shall have the court photographer take one specially for you. Then he will destroy the negative.'

'Do you have a court photographer too?'

'Naturally. Count Otto smuggles my pictures back to Althenia whore they are sold. More than half of all my subjects have bought one.' He added thoughtfully: 'It pays very well.'

Eve laughed. 'That yacht must be a hive of industry! I'd no idea that you were such a going concern.'

'Even a King must live. All our estates were confiscated when Leonardo Manetti. . .' he stopped.

Leonardo Manetti: the name fell and seemed to lie on the silence that followed it. Eve turned her head away with a sudden movement of shock. Avril crushed out her cigarette and stood up.

'Do I have to ask someone to dance with me?'

After only an instant of hesitation Anthony joined her. 'I'll risk it,' he said.

It was as easy to dance with Avril as to look at her. Presently she looked up at him and smiled.

'Still jealous?'

'No, and you?'

'No, I think I like being given away.'

He smiled. 'It's nice having you. How long am I supposed to keep you?'

'I've no idea. Maybe we should ask Rudolph.'

'Do you love him?'

'Oh, heaps and heaps, but I've got used to it. Then there's the fact that I've grown up.'

'Really, I shouldn't have guessed it, you know. You look very much of a little girl from this angle; quite an adorable one, in fact.'

'I must admit that I'm not bad, but not exactly the type I'd have chosen if I'd been designing myself.'

'Oh; what exactly would you have had in mind?'

'Well, something along the lines of that golden girl of yours. She's lovely, isn't she?'

'Very, but I still think you are pretty good yourself. I'll even take your word for it that you are grown up. What, by the way, has growing up to do with your love for Ticker?'

'Well, he hasn't. In fact, he'll never grow up.'

'He's very much wiser than he looks.'

'I know, that's what's so maddening about him. He's spoiled.'

'Who wouldn't be?'

'Born to be a King. It's something you can never live down.'

'He seems to do his best to forget at times.'

She shook her head. 'Not really. He'll never rest till he goes back to Althenia.'

He looked at her in surprise. 'Do you think he will go back?'

'Yes, soon, most of the people have always wanted him back. Some day there will be one of those Royalist plots and there will be lots of bloodshed, and that will be that.'

'I shouldn't think he'd want his own people to start killing each other for his sake.'

'On the contrary, that's just what he would want. Down with the vile traitors, Long live the King. The sound of the guns would be music in his ears.'

He looked down at her tense upturned face and said gently: 'You are a serious little thing, aren't you?'

'I hate it so! I was almost brought up with Rudolph. I used to laugh at all that Divine Right business, but to him it was absolute reality. He thought of his people as if they really did belong to him. And the funny thing is that most of his subjects thought so too. When I used to see his cavalry clearing the street for the Royal coach, their methods used to make me furious. Everyone else seemed to think it was the most natural thing in the world.'

'Well, it was backed by their traditions, certainly.'

'I used to raise hell with Rudolph, but he only laughed, and if I kept it up he would go all cold and royal.'

Anthony smiled. 'You must have had fun!'

She too smiled suddenly. 'It was a bit like a fairy tale.'

'And you'd like to go back when Rudolph goes?'

She shook her head, serious again. 'I don't know, perhaps the fairy tale is finished. Next time the fairy prince might be the demon King.'

The dance finished and they strolled through the long windows on to the balcony above the sea, and leaned together against the railings. The lights were on across the bay and were sending reflections like mysterious fingers, exploring the dark shadows of the sea. Softly the unseen waves were sighing and dying on the sand below them.

As if there had been no break in their conversation, Anthony asked: 'Then you think he will go back?'

'Rudolph? Yes, I'm sure he will.'

'Soon?'

'Why yes, now that Leonardo Manetti is dead. . .'

He asked sharply: 'How did you know that he was dead?'

She gave a little gasp and then asked in a carefully controlled voice: 'Is it a secret?'

Equally carefully he replied: 'I just wondered who told you.'

'Rudolph. . . at least, I think it must have been.'

'Did he make any suggestions as to who may have been responsible?'

'No, but naturally I assumed it was one of the Royalists.' She gave a brittle little laugh. 'It's one of those things they do well.'

'Did you know him?'

'Yes. He actually asked me to marry him. It's odd that one should feel insulted by an honourable proposal.' She turned swiftly to face him. 'Can't we talk of something a little more appropriate to the setting?'

He leaned toward her, smiling into her eyes. 'I say, I really am sorry. I should be telling you I love you.'

'But you love Eve.'

'Do I?'

'Well, don't you?'

He paused and said: 'That is difficult to answer. We don't see each other a lot, we like each other when we meet.' He laughed. 'But is it important?'

'Well, it is rather.'

'Why?'

She looked up at him, amusedly speculative. 'I think we'd better go in before I say something immodest.'

He reached out to catch her hand, but she turned and walked through the window.

Eve and the King had left the terrace and Avril and Anthony found them in the roulette room. Eve was playing and Rudolph was standing behind her chair. It looked as if she had luck on her side. She looked up at them and smiled. She seemed oddly excited. Anthony whistled softly as another pile of chips came sliding across to stop in front of her.

'Lucky lady.'

Eve shook her head. 'It isn't my money; I'm just lucky for someone else.' She jumped up from the table. 'That noted authority, Francis Raymond, my father, says the great thing about roulette is to know when to stop.'

They helped her to gather up her chips and carry them to the cash desk in the corner. Anthony hardly noticed the amount as the cashier counted out the notes. He should have done, because to win fifty thousand francs in twenty minutes was quite good. He was thinking instead of the name Francis Raymond. It was odd that Aunt Ethel should have asked him to inquire about Raymond's first name, odder still that her guess should have been right. Obviously somewhere a long way in the past she had known somebody named Francis Raymond. Even so, there were plenty of Francis Raymonds in the world.

Eve and Rudolph were disputing over their winnings. Rudolph was trying to insist that she take the lot; Eve was refusing indignantly to take any. Avril suggested that they divide.

Eve's face was slightly flushed. It was difficult to guess whether anger or excitement were the cause.

Rudolph took her handbag, counted half the winnings, tucked them inside and handed the bag back to her. 'Soon,' he said, 'I may be playing for really high stakes. I may ask you to be my partner again.'

Eve looked at him queerly: I wouldn't let the gambling fever get into my blood, if I were you. I don't think you are cold-blooded enough.'

He laughed and lifted his head arrogantly. 'You would not say that if you knew anything of the history of Althenia.'

It was quite obvious to Anthony that Ticker had taken one of his periodic plunges into infatuation. When Rudolph the Third concentrated on a girl he concentrated very emphatically and he cared not in the least who knew it. When Eve danced with Tony he sat and waited, watching till they had finished. As to Eve, it was difficult to know what she was thinking. She was flattered, of course.

'I will say for Ticker,' Anthony said, 'he's quite open about his feelings.'

Eve smiled. 'More than you are, for instance?'

'I'm merely frustrated, darling.'

'I shouldn't have noticed it. When did you find out?'

'Tonight, for instance. I can't make up my mind whether to be jealous of you or make love to Avril.'

She hesitated and then asked without looking at him:

'Have you consulted Avril?'

'Certainly.'

'Doesn't she find it a little galling having you undecided like this?'

'No, no; she doesn't think it's at all urgent.'

'That either shows a lack of enterprise or a great deal of confidence.'

'Lovely girls like Avril Pares never lack confidence. Why should they?'

'Well, Rudolph, for instance. . . I wouldn't say he was exactly grovelling at her feet, you know.'

'I gather that she has been watching Rudolph in and out of these experiments of his ever since they were kids. He probably comes to her to be rescued.'

'I think you're jealous.'

'Yes, darling, I think so too, but of whom?'

'I think he's rather wonderful... I mean exciting.'

'Is that what you like, excitement?'

'Yes, yes, I think it is.'

Anthony looked across the room and saw the little manager trying to attract his attention. His face was very white.

'Excitement,' Anthony said softly, 'I think, darling, you may be going to have some.'

She looked at him quickly. 'You said that in a funny way Tony. What is it?'

He shook his head and danced with her in the direction of their table. He left her with Avril and the King, and walked away. Avril watched him speculatively.

'That man has something on his mind,' she said. She smiled suddenly and added: 'I wish it was me. How long have you known him?'

'Oh, years and years.' Eve could not have explained why she resented answering questions about Anthony, but she did.

'Lucky girl.'

'Why lucky?'

Rudolph interposed. 'Yes, why lucky? Anthony is all right in his place, one presumes.'

Avril laughed, a sudden outburst of irrepressible mirth. 'Rudolph, you are marvellous!'

'Have I said something funny?'

'No, no. You never do when you are in love, but you are still marvellous.' She laughed again.

Rudolph looked at her coldly. 'I am not accustomed to being laughed at, Avril.'

She made bogus soothing noises. 'Of course, you're not, you great big spoiled schoolboy. We'll both love you very much, Rudolph dear... when you grow up.'

He did smile then and said apologetically to Eve: 'The trouble is, she knows me too well, you mustn't mind what she says.'

Eve answered: 'I don't mind a bit what she says,' and after a fractional hesitation which both women were aware of and the man was not, 'about you.'

Half smiling, Avril contemplated her cigarette. 'But we didn't begin to talk about you, Rudolph dear, we were talking about Anthony. Eve and I are both wondering why he left us so suddenly.'

Anthony walked slowly back to where he had seen the manager. Jean Baretti was waiting for him and unostentatiously led the way to an alcove off the cocktail bar.

The little man had lost much of his assurance. His hands were not steady and his face was very white. He plucked the flower from his buttonhole as if he were divesting himself of his office.

'I am ruined,' he said.

'I'm sorry. Surely it isn't quite so bad as all that?'

'It could not be worse. If only you had stayed away!'

'I?' He looked politely surprised. 'That is not very hospitable of you.'

'No, no, not you alone, Mr. Tolworth. All of you, the King, your party.'

'This is getting mysterious.'

'They have come for Miss Raymond.'

Anthony knew now that this was what he had been waiting for, but his voice indicated only vague faintly puzzled surprise.

'They?'

'The police, not our own people this time, Mr. Tolworth, but the authorities from Nice. They have been instructed from Paris.'

'How very complicated. So they have been instructed from Paris to call for Miss Raymond; whatever for?'

'Mr. Tolworth, Mr. Tolworth, please; this is serious, desperate. We have all been accused of trying to hush this matter up, to avoid a scandal.'

'My dear chap, what matter? What scandal?'

'The murder of Leonardo Manetti.'

'Ah, so it has been decided that he was murdered?'

'Of course. Now there must be action, developments, an arrest.'

'I see, and so they have decided to arrest Miss Raymond?'

'Question her.'

'Here? Well, why not?' He half turned away.

'No, not here, they have decided to take her to Nice.'

Anthony turned back thoughtfully. 'That, of course, is not quite the same thing, is it?'

'But they insist, Mr. Tolworth.'

Anthony shrugged. 'Well, if they insist tell them I'll bring Miss Raymond into Nice myself in the morning.'

'They cannot wait, their instructions are to report progress to Paris tonight; progress is expected.' He added with a gleam of hope: 'I have persuaded them not to intrude on His Majesty's party. They are prepared to wait a reasonable time.'

'I see, so His Majesty is to dance away knowing that when it is all over one of his guests is to be arrested for murder? Delightful memory for him.'

'But Mr. Tolworth, need he know?'

'Ask yourself.'

The little man clasped his hands in distress. 'I have, I have.'

'May I ask what this extraordinary conspiracy is?'

Jean Baretti started, and when he saw Rudolph the Third at his elbow, he retreated a step.

'Your Majesty.'

'I was just explaining to him,' Anthony said dryly, 'that it is quite difficult to keep Your Majesty in ignorance of anything concerning himself.'

Rudolph leaned forward, a lock of fair hair fell romantically over his forehead. He looked down at the little man with detached curiosity.

'Now what could he possibly have wanted to keep from me?'

'I have done my best to be discreet, Your Majesty. I will be ruined.'

The ruin facing Jean Baretti did not seem to register with the King.

'No doubt,' he said, 'I'm sure it's very important. What is he talking about, Anthony?'

'Well, it seems you are about to be embarked in a bit of notoriety.'

'Ridiculous. I've never behaved better in my life.' He took a tie-pin with the royal coat of arms from his pocket and said: 'Give this to somebody or other with my compliments and let's forget the whole thing.'

'It's not so simple as all that, I'm afraid. In fact, it is not simple at all. The police have come to question Eve about the death of Leonardo Manetti. They are determined to do it tonight.'

Rudolph turned on the manager. There was cold hauteur in his voice. 'Have you informed these people that Miss Raymond is my guest?'

'Yes, Your Majesty, but . . .'

'Where are they?'

'In the . . . in my private office, Your Majesty.'

'Lead the way.'

Jean Baretti opened his mouth, closed it without saying anything and led the way to an unobtrusive door in the corner of the room.

Four men smoking crumpled cigarettes were waiting for them, or rather waiting for Eve Raymond.

The senior of the four of them, a thin man with a pinched yellow unfriendly face, raised hooded inquiring eyes as they came in.

Jean Baretti turned sharply aside and said impressively: 'His Majesty, King Rudolph of Althenia.'

With reluctant courtesy they shuffled to their feet, but they were not impressed.

Rudolph surveyed them coldly. 'Do I understand that you wish to interview one of my guests?'

The thin man inclined his head without feeling the need to speak.

'And that to do so you propose to take her to Nice?'

'That is our intention.'

'Nonsense.'

The police official shrugged without speaking. Obviously he was a man of few words.

Rudolph went on coldly: 'I assume that you are doing what you conceive to be your duty?'

'Precisely, Your Majesty.'

'In that case I am prepared to bring Miss Raymond into this room. We will remain with you for ten minutes. That will be quite sufficient.' He turned to go.

'Not quite.'

He swung back. 'What's that?'

'We are taking Miss Raymond back with us to Nice.'

'Why?'

'I can say only the reasons are sufficient.'

'Supposing she refuses?'

The thin lips compressed and the shoulders were raised in a just perceptible shrug.

'Since you take that attitude, I tell you that she does refuse.' Rudolph was angry and as Anthony could see was behaving foolishly.

The official looked at him coldly. 'I have to remind Your Majesty that you are now in the Republic of France.' As he spoke this untidy unprepossessing man seemed to grow in dignity and stature. He turned to the manager.

'M. Baretti, would you please be good enough to bring Miss Raymond here to us in this room. Have the attendant bring her wrap.'

Anthony, who had been leaning against the closed door, did not move aside. He looked at the little manager with an odd smile. 'You don't want a scene on your hands, do you, Mr. Baretti?'

The little man was horrified. 'My God, Mr. Tolworth, you don't suggest. . .' He couldn't go on.

Anthony's smile widened a little. 'Miss Raymond is a very temperamental girl. If there is one thing she loathes above everything else it is being ordered about.'

'But. . . but I am not ordering her about!' He turned piteous eyes on the officials.

'Perhaps not,' Anthony answered. 'But she may think you are.'

'But how well I know it! That Miss Raymond, her eyes flash.'

Rudolph did not improve matters by throwing back his blond head and laughing heartily. 'Why don't we all have a scene?' he said.

The thin police official for the first time looked vaguely disturbed. He was a ruthless and cold-blooded policeman, but also he was a Frenchman who had lived his life and made his career in the resorts along this coast. He understood the meaning and importance of quiet unruffled decorum, no matter what was happening underneath. Jean Baretti, who was part of the Casino façade, and Leon Picoy, burrowing in the criminal background, were really very much akin. But his hooded eyes were blank. He said nothing. It was Anthony who guessed.

'I suppose a lot of people would know that that car of yours outside is a police car?'

'They know, yes.'

'There will be comment if Miss Raymond drives away in it.' The other shrugged, accepting the likelihood.

'On the other hand, if I were to drive Miss Raymond to Nice.' Out of the corner of his eye he could see the manager looking at him with a dawning hope.

'But she is not going to Nice,' Rudolph was angry again. Anthony caught his eye and looked at him steadily.

'Your Majesty would be doing a disservice to Miss Raymond and the hospitality of France if he were to interfere.' He could sense the approval of the others in the room.

Rudolph was looking at him in doubtful inquiry. Then he shrugged. 'It is against my instincts . . .' He shrugged and said no more.

'As I said,' Anthony repeated, 'it would be quite easy to drive Miss Raymond to Nice.'

'*If* you drove her to Nice, Mr. Tolworth.'

Anthony looked at him coldly. 'I am not accustomed to breaking my word, Messieurs. His Majesty, also, will guarantee that we will go direct to the Police Judiciaire.'

He looked hard at Rudolph who hesitated and then said: 'Very well, you have my word.'

The official hesitated. 'I see no objection to your driving Miss Raymond in to Nice. Naturally one has no wish to involve the Casino in notoriety.'

Jean Baretti sighed windily; Rudolph was still looking puzzled and angry, but he kept silent.

'Very well then; you realize, Mr. Tolworth, that our car will be following you?'

Anthony smiled. 'Oh naturally, I didn't expect you to trust us quite alone.'

'When will you be ready to start?'

'Shall we say in half an hour?'

The police official stood up. 'We will be waiting in our own car and will follow you as you move off.'

Anthony nodded and opened the door and waited for Rudolph to walk through.

'Now what sort of a mess have you made of things?'

'I thought I did rather well.'

'Oh beautifully, but what are you going to do next?'

'Why, drive Eve to the police headquarters at Nice.' Rudolph turned on him. 'I see. You take Eve and hand her over to the authorities in Nice and I sit quietly on the yacht and do nothing at all.'

'Oh no, you are going to be busier than any of us. Listen . . .' Rudolph listened and, as he did so, he brightened considerably.

They made their way back to the table. Avril was chattering inconsequentially. Eve was looking straight ahead. She nodded now and then, but Avril knew that she was scarcely listening. Suddenly Eve swung round to her impulsively.

'Please don't try to help!'

'Don't mind me,' Avril said. 'I'm only keeping up appearances. The trouble about dining out with a King is that everyone looks at you.'

'Are they looking at us now?'

'Goggling, dearest.'

Eve said bitterly: 'I suppose I'll have to expect plenty of that from now on. Only their looks won't be envious.'

'Why should they look at you? Are you going into politics or a circus or something?'

'I think I'm going into gaol.'

'Oh I say, you poor child. You must ask Rudolph to do something about it. It's amazing the things he can get done.' It was typical of Avril that she could give her sympathy and help without asking for details.

Eve said, 'I think I'd like to go home. I wonder where they have gone to?'

'Rudolph and Tony? Oh, they'll be either propping up the bar or getting some money out of somebody, or maybe both.' But she was not so convinced as she sounded. She knew that it was not in Rudolph's make-up to neglect his guests.

Then they saw the two men come back into the room. Rudolph had regained his good humour. He was every inch the romantic young King again.

Avril said lightly: 'Where have you been? The women round here have been having a lovely time feeling sorry for us.'

'As a matter of fact,' Anthony said carefully, 'we have been arranging to take Eve for a drive.'

Eve picked up her glass, looked at it vaguely and replaced it on the table. It was an odd gesture of helplessness and resignation.

Avril tried to keep the conversation on a lighter plane. 'Didn't anyone arrange to take me for a drive?'

Rudolph stood up. 'I'm going to take you home,' he said. Avril looked at him in astonishment. 'Rudolph, how very unlike you. What causes it; pity?'

He laughed and the lights were dancing wickedly in his eyes as he leaned down and said in a low voice: 'You are part of the plot. Come on.'

As Eve had come in Avril went out, on the arm of the King. Faces turned and eyes followed them as they went out. The little manager, reprieved at the last moment, was bouncing ahead of them towards the doors.

Eve turned back to Anthony. Her eyes were piteously afraid. 'Well, Tony, when do we start?'

'We have to wait for the car to come back.'

'Where are we going, or shouldn't I ask?'

'I'm drawing you a plan.' He was making swift clear lines on the back of a menu card. He tossed it across to her, deliberately casual. Look at it very carefully, Eve.'

'I am, but what is it?'

'A corridor. Or rather two corridors.'

'Oh, I see now, but where is it?'

He said lightly: 'Police Headquarters, Nice.'

There was a long silence and then, in quite a steady voice, she replied: 'You must know it well.'

'I've had to go there several times on Ticker's business.'

'What do I do with the plan, keep it as a souvenir?'

'Memorize it.' He waited while she studied it and then he took it away from her. 'Now, how many doors do you pass on the right?'

'Four.'

'How many corridors do you pass before you turn right?'

'Two. I have a good memory.'

'Good . . . sure you won't forget?'

'Positive, but what is it about?'

'I'm driving you to there. The police are going to follow us in their car.'

'Must I go, Anthony?' The appeal in her voice was pathetic. He nodded. 'I gave them my word that I would take you there. I thought you'd prefer that to going in the police car.'

'I suppose I should say it's very chivalrous of you,' her voice trembled, 'I'm frightened, Tony. Everything is so, so dark. I can't see ahead, not anywhere.'

'Don't try.'

'What was it you said about women in France? They don't kill them for crimes of passion.'

'No, they don't make a habit of it. However, if you are thinking of confessing on that account, don't.'

'It would save the authorities a lot of time and my friends a lot of worry, wouldn't it?'

'On the other hand, the real murderer might feel that he had to come forward and give himself up.'

Her eyes dilated. 'I don't know what you are talking about.'

'Don't you, darling?' He looked at her quietly. 'It will be time enough to talk about confessions when we find out how much they know.' He grinned. 'If you aren't careful you'll have Rudolph confessing. He gets such heavy bouts of Danubian chivalry there are times when he is capable of anything.'

She shook her head. 'Funny, isn't it, a few hours ago I was thinking that this was the most wonderful evening of my life. Turned out to be a Cinderella story with a new twist, didn't it?'

'I didn't know that Ticker could stir up so much romance.'

'You were there too, weren't you?'

'I'm still here.'

'You'll soon be rid of me.'

'In this life, my angel, you never can be sure of anything. I may even have myself arrested just so that I can be in the same gaol.'

'That doesn't sound very funny. I suppose I'm losing my sense of fun.'

'It could be that. Or perhaps you'll only see the funny side when you find out that it's true.'

'Please don't, Tony. I know you're trying to be amusing . . .' She broke off and pressed her clenched hand against her lips.

Tony looked quickly away. 'God,' he said with sudden savagery, 'how much longer is that damned car going to be?'

In fact, at that moment, the little manager was making his way to their table. When he spoke his voice was solemn and subdued.

'The car is waiting, Mr. Tolworth.'

Eve forced herself to laugh. 'You sound as if you had summoned a hearse, Mr. Baretti.'

The little man was obviously deeply stirred.

'I hope some day you will forgive us all. I assure you, I promise you that nothing serious will come of this.'

Eve found herself feeling sorry for the manager, which was ridiculous. Obviously it should have been the other way round.

She held out her hand to him. 'It's been a marvellous evening. Whenever I feel depressed, I'll remember it.'

She slid her shoulders into the cloak that Anthony held for her and picked up her bag. The glances that followed her as she walked out remained envious. Her head was held high, her lips were slightly parted. She was still the lovely girl who had danced all the evening with the King.

Little Jean Baretti bowed them out, then he hurried to his office, locked the door, and threw himself down on his desk and sobbed.

CHAPTER 6

ANTHONY and Eve went to the car with the same air of casual departure that they would have affected on leaving any party on any ordinary night. Anthony gave the doorman a tip that made his waxed moustache bristle with professional satisfaction. He bowed, saluted, and shut the car door with one graceful coordinated flourish.

'You wouldn't believe it possible unless you saw it done,' Anthony said thoughtfully as the car moved off.

'You were referring to?'

'The commissionaire. Do you know that my father used to over-tip that man thirty years ago? He was outside Maxime's then. He has been outside every fashionable door in France; sombre thought, isn't it? He told me the other day that he took this job because he wanted to be near his property. He owns the Grand Hotel.'

He was talking idly, but through the mirror he was watching the police car. Unobtrusively it had slid out from the curb and now it was following a hundred yards behind them. He glanced at Eve. She was sitting very still, her eyes steadily on the road ahead.

'I'm sorry,' he said casually, 'that I had to be so crudely hearty while we were waiting for the car to come back.'

'Were you?'

'Of course.'

'Then of course you had your reasons.'

'I wanted you to look the part.'

'What part?'

'The part of the poor girl who has learned that she is going to prison.'

'And did I? I hoped at least that I hadn't made an exhibition of myself.'

'You were marvellous. I could see those four coppers peering at you with overacted unconcern while we were waiting for the car.'

Suddenly at breaking point, she beat her hands on her knees. 'Oh God, Tony, must you go on being facetious even now that we are alone? I can't bear it, I tell you, I can't bear it!'

'Eve, really I'm ashamed of you. Did you think for one second that I was going to leave you to be shut up in their miserable gaol?'

She turned, her eyes startled. 'But we are going there. You said so.'

'Yes, I didn't want you to go dancing out of the Casino like a young lamb. The police might have thought we were too jolly for the occasion. As it was, you looked,' she heard his soft laugh in the darkness. 'like an aristocrat going to the guillotine . . . just right, in fact.'

'But you told them you were taking me to Nice.'

'Yes, what I didn't tell them is that I'm not leaving you there.'

Eve shivered. 'I'll never get away from there. They will question and talk and hint and suggest till I have forgotten what I said last. Then in the morning they will begin again.'

He put a hand on her knee. 'You won't be there in the morning. In fact, you are paying the world's shortest visit. You remember the plan I drew for you?'

'Yes, but. . .'

'Just concentrate on that. It shows you the way in and the way out. Now repeat again. You go in, what next?'

'On my right I pass four doors and two corridors. Then I turn right.'

'Correct. At the end of that corridor there is another door. It has a Yale lock. You open it, go through, pull it shut after you . . . and your visit to the Judiciaire is over.'

There was a pause and she said: 'Then the manhunt begins.' He answered: 'That's right.'

'I begin to run.'

'No; you stand in the shadow of the wall.'
'Is that all?'
'Nothing more, nothing else. I'll collect you.'
'Tony, this is insane. They'll catch us both; they'll hold you too as an accomplice.'

He laughed. 'Catch us, with five minutes start? Ridiculous!' But she caught his arm. 'Please Tony, I don't want to drag you into this.'

'Why not?'

'It's not your affair . . . and I—well, I'm too fond of you.'

'Eve, you darling, you couldn't keep me out of it. This is the sort of thing I live on. It's nothing but a busman's holiday, you silly child. Now be an angel and look back and see where the car is.'

'It's still there, about a hundred yards behind.'

'That's fine.' They slid through the silent streets and down on to the sea front. The Rolls-Bentley was running so silently that they could hear the racing engine of a speedboat away out of the bay.

'I think,' Anthony said, 'we might fluster our pursuers a little.' He pressed the accelerator and the car swept up to eighty miles an hour.

The police car dropped back, but presently it reappeared again, being driven furiously. Tony laughed and stepped up his speed to a hundred miles. The following car disappeared again, and that, till they were at the door of the police headquarters, was the last they saw of it.

Anthony gripped Eve's hand. 'You're not scared?'

She returned the pressure. 'Not any more. . . excited, that's all.'

'Good . . . you remember the way?'

'Yes.'

'Keep cool.' He opened the door and she got out as the headlights of the following car turned into the Rue Gioffredo. Tony said softly: 'Face toward them, let them see you clearly. Right. . . now turn and hurry inside. . . . Good-bye.'

Breathlessly she replied: 'Good-bye, Tony.' Then she turned quickly and walked through the doorway.

The police car drew in behind the Rolls-Bentley. The four men got stiffly to the pavement. The leader passed his handkerchief across his brow and walked to the Bentley.

'That was not funny, Mr. Tolworth.'

'Funny?'

'I could arrest you for breaking the speed laws.'

'I say, I'm most frightfully sorry; was I going too fast?'

'Much too fast.' He was looking with reluctant approval at the sleek docile shape by the curb. 'Much too fast. I thought you might have had an idea of getting away from us.'

'Oh, but I wouldn't have dreamed of it.' He added with dignity: 'I gave you my word that I would bring Miss Raymond here.'

'Very well. In future be good enough to keep the speed of this car under better control.'

Anthony smiled. 'When next you follow me, Monsieur, you will find me a model of decorum. As a matter of fact, I thought you were in a hurry.'

There was something quietly suggestive in the reply. 'We have ample time to question Miss Raymond, now that she is here. But you, Mr. Tolworth, we will not detain.' Without waiting to say good night he led his followers through the high doors of the building.

At the same moment the Rolls-Bentley moved off as quietly as a phantom.

Anthony turned the corner and saw a gleam of white in the shadow of the wall. He swung open the door as he approached.

Eve ran across the pavement and jumped in beside him. He was travelling at fifty miles an hour before Eve had given way to her first shiver of relief. Or it may have been excitement, or both. She was unable to resist turning to look back. There was no sign of alarm behind them.

Tony laughed. 'I told you we had at least five minutes. They aren't in a hurry. They took time off to give me a word of warning, about my driving, which I expected. It gave you time to get out the back door.'

She gasped. 'Tony, I couldn't open it. There was a bolt that I hadn't noticed at the top. I thought I'd die!'

'But you didn't?'

'Hurry; can't you go any faster?'

'Don't worry, Eve. I'll tell you what they will all be doing now. Among other things they'll be washing their hands and brushing their hair. After all, they are men, and you are a pretty girl, darling. Why should they hurry? Their work is only just about to begin, they have the whole night before them. At first they will merely think you have wandered into the wrong room. You did go there of your own free will. If you were going to try to get away, surely you'd have done it when we lost them on the road. Oh no, it will be at least five minutes before they even begin to gesticulate.'

'But we are still in Nice; what can we do?'

'We have almost done it. Look.'

The car slid quietly to a stop on the cobblestones of the yacht harbour. Peering up from a flight of stone steps was Rudolph. She could see the light shining on his blond head. He was wearing a suit of very dirty white overalls and he was grinning like a schoolboy.

Anthony patted her shoulder. 'Five minutes are nearly up,' he said. 'Run.'

As he turned the Rolls-Bentley to drive away, he saw the dark shape of Rudolph's speedboat slip quietly away and lose itself in the gloom.

He parked his car in the shadow of the covered space that houses the vegetable market. Then he strolled idly across to Chez Joseph. The restaurant was empty, madame and the chef were sitting at a table at the end making the inevitable plans for tomorrow's menu.

She exclaimed when she saw Anthony and came running with both her hands held out.

'M. Tolworth, what a pleasure! Wherever have you been?'

He smiled at her, giving her his attention as if she were the most lovely girl in the world. 'I have been all over the world, madame, and always too far from Chez Joseph.'

'You mustn't flatter me, it goes to my head.' She gave a girlish little laugh.

The chef came forward, wiping a thumbless right hand on his apron.

'M. Tolworth, we had despaired of seeing you.'

Anthony shook hands. 'Nonsense, you old rogue, till I came in the door you had forgotten that I existed. Can you still make a Lobster Vanderbilt?'

The old fellow grinned. 'For those who can appreciate it, yes.' He added bravely: 'You wish for one now?'

'No, no, you have had quite enough for one day. The trouble with you is that you work too hard. You've got pads under your eyes. Or is that the ladies?'

The old man pulled a wispy end of his moustache and leered. 'Ah, monsieur, I am an old man . . . but still, one is never too old.'

'Be off with you,' Madame said. 'M. Tolworth does not wish to listen to your innuendoes. Also if he wishes a Lobster Vanderbilt it is by no means too late.'

'Thank you, madame. If there is some coffee I'll have a coffee and liqueur, if not I'll just have a liqueur. Armagnac please, if you have a good one.'

She brought the liqueur herself and left the bottle on the table. 'Please help yourself, monsieur, we are so happy to see you back again.' She chatted a while and only when Anthony protested that he was keeping her from her work did she go back into conference with the chef.

Anthony had begun his second liqueur when the police chief arrived. He walked up to the table and without removing his wide-brimmed black hat, he sat down.

'Alone, Mr. Tolworth?'

'Naturally, won't you join me in a drink?'

'No thank you.'

'I see, so it's a business call.'

The other man raised his heavy lids and let them drop again.

'Miss Raymond has disappeared.'

'Disappeared? You mean you've lost her?'

'Yes.'

'I say, that was very careless of you, wasn't it?'

'Perhaps; if by that you mean that I should have driven her to Nice myself.'

'I don't see the connection, I'm afraid.'

'Where is she?'

'My dear chap, I delivered Miss Raymond to the Judiciaire. Surely you saw that yourself?'

'It seems now that you were altogether too eager to bring Miss Raymond to Nice.'

'The idea was to avoid a scandal. I thought that was agreed.'

'There will be a far worse scandal when we find the person who helped her to escape.'

'Escape from what? Was she under arrest!'

'At the time, no.'

'Well, she must have decided to go home.'

'Unless she had wings, that decision could not be carried out.'

'It sounds exciting. Tell me more.'

'You detained us several minutes at the door, Mr. Tolworth. When we went in Miss Raymond had disappeared.'

'There is one little flaw in that statement,' Anthony said. 'It was not I who detained you. If you remember it was you who detained me; a little matter of speed, if you recall.'

'Where did you go when you left the Judiciaire?'

'I came here.'

The thin man beckoned to Madame. She came reluctantly; obviously there was no love lost between them.

'What time did M. Tolworth arrive here?'

'Thirty minutes ago, Monsieur. At five minutes past two.' The thin lips drew back sceptically. 'Very precise. Did he draw your attention to the time?'

'Monsieur,' her voice was wearily contemptuous, 'when you are very tired and the restaurant is at last empty and a customer arrives, you naturally look at the time. My chef and I had begun on the menus. We saw a car draw up opposite. You may be sure we both looked at the time.'

'But tired as you were you served him and permitted him to stay till now.'

She folded her hand across her waist and looked the police officer in the eye. 'I am honoured to think that Mr. Tolworth is a friend of mine. A friend of mine is welcome to sit here all night if he is so disposed.' She looked at him meaningly. 'I said a friend, Monsieur.'

'I suppose you were too good a friend to notice if a lady was with him?'

'He was quite alone.'

'You would be astonished if she were discovered to be upstairs, for instance?'

She threw up her head indignantly. 'I do not know what you are implying, Monsieur. Ladies do not go upstairs in this establishment with, or without, my consent.'

They understood each other, these two, in spite of their clash. There was no doubt in his mind now that Anthony had been alone when he arrived.

Anthony was looking from one to the other. Obviously he was enjoying himself.

'As a matter of fact, madame,' he said, 'he thinks that I abducted a lady, and hid her somewhere. But what defeats him is that I had only five minutes to do it in.'

She laughed then and she made no pretence that she was not laughing at the thin grim man who had been questioning her.

'I can assure you, from what I have seen here, Monsieur, that Mr. Tolworth has no need to abduct his ladies. Oh no! If you had come here and said a lady had abducted Mr. Tolworth . . .' She gave Tony a look which he chose to interpret as motherly, then she turned back to the official. 'Perhaps Monsieur would like to order a coffee? It is fifty francs.'

The thin man stood up. He contemplated Anthony, without enthusiasm. 'I will question you again,' he said, and added: 'The interests of everybody would be best served if Miss Raymond gave herself up in the morning at the latest.'

Anthony raised his eyebrows. 'Gave herself up?'

The other nodded coldly. 'Tonight I have issued an order for her arrest, on a charge of murder.'

Anthony looked thoughtfully at his cigarette.

'That was a mistake,' he said. 'You will regret it.'

The other's voice was thinly sarcastic. 'Perhaps you can tell me who the murderer is?'

Anthony stood up. 'Perhaps. You may even find yourself with a glut of murderers. Good night.'

He kissed madame's hand and strolled out to his car.

The drive back was quite different from the journey in the other direction. This time he was in no hurry, but he was amused to notice that a car, which had been parked at the other end of the market, slid in behind him and followed him when he turned out into the Promenade des Anglais. He was not in the least worried about the police. In fact, he was only too happy to be engaging their attention.

Halfway home he was stopped again. This time they searched the car, explaining, of course, that it was a routine check-up. They found nothing, and with the other car still quietly following, he drove home. He left the car in the public garage they patronized, smiled, gave an ironical salute to the occupants of the car that had followed him and strolled down past the now darkened Casino, walked down on to the jetty and hailed the King's yacht. The launch slid away and five minutes later he was on board.

There was no sign of life on the darkened deck. He thought everyone had gone below, but Rudolph's voice called him as he was about to go down.

'That you, Anthony?'

'Oh, hello, I thought everyone had gone to bed.'

'No, we waited up for you.'

'We?' He came nearer and saw that Eve and Rudolph were reclining side by side in two lounge chairs.

Rudolph explained unnecessarily. 'We are sitting in the dark because, naturally, I don't want Eve to be seen from the shore.'

Anthony said: 'Yes, that would be too much after all the trouble we've been through.'

'Don't be sarcastic, old boy,' Rudolph said plaintively. 'We're only doing our best.'

'To do what, catch cold?'

'I'm all wrapped up in a rug,' Eve said. 'Didn't you want us to wait up for you?'

'There is a drink on a table somewhere if you care to grope in the dark for it.'

Anthony guardedly struck a match and poured himself a whisky and soda. Then he pulled up a chair. 'If we're all going to sit up all night there's no reason why I shouldn't be comfortable.'

'You're tired,' Rudolph said solicitously. 'Why don't you pop off to bed?'

'I wouldn't dream of being so churlish. Tell me, what sort of trip did you have?'

It was Eve who replied. 'It was marvellous, Tony, absolute heaven!'

'What, in a speedboat on a dark night?'

'It was the dark that made it so wonderful.'

'Ah yes, of course, the dark. At least I hope nobody saw you.'

'Not a soul,' Rudolph added with satisfaction. 'That was quite a good idea of ours, wasn't it?'

'Ours?'

'All right, yours.'

'What does your mother think?'

'Well, she hopes there won't be a scandal.' He added casually: 'You know what Queen Mothers are like. They've learned to have very little faith in Kings, I'm afraid.'

'These little Kings are sent to try them.'

Rudolph stirred in his chair. 'Sometimes, Anthony, you are damned impertinent.'

'Forgive me, Ticker, it was a stupid remark, and anyway, I don't include you among the little Kings. You are quite big; definitely outsize, in fact.'

Eve broke in: 'Tony, how did you get along?'

'Everything went more or less according to plan.'

'You don't think they saw us?'

'I'm sure they didn't, otherwise they would have been here long ago. When that old turtle face Picoy caught up with me I was sitting in Chez Joseph guzzling Armagnac without a care in the world.' He smiled in the dark. 'Picoy thought I might have hidden you upstairs. Madame seemed to take that as a suggestion that she was keeping a disreputable house. Her outraged dignity was very impressive indeed. The old sleuth was convinced.'

Eve said softly: 'You are a darling, Tony.'

'Picoy doesn't think so. Nothing could give him livelier satisfaction than to see me in two parts, one on either side of the guillotine. As a matter of fact, Eve, he must have thought I had you up my sleeve or something, because when I left the restaurant they followed me and they searched the car on the way home. I'll bet anything you like they are strolling up and down over there just in case I come ashore again.' He sighed. 'It looks as if I'll have to behave very correctly for a day or two.'

Rudolph said: 'All this is absolute nonsense. Tomorrow we'll up anchor and go somewhere where we can have some peace. Eve, let me take you shopping in Cairo.'

'There is one thing about you, Ticker,' Anthony said, 'you do tackle your problems with a great deal of simplicity.'

'What is wrong with the idea?'

'The only thing to do is to find out who did kill Leonardo Manetti. We can't do that by taking a shopping trip to Cairo.'

'I am quite prepared to leave you behind to clear the matter up,' Rudolph said. 'In fact, it might be a very good idea.'

'But it would not be quite such a good idea for you to be seen on a shopping tour in Cairo with a pretty girl who was wanted for murder in France. The more pious among your devoted followers might think it a little odd.'

'It is not the habit of the people of Althenia to question the doings of their King,' Rudolph said with dignity.

And without dignity Anthony replied: 'That's what *you* think.'

Eve said flatly: 'He is quite right, of course, we can't go on like this. It's like living in a vacuum. I'll still have to go to the police, I'll still have to be questioned. I'm not afraid of that; I'm afraid . . .' She stopped, with a quickly indrawn breath.

'What are you afraid of, Eve?' Anthony's voice was quiet in the dark.

'I can't tell, that is, I don't know.'

'Of course not. Once upon a time I was afraid of the dark. It's like that, isn't it?'

Rudolph said irritably: 'Listen, Tony, this is quite simple; we've rescued Eve from these ridiculous people, the obvious thing is to take her away and keep her away till it's over.'

Eve said wearily: 'There is my father too; I couldn't possibly go away and leave him alone.'

'Your father will be all right, Eve,' Anthony said. 'I telephoned him as soon as I left the manager's office at the Casino tonight. I told him you would not be home. I told him I was taking care of you.'

'Was he worried?'

'Not at all. He said that as long as you were with me it would be perfectly all right. Unflattering, wasn't it?'

'Well, trusting.'

Rudolph said: 'The main thing is that he is not worrying.'

'He will be in the morning, when he heard what happened tonight.'

'I told him I would get in touch with him in the morning.'

'I can't go any farther away than this,' Eve said. 'He's so terribly helpless, he couldn't possibly get along alone.'

'I've heard that said of a lot of people,' Anthony told her. 'But they do manage to survive, you know. They may not be able to look after themselves, but they are pretty good at finding someone to do it for them. In his case it happens to be you.'

'You really don't know him, Anthony.'

He sighed gently. 'Perhaps not. I also wonder if you do.'

'Oh no, I'm only his daughter!'

Tony stood up. 'We'll see what happens tomorrow, or rather today. I'm going to bed.'

'Good night,' Rudolph said.

'I think I'll go too.' It seemed to Anthony that her voice sounded faintly reluctant.

'Why hurry?' Rudolph stretched out luxuriously. 'You won't be able to appear on deck in daylight tomorrow.'

'I don't think I want to see tomorrow.'

'Then you shan't. We'll stay here till dawn and then you can go to bed and stay there till the day after tomorrow.'

'That sounds marvellous.'

Rudolph laughed. 'No, no, it's just simple old Badenburg hospitality.'

'He means they try to keep their women in the dark,' Anthony said.

He spoke lightly enough, but as he walked away he was annoyed at the idea that he should be annoyed. In the circumstances that made him more annoyed than ever.

Eve called him softly, but he closed the door without hearing her.

CHAPTER 7

WHEN Anthony came ashore to the beach, it was still not quite nine o'clock. His Aunt Etheldra was there stretched out on the damp sand.

'Been out all night?' he asked her.

'No, I'm still alive.'

'I hope you keep it up. Still drawing inspiration from Manetti's last resting-place, I see.'

'The sand is nice and cool.'

'So I presume is Leonardo. Has that terrifying brain of yours solved the mystery yet?'

'No, those damned boys are helping me.'

'Dear, dear; why don't you tell them to go away and annoy someone else?'

'I don't tell children what to do when I am on holiday. They would consider it definitely unfair.'

'Don't tell me you value their opinion, Aunt Ethel.'

'I do, very much indeed. I am afraid of them, of course, like any other intelligent adult. That is why in term time I strictly limit their activities to channels in which I can unfairly compete with them. It's cheating, of course, but they are tolerant enough to put up with it.'

'But here you let them do what they like?'

'My dear Anthony, has it not occurred to you that by and large they and I like the same things? I have explained why I cannot indulge my girlish fancies in school, but here I find we have a great deal in common. We share, for instance, a very low opinion of adults. Also we only deceive ourselves and each other for our own entertainment and then only for the moment.'

He seated himself on the upturned keel of a red canoe.

'Mr. Raymond's Christian name,' he said casually, 'is Francis.'

'I was afraid it might be.'

'Do you think that you could spare a little time from materializing Manetti's ghost and go and see him?'

She was building up a little cone of sand and for a little time made no reply.

'I am afraid, Anthony, that a visit to Francis Raymond would only cause embarrassment to both of us.'

'It might help if you did go.'

'Why not go yourself, or is any action as simple as that beyond your grasp?'

'But it's not so simple as that. If you look along the sea wall you will see a local inhabitant leaning there looking pensively out to sea.'

'Why not? It's his wall, isn't it?'

'He has been put there to watch me.'

'Nonsense; you have delusions of grandeur.'

'No, I assure you: if I go to visit Eve's father he will follow me.'

'Why on earth should he do that?'

'Eve has disappeared.'

'Does he think that you will disappear too?'

'No, but he has been led to believe that I know where she is.'

'And do you?'

'Yes.'

'Anthony, one day these romantic notions of yours are going to get you into trouble. Do the police want to arrest the girl?'

'More or less.'

'Then why not let them get on with their duty? If the girl is guilty she must take her punishment. If she is not guilty she has nothing to worry about.'

'In this country she has to prove that she is not guilty.'

'Is that what you are trying to do now?'

'In an amateurish sort of way, yes.'

'What am I supposed to say to her father?'

'You might tell him that she is quite safe and well.'

She looked at him shrewdly. 'Do I say where she is?'

'No,' he smiled. 'As you don't know yourself, that would be a little difficult, wouldn't it?'

She snorted disgustedly and then said: 'Would you say that that little manager friend of yours was much of an athlete?'

He gave her a surprised glance and then hesitated before replying. 'You never know with these Frenchmen. It's surprising how serious some of them are about keeping fit. Why do you ask about Jean?'

'He was putting up a very good performance this morning.'

'What, exercising?'

'I think, as a matter of fact, he had been swimming round that yacht of yours. It's quite a long way.'

Anthony looked startled. 'Why on earth should he do that?'

She grinned. 'How should I know? Unless, of course, he thinks what I think.'

Anthony fixed her with an eye. 'And what, Aunt Ethel, do you think?'

'I'll tell you what I don't think. I don't think your little friend swam out to the yacht because he felt he needed the exercise.'

'I see. And what time did all this take place?'

'About seven o'clock this morning. I was out for an early morning walk. He swam in, popped on his beachrobe and walked off looking businesslike. I half expected him to have a dispatch case in his hand. At least I'd have expected him to stop and dry himself. What do you make of it?'

'I think Jean Baretti hurried down to the beach, had a nice long swim and hurried back to his room to have a fresh-water bath and dress himself. What do you make of that?'

'Possibly you're right,' she said. 'As a girl I was a very determined swimmer. I never once came out of the water without turning round and looking with virtuous satisfaction at the expanse of water I'd covered.'

'Perhaps,' Anthony said sourly, 'Jean Baretti is not so virtuous as you were in those days. Why on earth shouldn't the wretched man have a swim in the morning if he wants to?'

'Anthony, when you begin a sentence with the words "why on earth" you remind me so much of your dear uncle whom I married that I see you wearing a monocle and spats.' She sighed deeply. 'I loved him in spite of them.'

'Aunt Ethel, must you rush off into these nostalgic memories?'

'Why not? He was the only husband I ever had. Let me tell you the only romance in my life since then was a discreetly worded proposal from a housemaster at Stowe . . . at least I think he was at Stowe. He told me he thought I'd get along swimmingly with the boys. Look out!' She ended on a shout of warning.

Tony leapt like a frightened stag. 'What's the matter?'

'Bassett and Carpenter! They're coming!'

With a look of pained protest he seated himself again. 'Good heavens, Aunt Ethel, those two kids are at the other end of the beach. Anyway, I thought you said you liked the little brutes.'

She scrambled to her feet. 'I do, I do, but if you don't mind, Anthony, I'll get away before they come. They've begun to follow me about and you do want me to call on Francis Raymond discreetly, don't you?'

'Of course I do, but . . .'

'Very well then, just chat to them for a while like a good boy, till I've dressed and got away.'

It could not with truth be said that she darted away, but she did disappear with commendable speed.

Anthony watched the two small boys making their way along the beach. Bassett ran round a beach umbrella and sat down. Carpenter ran round the beach umbrella and sat down. They both got up. Carpenter ran round the umbrella, shook the handle as he passed and sat down. Bassett ran round, shook the handle as he passed and sat down. The umbrella toppled over. The boys got up and continued their walk.

They said good morning politely and sat down.

'I've got the best mummy and daddy in the world,' Bassett said.

'No,' said Carpenter. 'I've got the best mummy and daddy in the world.'

'No,' said Bassett without rancour, 'I've got the best mummy and daddy in the world.'

Anthony thought the conversation monotonous, but he consoled himself with the thought that he was not involved and that the time asked for by Aunt Ethel was passing.

After a while they left the argument unfinished and Bassett asked Anthony if he would care to take them out in a boat.

Anthony said 'No.'

'Are you a sailor?'

'No.'

'Are you a soldier?'

'No.'

'Oh.'

As this line of inquiry seemed to have petered out Carpenter asked Anthony if he had ever seen a fish ten feet long.

'Yes.'

'Have you seen a fish a hundred yards long?'

'Yes.'

'Have you seen a fish a million billion trillion dillion miles long?'

'Yes.'

'Where did you see it?'

'In a pond.'

'Was it a big pond?'

'Quite big.'

So much for the fish. They sat and thought of it for a while, but they seemed to find that its possibilities were exhausted.

Bassett said: 'Mrs. Truman is going to find out who killed the fat man.'

Anthony considered this and said: 'I thought we were talking about fish.'

'She is your aunt,' Carpenter said as if he had unearthed a guilty secret.

'What, the fish?'

'No.' The idea made them laugh so much that it became a burden.

'No.' Bassett said. 'Mrs. Truman is your aunt and John and I are helping her.'

'Did she say she wanted help?'

'Old ladies always want help. They can't run.'

'I see; so the idea is that you are doing the old lady's running for her?'

Out of the corner of his eye he saw his Aunt Ethel come out of her cabin and slip into the passage leading past the Casino.

Anthony brightened at the thought that he could now dispense with the gay little helpers. But his pleasure was short-lived.

Picoy, looking even more funereal in the bright morning sun, was walking toward him along the beach. Anthony grinned at him affably.

'Good morning.'

The thin lips opened grudgingly to reply.

'Have you found the lady?'

'I shall find her. It was a mistake to run away. She was badly advised.' He raised his turtle lids to look coldly at Anthony. 'It was not the act of an innocent person.'

'I thought you said she was advised to do it?'

'By someone, one supposes, who knew she was guilty. Why else should she run away?'

'She may have found the atmosphere depressing; maybe she just felt that she would like to go home.'

'She did not go home.'

'You verified that?'

'Naturally. I was at the villa a few minutes ago.'

'How was her father? Upset, I imagine.'

'On the contrary,' the thin voice was vicious, 'what I had to say was not news to him.'

'Well, well.'

'He had been told of Miss Raymond's disappearance, Mr. Tolworth, before she disappeared. That is strange, is it not?'

'Amazing, like second sight, isn't it?'

'Or as if someone knew in advance what was going to happen.'

'Same thing.'

'Are you gifted with second sight?'

'Me? Oh dear no!'

'Then one must assume that you had some other means of knowing what plans had been made for Miss Raymond.'

'Really, M. Picoy, you alarm me. Did Miss Raymond's father tell you that I was going to snatch her from the very vitals of your headquarters?'

'He told me, Mr. Tolworth, that he was quite undisturbed as to his daughter's whereabouts, because you had assured him that she would be all right. Then, in the calmest possible way, he endeavoured to draw me into a discussion about the psychology of gambling. When I insisted on knowing where his daughter was he suggested that I should ask you. I am asking you.'

'Really, M. Picoy, why ask me? Since I left you last night after you saw me deliver Miss Raymond at your headquarters I have accounted for every minute of my time . . . at least you have. Your men followed my car home. They stopped me on the way and looked everywhere for Miss Raymond but in my pockets. They watched me leave for the yacht. That idle gentleman on the parapet up there has been watching me ever since I came ashore this morning. The topic is beginning to bore me.'

'You could have had a confederate.'

'Ah yes; so all you have to do now is to find the confederate.'

'Why did you tell Miss Raymond's father that she would be all right?'

Anthony put his head on one side and smiled amiably at his questioner. 'I trusted you. I had your word for it.'

'Or did you trust your own ability to get her away?'

'Quite a problem for you, isn't it? On the one hand, if I deny it you don't believe me, and on the other you can't reasonably expect me to admit it even if I did take her away. What is more, my dear chap, you can't for the life of you see how I could possibly have got her away. I'm really sorry for you.'

'The time may come when you will be sorry for yourself, Mr. Tolworth.'

'Oh yes, I'm sure I will. How long can I look forward to being followed about by that gent up there on the parapet?'

Picoy said sourly: 'For as long as I think necessary.'

'Poor chap. I must try not to tire him out.'

Picoy turned away and then back again. 'I have it in my power to make things easy or very difficult for Miss Raymond. She can be shown as the victim of the dead man or as a woman enraged at the collapse of a sordid love affair.' His voice was without emotion. 'What I decide to do depends on how soon Miss Raymond keeps her broken appointment.'

'All this, of course, regardless of whether Miss Raymond is guilty or innocent?'

Picoy nodded. 'I do not like people who try to be clever at my expense, Monsieur. I do not like you, in fact.'

Anthony laughed. 'What a thing it is not to be loved.'

But as he watched the policeman making his sober way back across the sand he had an uncomfortable feeling that Picoy meant what he said and that he was the kind of man to take his dislikes seriously. He saw Picoy beckon to the man at the parapet and together they walked away.

He had forgotten altogether the two small boys. But they were still there and they had been as absorbed in the interview as if they had known what was being said.

'Was that a policeman, Mr. Tolworth?'

'It was.'

'Is he going to take you away?'

'He is not.'

They registered faint disappointment.

'Is he going to take away the man who killed the man who's dead?'

'If he can catch him. If not I imagine he will console himself with someone else.'

'Would he take us?' Bassett asked.

'No.'

'Why?'

'Because you would be too much for his peace of mind.'

'Which piece?'

'I beg your pardon?'

'Which piece?'

Anthony asked desperately: 'Which piece of what?'

'Piece of mind. Which piece of mind?'

The adult member of the trio swallowed and said: 'I don't know.'

'We'll ask your aunt, Mrs. Truman,' Carpenter said as if he were tired of dealing with underlings.

'That's a good idea, she'll love that.'

'Perhaps,' Bassett said, 'the policeman will take Mrs. Truman away.' He seemed determined to keep the matter in the family.

'Why should he do that?'

'Because she told him he was a poppycock.'

Anthony's eyebrows shot into the air. 'Did she indeed? I didn't know that she knew him.'

'She called him one.'

'I wonder what made her say poppycock?'

His astonishment grew. 'I did?'

'He said you were foolish to have Mrs. Truman working for you and she called him a poppycock.'

'So he is,' Anthony said. 'Mrs. Truman is not working for me.'

They looked at him almost with pity. Much experience had taught them that when Mrs. Truman said she was doing something she was doing it.

'Anyway,' Carpenter said, 'Mrs. Truman told him they should find the murderer instead of annoying people. Roger and I thought he was going to get into trouble.'

'You mean you thought Mrs. Truman was going to get into trouble.'

They stared at him in astonishment.

'Mrs. Truman is the head of our school.'

'My goodness!' Bassett said, 'I think you'd better be careful.'

'Yes,' Anthony answered. 'Yes, I expect I had.'

'Yes,' echoed Carpenter. 'That man had better be careful too. Mrs. Truman is a very important woman. Even teachers do what she tells them.'

'I'll try to remember,' Anthony said. He got up and walked away, quite aware that their indignant glances were following him.

CHAPTER 8

ETHELDRA MARTHA TRUMAN was not one to shirk a duty because it was unpleasant, but she certainly had no liking for the duty that was ahead of her now.

She climbed the last steps to the terrace of the Raymonds' villa and arrived panting slightly and uncomfortably hot. Her weight and gait were all very well in a country where you had to keep moving to keep warm, but not here. She took a handkerchief powder puff from her pocket, unrolled it, and made a couple of resentful jabs at her nose. Then she rang the bell. Antoinette's round black head shot through a side window, was snapped back again and her footsteps came pattering to the door.

Mrs. Truman could see Francis Raymond sitting at his desk and equally clearly he could see her standing at the door. But the presence of Antoinette was required to bring her over the threshold.

Presently he came forward courteously formal and obviously with not the slightest idea who she was.

'How do you do, Mrs. Truman?' He glanced down at her card. 'You have come from England. I have not been there for many years. Won't you sit down, or shall we go out on the terrace where you can see something of our view?'

'That would be very nice.'

He drew up chairs and waited for her to sit down. Then he settled himself and looked with satisfaction out over the bay.

'What a change it is from England.'

She glanced at him and saw the outward appearance of a man at ease, serene and the master of his destiny. But he had always been like that.

She asked: 'Do you prefer this to England?'

He answered in his quiet voice: 'Well, you see this is where I have made my home.'

She forced herself to say: 'Yes, it would be a strain to be uprooted a second time, wouldn't it?'

He looked round at her sharply, and it seemed as if his protective covering had fallen away from him.

'But you haven't told me what you came to see me about, have you, Mrs. . . .' he hesitated and then finished as if the name registered for the first time, 'Mrs. Truman . . .'

She shook her head slightly. 'Do you give me to understand that my name means nothing to you?'

'Truman,' he repeated. 'Truman. There are many people of that name in the world.'

'My nephew used almost the same words with regard to the name Raymond.' She added softly: 'You haven't changed very much, have you, Francis? and you still haven't learned to face unpalatable facts.'

He sagged wearily in his chair. 'It's all so long ago. I had hoped most people would have forgotten me.'

She answered that with grim practicality. 'They will be reminded of you forcibly enough if this beastly mess in which your daughter is involved is not cleared up.'

He brightened at once. 'Oh, but Eve is being taken care of.'

'You mean by my nephew?'

'Is young Tolworth your nephew? I say, I'm so glad. It is a small world, isn't it?'

'It is much too small for your daughter to hide in for the rest of her life.'

'But really, there is no question of her hiding.'

'I don't know how else to interpret this crack-brained adventure that Anthony has involved her in.'

'The police came here this morning and told me some ridiculous story about my daughter escaping from them. I told them that I was quite sure that my daughter was in good hands and that any further discussion of the matter was a waste both of my time and theirs.'

'For the moment she's safe. I know very little about police methods here or anywhere else, but I do know that if they want to talk to your daughter about this man who has been murdered they have their own good reasons for doing so.'

'Eve disliked the man naturally.'

'Then why on earth was she working for him?'

He turned his head away and said: 'Because he insisted.'

'Insisted, my dear man! What an extraordinary thing to say!'

'You see, Manetti had us in his power. At least he had me in his power and as far as he was concerned that meant both of us.'

Ethel Truman sighed. 'The police will think that a very good reason for killing him.'

'My daughter is not a murderess.'

Mrs. Truman regarded him thoughtfully. 'We aren't all so civilized as we think. Your daughter must have her maternal instinct pretty highly developed or she would not be so devotedly looking after you.'

'Looking after me: I assure you, Mrs. Truman, it is quite the other way round.'

'Bosh,' said schoolmistress Etheldra. 'You are no more capable of looking after yourself than a child of four. I am quite sure that your daughter knows it. I've seen her picture, and although she is far too beautiful she looks a very strong-minded child.'

He was not interested in her diagnosis of Eve's character, but he was definitely incensed at her suggestion that he was not the calm and deliberate man of affairs he considered himself.

He said dramatically: 'I would kill any man who injured my daughter.'

'Oh yes,' she agreed with him quite readily, 'I'm sure you would, impulsively and like a child, quite regardless of what happened next.' She regarded him pensively. 'You were responsible for just such an impulsive act about twenty years ago, if you remember.'

'If I did,' he said, 'I have paid for it. Why are you torturing me with the past?'

She answered patiently: 'I'm not torturing you with the past. Unfortunately the past has overtaken you.' She added flatly: 'What we have got to consider now is how much the past is going to mess up the future. Why not start with the past?'

He tried to stand on his dignity. 'I'm afraid I don't understand you, Mrs. Truman.'

'Utter rot. You stole some money.'

The colour went out of his face. 'You don't understand the predicament I was in.'

'I do. I understand it perfectly well. Your wife was ill.'

'Dying.'

'She was a lovely girl. We were all very sorry.'

'The doctors told me there might be some hope for her if I could take her to Switzerland. Switzerland . . . it seemed as remote as the moon, and yet . . .' He paused looking out over the bay.

'And then the money was actually placed in my hands,' he resumed presently. 'In notes by the secretary of the Golf Club. Do you remember him? His name was Coombs, a big jolly man with freckled hands. He was always organizing something or other. This time it was a sweepstake on the Grand National. He and the members had already sold tickets worth five hundred and thirty pounds. "Look here, Raymond," he said to me, "I'm getting a bit nervous about keeping all this in the club safe. I think we ought to pop it away somewhere, don't you?" "Very well," I replied. "I'll look in in the morning on the way to the bank and take it with me." "That's very decent of you." He always said, "that's very decent of you," no matter what little thing you did for him. I remember how the next morning we counted the money. As a bank clerk I had counted money for hours a day. But the feel of this money under my fingers was strange. In a kind of way it felt alive. I can still feel those notes flicking eagerly under my fingers. We both checked them; he, of course, was slower than I was. Then we put them into an envelope, sealed it, signed it, and I gave him a receipt, which he put in the safe. He came with me to the door and said, "See you at the weekend," and I was almost surprised to hear myself say: "No, I'm afraid not. As a matter of fact I have to take my wife to Switzerland."

'All our friends knew how ill she was and he was sympathetic. "You know, Raymond, that if there is anything I can do to help I will be only too happy to do it. I don't know how you are placed financially, but I do know that this business must have put you to a lot of expense." Then he added: "I haven't much myself, but I'm sure if I mentioned it in confidence to one or two members we could quite easily help you out."'

Again there was a long pause.

'I had always tried to keep my head up,' he resumed. 'I think most people had the impression that we were comfortably off.'

'The impression we did have,' Etheldra said, 'was that you were living beyond your means. And so because of your wretched vanity you chose to steal rather than admit your difficulties.' She added: 'It is a thing that children commonly do.'

He was not resentful. He seemed to be making an honest endeavour to explain. 'No, you see, when Coombs made the offer I had already stolen the money. I had been through the whole experience of theft. For the sake of my wife I had made myself a criminal. I can't explain why, but in an odd sort of way, I felt exalted.'

And then the child in him appeared again, for he said pathetically: 'And, you see, I knew the money would not be missed for three weeks and in that time I had a chance to pay it back.'

When Etheldra made no comment he went on: 'I did want to keep the good opinion of my friends.'

That stirred her. 'You wanted to keep your good opinion of yourself,' she said sternly. 'You wanted to be the outward symbol of the popular young suburban husband, who played tennis better than the others and who was the scratch golfer they were all so eager to play with and yet who was devoted to his poor sick wife.' She sighed. 'It would save such a lot of trouble if we could all get rid of this idea of keeping up appearances. Yet here you are still doing it after all these years. Well, get on with your story.'

'I took the money with me and went to work as usual at the bank. I was second in command there. The manager was not a very pleasant man; but when I asked him for two weeks' leave to take my wife to Switzerland he could not refuse. He expressed surprise that a man in my position could afford what he called these fashionable cures. I wanted to tell him that a man in my position was so desperate that he could afford anything. I took Jane to a sanatorium in Switzerland and put my little daughter in a nursery school, nearby. I paid for everything several months in advance and I had two hundred pounds left and four days of my two weeks' leave. I went to Monte Carlo. You see I did have a plan for paying the money back. I felt sure that just for once after all I had been through fate would be kind to me—just for once. It was not asking much with two hundred pounds to win six hundred. People were doing it time and time again.'

Etheldra sat watching him, her expression yielding from censure to pity.

'I was sure, absolutely sure, that everything would be all right. It very, very nearly was. I increased my stake to five hundred and fifty pounds,' he paused, living it all over again. 'It would have been enough, but the idea of stopping then barely crossed my mind. Six hundred was the arrangement I had with fate. I began to lose, and much more quickly than I had been winning. It was terrifying, inavertable. Whatever I did was wrong.' He pressed his hands together in an agony of recollection.

'Then there was that last frightening picture. I looked down at the table in front of me where my chips had been. It was bare, quite green and quite bare. In my hand I was holding one chip. It was a red one, for twenty francs. A hand other than mine seemed to be reaching out to place it. It went on red. Black turned up.'

His body relaxed. His tense hands fell limp on to his thighs.

Etheldra gave a brief sigh and said softly: 'So that was that. It would be wrong to wish you had won, but . . .'

'I went out on the terrace, we all do, we losers. You must get away, you must be alone. You cannot bear to be seen in final defeat. It was then that I met Leonardo Manetti for the first time. I heard him speak. He spoke English in a soft voice with a foreign accent. I can remember the conversation word for word. "I should not jump over there if I were you," he said. "It is not worth while. It never is." I didn't reply. I couldn't. "You had a bad night? Have you never gambled before?" "No," I don't know why I talked to him. "I have never been here before." "There are only two kinds of people who win here," he said. "Those who are rich, and those who are ruthless." I noticed even then how he used the word "ruthless," as if it excited him.

'I did not answer that and he asked: "Do you know why you lost?" I had to say "No." "Because you had too much at stake," he said. "I suppose two hundred pounds is a lot of money." "Two hundred pounds," he said scornfully. "Two hundred pounds is nothing. But you . . . you were playing as if it meant life or death." I heard myself saying: "Perhaps it did." "I thought so. But of course you were wrong. Two hundred pounds is never a matter of life and death. That is your imagination." "I'm afraid," I said, "it's more than that." He was so confident. He spoke so contemptuously of what I regarded as my tragedy, that I found myself wanting to talk to him. "Of course," he said, "it would be rather worse, wouldn't it, if the money did not happen to be your own."' He paused again.

'You'll find it hard to believe, I know, but I who had been too proud to appeal to my friends found myself telling this stranger the whole wretched story. Perhaps it was because I was beaten. Perhaps if I had not told somebody, I should have jumped over that parapet as others had done before me. I shall never know, of course, but whatever the circumstances, I presently found myself discussing my predicament with this man as if we were talking over an ordinary matter of business. You won't believe it, but I even began to recover some of my pride.'

He had no idea what a vivid picture those last few words had given Etheldra Truman of the man she was visiting. Some of his pride . . . She could imagine the straightening shoulders, the returning confidence in his voice as he talked to Leonardo Manetti as man to man.

'He showed me that what had happened to me might have happened to anyone, and persuaded me that it was not what had happened that mattered, but what was going to happen next. He asked me to go with him to his hotel so that we could talk it over. I did not need to be invited. I was clinging to him then in a way that has left me with another humiliating memory. He had a bedroom and sitting-room in a small hotel overlooking the port. It was a small place, as I said, but he was quite obviously doing himself well. The rooms were quite delightful, and the man himself impressed me favourably,' he smiled apologetically. 'Of course in the circumstances I was easily impressed. He was younger than I was, heavily built, well dressed, too well dressed for my taste. He had high cheekbones, a rather flat nose, full lips and bold eyes. I have described him as he was then because the memory of him standing there being my host is still so vivid.' Once again he gave his rather attractive deprecating smile. 'I can even remember the slightly irritating thought that came to me that he would appeal to women.'

Etheldra smiled with sudden humour. 'Considering your predicament you do seem to have had an odd assortment of thoughts that night.'

'Ah, but you see by this time I had regained a great deal of my poise.'

She replied grimly: 'But you still hadn't repaid the five hundred pounds you pinched from the golf club. I'm still wondering how this boy wonder managed that.'

Francis Raymond recalled himself sharply to his narrative. 'He took charge completely. He gave me a drink and as we sat down he set himself to discover every detail of my life. I'll never forget that great surge of gratitude I felt when at last he said: "I think you'd better leave this to me." Everything he asked me to do then I did, feeling that I was in the hands of a strong and dependable friend. First of all he said he was going to provide the money to replace what I had stolen from the club. Just as I know now he expected me to, I told him that I had no assets to set off against the loan he was making. He laughed and said he could settle that with the greatest of ease. "Go and sit down over there," he said, "and write out a full confession. I'll keep it and then when you pay me back we'll have a drink and we'll tear it up. You talk of assets, what better guarantee could I have that you'll pay me back? My dear chap, of course you'll pay me back." And then he added: "Mind you, I'm not going to let you off without interest."'

He shook his head. 'People are such utter fools. Do you know it was the mention of interest that gave me the confident feeling that I was dealing with a business man. Here was his proposition. I put in my confession as a guarantee. He got me out of trouble, collected his money plus the interest . . . and I hoped it would be a stiff interest as a lesson to me . . . and that would be that. I walked over to his writing bureau and wrote to his dictation, signed it, folded it and handed it to him almost with a flourish.' He passed his hand across his forehead. 'And at that moment I made myself his servant for the rest of my life.'

'No,' Etheldra said, 'that was not clever of you: not clever at all.'

'He told me that he was going to London on business next morning and that I should give him a note to the Secretary of the Golf Club saying that as I was detained abroad I had asked a friend of mine to hand over the money. He also invited me to notify the bank that I was not able to get back, because he said it was better to be on the safe side and make sure that everything was all right before I put in an appearance. I was even glad to do this because after all that had happened I didn't feel ready to face my friends at home. He loaned me ten pounds to get me back to Switzerland and I left feeling like an envoy who has negotiated successfully a delicate piece of diplomacy.

'When I got back I found that my wife was better than she had seemed for months and our little girl was quite happy at school. I was so confident that everything would be all right that I wrote to the manager of my bank and explained that I was held up but I had hopes that the delay would not be a long one. It was quite a confident letter. The reply I got back was astonishing. It was definitely cordial. The man who was relieving me was a very capable man, everything was going along nicely, and I was to stay away as long as seemed necessary. Then followed the news that a firm of solicitors had been making urgent inquiries, for they had something 'very definitely to his advantage" to communicate. That I guessed inspired the cordiality of the letter. I wired the firm at once and two days later their representative came to see me. I found that I had inherited twenty thousand pounds from an aunt I had almost forgotten.

'It was wonderful. It meant that all my troubles were over, and it meant too I was in a position to stay with my wife in Switzerland. I wired to the bank that I was not returning and followed this up with a letter of resignation which was accepted with cordial regret. Then when the money was lodged in my Swiss Bank I took myself off to Monte Carlo again, not to gamble this time but with the virtuous determination to have done with my last squalid obligation.

'Of course, Manetti had been very nice to me in my hour of need, but he was not my type and I wished to deal fairly with him and have done with him. I went straight to Manetti's hotel and told him I had brought the money. He laughed and asked if I had had better luck than last time. Something in his tone and the way he laughed made me afraid. But I told him that where I got the money was not so important as the fact that I had it. I counted out five hundred and ten pounds. Then I added a hundred pounds which I told him I was giving him for his trouble.'

He paused once again.

'He folded the notes together and put them in his pocket almost contemptuously. He was watching me half smiling. "For my trouble?" he said. "But I have not taken any trouble." I tried to sound casual. "At least," I said, "although I know you had your own business to take you to London, you did have to go to the Golf Club." "Golf Club, London?" He pretended to be quite bewildered and I knew he was laughing at me. "Really, I have not been in London for months, and when I do go there I certainly do not go to small suburban golf clubs." I could scarcely speak. "You mean that you have not paid the money?" "The money you stole?" he was sneering at me. "Did you seriously think I was going to give away five hundred pounds of my own money with no guarantee but the word of a thief? . . . My dear chap, as you English say."

'I must have amused him; my poor protests were so bewildered. "But you promised, you offered to help me, I wrote that confession as a guarantee." I said all that and more. He looked at me contemptuously. "What I really did was to save your wretched life. You would have jumped over that parapet and you know it. Whatever else has happened to you you are at least alive." "My God," I shouted. "You have made me a criminal." But he said, "No, I have not made you a criminal, I have merely decided that to keep you alive was enough without attempting to rescue you from your folly.

Surely your life is worth more than this six hundred pounds you have given me?" He laughed again and said: "Not that I personally think it is worth anything, but we must think in terms of your own valuation."

'I saw the whole thing clearly then. I saw it was no use pleading, no use arguing, or threatening. I saw that this was his trade. I remember wondering how many other poor devils he had followed out on to the Casino terrace and offered his sympathy. I did not speak again. I picked up my hat and coat and walked out of his apartment. I think that is one of the few things I have done of which I need not feel ashamed.'

He was silent for a while, and then said quietly: 'As I walked down the stairs that night I realized that one day I might have to kill him.'

'And did you?' Etheldra was astonished that her question should have been asked so conversationally.

He smiled at her. 'If I confess, Mrs. Truman, I think it should be to the police.'

She looked at him speculatively; so handsome, so dignified, and yet so weak; weak and still able when and if the time came to confess to a murder. She found herself wondering if Leonardo Manetti had underestimated him; probably he had felt for Francis Raymond nothing but contempt. In doing so, he would be wrong. Aloud she said: 'And so you went back to Switzerland?'

'Yes, I went back to Switzerland. The cold had descended on my life again. In all my life I have never felt such bitter despair.' He shivered. 'Perhaps life still has something worse in store for me. I have had several years of happiness, perhaps that is too much for a man of my type.'

'Too late to start being sorry for yourself now, old feller,' Etheldra said in a hearty voice. She paused and added as one accepting the inevitable: 'I take it that you still refused to face the facts?'

'You mean you think I should have gone back and taken my punishment?'

'I should have thought that by that time you would have learned that your little evasions had got you just about up to the neck in the soup. Any reasonable man at that point would have preferred six months in gaol to a lifetime under the domination of this Manetti creature.' She added with wrathful impatience: 'You, of course, had some other crackpot idea.'

'No,' he answered. 'I had no other ideas. I only knew that if I went back and the whole sordid story came out, it might kill my wife. You see,' he added pathetically, 'she took me at my own valuation.'

Mrs. Truman nodded her understanding. 'You are probably right. I admit you were the sort of man who could easily have been a hero to his wife.'

'At least she was spared knowing the truth.'

'You did not go back?'

He shook his head. 'She was not getting better as I had hoped. Even the doctor had to admit that she was not going to get well again. Whatever the future held for me, I knew that I could not go back . . . not then.'

Etheldra had an overwhelming sense of pity for him at that moment . . . more than twenty years in a trap of his own making . . . it was too long.

She said softly: 'If only you had gone back.'

'But I could not go back.'

'But you could,' she sighed. 'That is what makes the irony of it so bitter.'

He turned slowly to look at her. 'How could I go back then and confess that I had stolen the money?'

She laughed. 'But you did not steal the money . . . you won it.'

'I what?' He could only stare at her.

'How much did you take?'

'Over five hundred pounds.'

'The first prize in the Grand National sweep that year was five hundred and fifty. You won it.'

'I won it. . . I won it,' his lips were trembling pathetically.

'Nobody thought for a moment that you had stolen the money. They went to get it from the bank, but there was no record of it there. They supposed you had put it in a safe deposit and forgotten to make a proper entry. They were cross with you, but they made allowances because you were so terribly worried. My husband said he would guarantee the prize, so that was that. When it was announced that you had won it was the joke of the season. Everyone said you must have had second sight.'

'The joke of the season . . . the joke of the season.' All at once his trembling body went limp. He bowed his head on his hands and sobbed.

Etheldra Truman would not have regarded herself as a sentimental woman, but she did then what she had done time and again for a heartbroken little boy. She knelt down by his chair and pressed his head to her bosom. There was nothing incongruous to her in the fact that he was grey-haired and thought himself a man of the world. To Etheldra all men were little boys and most boys were little men. She simply comforted him till he was quiet. To an onlooker it might have been an amusing sight, but there were no onlookers and presently she got quietly up from her knees and walked over to the corner of the terrace. She was angry again now, angry at the folly and weakness of mankind. She wondered how often in the silences of those years he had tried and condemned and punished himself. There is no punishment so severe as that which is self-inflicted.

Presently she heard his voice beside her. He spoke quite calmly now. 'You must forgive me for that exhibition, but. . . but after all these years, the realization that if only I had had the courage . . . only a little courage.'

'I don't know, perhaps I shouldn't have told you.'

'I'm glad.' Characteristically he added a little pompously: 'It is a comfort that after all I have not lost the esteem of my old friends. They never knew.'

'I think,' Etheldra said slowly and honestly, 'I think now, looking back and after what you have told me, I believe that my husband did know. That,' she added, 'may teach you to realize the kind of friends you might have had.'

'I do realize it.'

'I have just remembered something that has puzzled me for many years; puzzled and annoyed me, because I am a martyr to curiosity. This is what happened. My husband and I had come in from the theatre. He was having a quiet drink by the fire when he looked up and said: "Ethel, today I took five hundred pounds of your money and my money and I invested it in a reputation. I doubt very much if we will get it back. Do you mind?" "Not if you don't," I said. "Also," he said, "I want you to promise never to mention it again." "All right, damn it, I said. "If you insist." I could have strangled him. He was the most lovable and the most irritating man I have ever known.' She grinned at him. 'So it was you who caused me to grind my teeth in a frenzy of frustrated curiosity. You owe me something!'

'I owe you a great deal,' he said seriously. 'Perhaps we should have a drink.'

'Very well, if you insist I'll have a beer.'

'A beer.' Already he had seen himself presiding at the cocktail cabinet. 'Are you sure you won't have something else? I have a rather interesting recipe of my own.'

'I'll still have a beer,' she said.

He gave up, and went to fetch her beer, and a gin and French for himself. He had quite recovered his poise again. He had passed through another cloud and was now sailing serenely in his own blue heaven. Soon she knew he would be thinking how skilful he was to have won the club sweep.

He settled himself comfortably with his drink and, after a pause, he said: 'You know, Mrs. Truman, the only regret I will have when all this is over is that I was not able to fling Manetti's offensive insinuations back in his face. The essence of the man was that he was no gentleman.'

That may have been his essence,' Etheldra said, 'but I should say it's his remains you have to worry about. Did he go on blackmailing you while he was alive?'

'For money? No, I don't think he thought I was worth it. But he never let me get away from his influence. He always implied that some day he might need me. When I came here to this quiet place I thought I might have given him the slip, but a few days after I arrived he called and was very friendly, but of course he let me see that it was foolish to try to hide from him in a little place like Europe. One thing he insisted on my doing for him was to supply him with details about the English visitors to the resorts along the coast.'

Etheldra sniffed. 'I shouldn't have thought you'd be much use to him there, considering that you hadn't been in England for over twenty years.'

'You are wrong,' he said. 'I have not visited the country, but I have not lost touch with it. Ever since I went into exile I have subscribed to English newspapers and followed the activities of the more important families. I have learned to recognize them from their pictures in the illustrated papers, I can remember their marriages, deaths, the scandals associated with them. I know who has inherited their money. I know as much about them as if they were my own relatives. They have become so much a part of my life that I feel I know them personally.' He added: 'I must say that since Eve began her newspaper work my knowledge has been a great help to her.'

'I'm sure it has. I wonder how much of a help it was to Manetti?'

'I did not inquire. I preferred not to.'

Etheldra said dryly: 'I'm sure you did.'

'Quite regularly he would ring up and ask me for a note on some person, or on a married couple. He sat here brooding over this coast like a spider. He grew rich and fat on the frailty of others. Even the numbers I recorded at the roulette tables interested him.'

'Numbers?'

He said like a connoisseur speaking of his art collection: 'I think I have the finest record in existence.'

'Do you mean to tell me that as the numbers come up at the roulette tables you make a note of them?'

'With the help of several loyal friends, yes.'

'Well, I'm damned,' said Etheldra. 'How long does it take that little hobby to drive you mad?'

'I assure you it's most interesting.'

'Well, I suppose if it interested this Manetti person there must be something in what you say. Did he have a collection too?'

'No, he would look over the figures and if they didn't interest him he would toss them aside. I was expected to draw his attention to anything unusual.'

'But what could be unusual?'

'Well, perhaps a certain croupier at a certain time might throw numbers in a certain sequence.'

'Could that happen?'

'I have known it to. That would interest him, of course.'

'I suppose it would interest any gambler, but I can't see why anyone should murder him on that account.'

'You haven't told me yet,' she said presently, 'how your daughter came to be involved.'

He passed a hand across his eyes.

'I find that more difficult to look back on than anything else. I have never told Eve anything about my past. Till three days ago she has never mentioned it. But perhaps she guessed there was something. Silence itself can be revealing, I suppose. She used to ask when she was a little girl why we never visited England, and I tried to give her the impression that without her mother the familiar scenes would be too painful to me. They would have been painful, but I am not so selfish that

I would have let my own feelings keep her from visiting her native country. Yes, I think she guessed there was something.

'I suppose later her own surmises were strengthened by hints from Manetti. He persuaded her to become a sort of social secretary. Eve is a popular girl and she knows most of the people who constitute our society down here. For that reason Manetti thought she would be of use to him. I did warn Eve against him, but she was quite sure that she was able to look after herself. Girls are, you know.'

Etheldra ignored this piece of homespun philosophy.

'And you both found out that she was not able to take care of herself, is that it?'

He looked shocked, and a little afraid. 'No, certainly not. I had warned Leonardo Manetti.'

'Warned him?'

'I told him that if anything happened to Eve, I would kill him.'

She looked at him thoughtfully and nodded. 'And, of course, he was quite unmoved.'

'He laughed as if I'd said something funny. Then he asked what on earth I thought would happen to her. I was too upset to answer him. But I meant it.'

She nodded again and stood up. 'You will have to curb that little habit of yours of acting first and thinking afterwards.'

He said slowly: 'I have been thinking of killing Leonardo Manetti for twenty years.'

Courtly as ever he walked with her down the steps to the villa garden gate.

Some day soon,' he said, 'I hope you will come and meet my daughter. It will be pleasant for her to know that I had some friends in my past.' Then he added as if the memory surprised him, 'I used to think you were very beautiful.'

Etheldra looked startled. She managed to stammer:

'Oh, rot,' and left. But she strode down the hill chiding herself for feeling so pleased.

CHAPTER 9

WHEN Etheldra Truman came on to the casino terrace, she came face to face with Jean Baretti. The little man started back, recovered sufficiently to bow and then he scuttled away. If M. Tolworth chose to have such aunts he must deal with them himself. She had been about to inquire about her nephew, so she watched his retreat in some astonishment. The man, she decided, looked positively guilty.

Anthony was not in sight but the eyes of Roger Bassett and John Carpenter were fixed on her over the parapet.

'Please can we have an ice-cream with you, Mrs. Truman?'

"You are always eating ice-cream, you little gluttons. All right, come up here.' She sat at a table and they took the two vacant chairs, sitting on their hands and wriggling.

'A man came for your nephew,' Bassett said.

'Yes, a policeman,' added Carpenter.

'With a long thin neck,' said Bassett.

'A policeman with a long thin neck came for my nephew. Bosh.' She put more emphasis on the word 'bosh' than her state of mind justified.

'Oh, yes, he did . . . shall I call the waiter for the two large chocolate ice-creams now, Mrs. Truman?'

'You will tell me about this policeman. What did he do with my nephew?'

'Nothing, because your nephew said he didn't take her.'

'Didn't take her?'

Carpenter was watching the passing waiters with hungry self-restraint. 'Two large chocolate ice-creams,' he muttered, and added experimentally: 'With strawberry sauce.'

'Madame?' A waiter was at their table at last.

'Two large policemen with strawberry sauce,' she said, and when they all looked startled she snapped: 'All right, do you or don't you want strawberry sauce?'

The waiter was not a great English scholar, but he was pretty sure there were no policemen on the menu.

'Policemen, madame?'

Bassett and Carpenter plunged their heads under the table. They knew by experience that it was indiscreet to giggle in front of Mrs. Truman, so they were compromising by giggling under the table.

'Did I say policemen?'

'Yes, madame.'

'All right, make it two large chocolate ice-creams and the same sauce as for the policemen. Damn it,' she added, 'I'm getting flustered.'

She looked at the two quivering little backs opposite. 'Very well, you two. You can continue your hysteria in the perpendicular.'

They reappeared, red in the face, nervous and by no means under control.

'You may laugh,' she said, 'for one minute precisely. That to my mind is doing ample justice to the joke.' She looked at her watch.

They were reduced to solemn attention in half the time. 'Now about the policeman.'

'Your nephew said he didn't take the girl away and the policeman said somebody did.'

Bassett chanted: 'Whom shall we have to take her away, take her away, take her away.'

And Carpenter added: 'We'll have the silly old policeman to take her away, take her away, take her away. We'll have the silly old policeman to take her away, on a cold and frosty morning.'

They stopped abruptly as the ice-cream was placed on the table in front of them. They forgot the policeman, Mrs. Truman, her nephew and the girl and stared at the delectable horror on their plates.

They were well-trained little boys. They did not put more on their spoons than they could get into their mouths, they did not slobber or make noises. They merely ate as fast as they could and their flashing spoons moved almost in perfect time. They took approximately four spoonfuls to each breath, which for little boys eating something they like is fairly normal.

Etheldra watched and waited till they had finished.

'Now,' she said, 'where is this nephew of mine?'

'He was on the beach,' Bassett said.

And Carpenter added: 'With a girl.'

'Hah. I think if you've finished ruining your digestion with that mess that was on your plates you might go and look for them.'

'Oh yes, Mrs. Truman.' They shot down the steps on to the sand and disappeared.

Etheldra followed them more slowly and presently she heard them shouting on the outskirts of the little *plage* that belonged to the Hotel du Monde.

'Here they are, Mrs. Truman. Here they are, Mrs. Truman.' She began to wish that they could do their work a little less dramatically.

It was a little time before Anthony realized that he was the object of all this commotion. He turned over lazily on his back and saw the two little boys pointing to him dramatically and shouting to his aunt, whose flowered robe was by now a distinctive feature of the beach.

She came within ten feet of the group and Roger said loudly, as if he had located a couple of whales: 'There they are.'

The girl lying beside Anthony sat up rather suddenly. She did not mind being identified in this dramatic fashion, but she was beginning to wonder what she had done wrong.

Anthony climbed to his feet. 'You've found me,' he said, 'what happens now, does someone else go and hide?'

'Don't be ridiculous, Anthony. I think the boys behaved most efficiently. I think ice-cream must sharpen their brains.'

'Avril,' Anthony said, 'may I introduce my aunt, Mrs, Truman?'

Avril scrambled to her feet and wriggled her tiny garments into place. 'Hello,' she said. 'How nice to meet you.' She thrust out a firm brown hand. 'Anthony has told me about you.'

'He regards me as a sort of ancient monument,' Etheldra said. 'A nice boy but unstable, like his father.'

'Aren't you swimming, Mrs. Truman?'

'Oh, dear no,' Etheldra said. 'I have to swim very early in the morning, so that I can spend the rest of the day running hither and thither doing errands for Anthony.' She looked speculatively at Avril. 'Are you the missing girl by any chance?'

Avril laughed. 'No, there's nothing remarkable like that about me. I just came here for a swim and met up with Anthony. Won't you sit down?'

Etheldra lowered herself to a sunbathing mat and tucked her gown neatly round her ankles. 'I must say it's more agreeable than toiling for Anthony.'

'You wouldn't miss it for the world,' he said. 'How did you get along, by the way?'

'We had a glass of beer and a chat. He is not the slightest bit anxious about his daughter . . . for the moment that is. It seems he trusts you. He prides himself on being a good judge of character. His experiences, I may tell you, have not borne out this view. The police, of course, have been to call on him. He thinks that he disposed of them with dignity and despatch.'

Avril said: 'I know you are speaking of Eve and her father. I've met him, and really, he's sweet. Oh, why can't the police leave them alone and find the real murderer?'

Etheldra looked at her shrewdly. 'Have you any idea where they should look?'

Avril Pares sat up. 'He was so detestable. I would feel it was treachery to help to find his murderer.'

Anthony said thoughtfully: 'I can understand how you feel, Avril, but you see we cannot have someone who did not murder him punished.'

'We all have our different loyalties, Tony.'

'You knew him in Althenia, didn't you?'

'He tried to know me because I was close to the Royal Household.'

'Rudolph said that anyone of his household would cheerfully murder him. That would include Rudolph himself.'

Avril laughed shortly. 'Rudolph's idea of getting rid of people like him is to string them up to the nearest lamp-post.'

'Avril,' Anthony said, 'would you mind very much telling me what Manetti actually did to the Royal Family?'

'It was quite enough,' she said shortly. She picked up a handful of sand and let it trickle through her fingers. 'They are so damned unforgiving, Tony.'

'Well,' Etheldra said abruptly, 'somebody killed the wretched man. Furthermore, I'm sure that the police are going to see that someone is going to answer for it. They would prefer a crime of passion to something that involved them in a web of complicated international politics. Anthony, what sort of girl is this Eve of yours?'

'She is not mine.' He said it so quickly that his aunt gave a snort of laughter. Avril had been about to gather up another handful of sand. Her fingers remained buried.

Anthony said slowly: 'I think you'd better meet her.'

'Where is she?'

'Don't ask questions.' He smiled at her affectionately. 'I think you'd better put on that startling nineteen nineteen dinner-gown of yours, or have you had it modernized again since then?'

'I have an excellent sewing woman, Anthony, and anyone who discards the genuine materials of thirty years ago for the poor imitations of this day would be simply a fool.'

He laughed, and Avril's small features dimpled with amusement. 'Very well, aunt dear, put on the worthy model and I'll pick you up at seven o'clock.' He turned to the girl. 'You'll come too, won't you, Avril?'

'Sure you want me to?'

'Quite sure.'

'Then, of course.' She uncoiled herself luxuriously back on to her mat. 'This is nice,' she said. 'It's uncomplicated.'

Anthony looked down at her, half smiling, half serious. 'That's what you think,' he said.

Etheldra struggled to her feet assisted by a last heave from Anthony. 'I think if you don't mind,' she said, 'I'll pop home and try on that frock of mine. I wore it at a teachers' conference two years ago, and I may have put on weight.'

'You have,' Anthony said and laughed. 'Have you got a piece of matching material to let into it?'

'Naturally,' Etheldra said, and marched off. The two little boys manœuvred about her like a couple of tug-boats. In fact, although she didn't know it they were pretending that she was the liner *Queen Elizabeth*.

Lady Anne Meaker walked sedately down through the Place du Casino from her little villa up on the hill above. It was four o'clock and the regular inhabitants of Monte Carlo were emerging from the lunch-time siesta. She knew many of them. Richard Weldon crossed her path on his way to tea at the Hotel de Paris. They had met at this point regularly for years. He raised his panama hat and walked on, tall, slender and stiffly graceful, his eyeglass swinging slightly outside his carefully-tailored grey suit.

'Heavens!' she thought suddenly. 'How old he's getting.' Her thoughts flew back to the time when he was such a menace in the stately homes of England. So dashing and so very careless . . . that awful affair with Diana Fenchurch . . . Good gracious, she must be sixty now.

She paused in the shadow of the Sporting Club to admire the flowers in the garden opposite. They were very nice, of course, but not so nice as at other times. Summer-time, in her view, was not a Monte Carlo season, however much nowadays they tried to pretend it was. Of course there were swarms of those odd people who went about more or less naked and swam.

Lady Meaker herself was far from naked. She wore a toque, more or less covered with a black veil, a dark coat and skirt with a scrap of tulle tied in a bow round her neck. She wore black shoes and her grey lisle stockings were just slightly wrinkled at the ankles. She was perfectly comfortable and quite unselfconscious.

'Hello, Lady Meaker.' She had been so absorbed in her thoughts that it took her a second to realize that the young man smiling at her from the highly-polished motor car was young Anthony Tolworth.

'Well, young man, what are you doing here?'

He jumped from the car. 'I was waiting for you.'

'Stuff and nonsense, nobody has waited for me for thirty years. And even then they showed no great endurance.' She looked at him shrewdly. 'You must want something.'

'As a matter of fact, I do.'

'Broke, I suppose.'

'Really, Lady Meaker!'

'Why not? Below the age of thirty you are merely broke. Beyond that age, you are poor, which is a different matter entirely. Well . . .'

'Are you awfully busy?'

'Of course, I'm busy. I'm going to the kitchen.'

He grinned. 'Gambling again, eh?'

'Certainly, I've been staring at the roulette wheel on my own particular table in the Casino for so long that I think it misses me when I'm not there.'

'Then I mustn't keep you from your friend.'

'What alternative do you suggest?'

'I thought you might have tea with me.'

'Hmm: well, at least you won't beguile me with an account of your ailments, which is generally my fate when I'm invited to tea. You aren't ill, are you?' she added suspiciously.

'Desperately, but I don't talk about it.'

'Very well, where do we go?'

'What about the Golf Club, it's a nice drive up.'

She looked at him in horror. 'Anthony, when I was a girl I rode up there on a mule with a young man in the Horse Guards. It ended a very promising friendship.' She sighed quite prettily. 'However, I am quite prepared to walk across the road.'

So they walked across the road and sat under a faded umbrella in the garden of the Café de Paris.

Anthony found himself wondering if the story of the ride on the mule was a fiction or was it that Lady Meaker was so tied to this minute corner of the world that she would not take even a drive of a few minutes. To the real habitués of Monte Carlo there is no other place, not even if it is just around the corner. It is a village, a tenement, a favourite public house. It is a shell which encloses and protects its denizens from the realities of the world outside.

Lady Meaker chatted idly and aimlessly about her little world, equally of events that took place yesterday and those of twenty years ago. There was no sense of time. Time was without significance.

'Well,' she said at last. 'You are not displaying all this patience without a reason, Anthony. How do I earn my tea?'

He said: 'I've got myself into a mess.'

'Naturally, I know that from your determinedly social behaviour. What form does it take?'

'A girl.'

'Then why come to me? I've almost forgotten what one is like. Do you love her or something, or do you want to get rid of her?'

'It's more complicated.' he said.

'There is nothing more complicated, that is, if those involved are to be believed. Why on earth they don't confine themselves to drink, or gambling, I can't imagine. I think,' she added, 'we might do better if you began at the beginning.'

'It primarily concerns Eve Raymond,' he said.

She nodded. 'Oh yes, I know her, she is a very charming girl. It was distressing for all of us to see her associating with that really dreadful man Manetti. I can't understand why she did it. Of course girls nowadays form strange attachments.'

'I don't know what caused this one,' he said, 'but there was no love involved in it—on Eve's side certainly.'

'And then, of course, they quarrelled.'

He looked at her quickly. 'How did you know that?'

'My dear boy, we old ladies feed on the affairs of this little community. They are our life. Between us we miss very little indeed. Of course, we knew they had quarrelled. As a matter of fact, Anthony, they were sitting at that table over there.' She pointed to one a few feet away. 'Odette Esme was sitting next to them. I know she exaggerated, but she said the poor child was terribly upset. She jumped up from the table and ran away. She was crying.'

Anthony said slowly: 'It makes me sorry that I didn't kill him myself.' The quality of his voice made the old lady look at him in shocked surprise.

'Anthony!'

'I'm so sorry. One mustn't be so ill-mannered as to be natural.' His slow smile took the sting out of his words. Then after a pause he added: 'I'm not being just inquisitive, but I wonder if you could tell me what they quarrelled about?'

'Odette was not listening, but suddenly the girl cried out: "How dare you! How dare you say my father is a criminal?"; the child was trembling so that she could not control her voice. She jumped up and said: "I will kill you, I will kill you!"' She stopped horrified at what she had said and added quickly: 'Of course the poor girl was so deeply hurt that she could not have known what she was saying.'

Anthony said bitterly: 'And when he was killed somebody, of course, ran along to the police to tell them what they had heard.'

'Tony dear, you must not expect people to think as you do about this. Of course there are lots of people who would tell the police. You see it would be important information, wouldn't it? And therefore it would make the person who brought it feel important too.'

'I expect so, but I wish to God people would mind their own business.'

She gave a little sigh. 'I suppose I must be included in that rebuke, Anthony. But there is so little else in our lives, you know.'

He reached over and patted her hand. 'Why, of course, I was not thinking of you. You're the most harmless little gossip in the world.'

But she could not let herself off as lightly as that. 'Not quite harmless, I'm afraid. It's so terribly tempting to pass on the story of something you heard or saw.'

'Well, I wish we could find someone who saw the murder of Leonardo Manetti.'

She looked across at him speculatively. 'Do you?'

He replied abruptly: 'Of course, I do. Why shouldn't I?'

'Heaven knows, my dear boy. For my own part I have no wish to be told who murdered that dreadful man. If nobody is arrested within a month the whole business will be dead and forgotten.'

'I wish I could believe you.'

'I really don't think you should worry so much. I think that if the police thought anything of those silly words of Eve's they would have done something before now.'

'They are trying to; but you see they can't find her. In fact, she escaped.'

Lady Meaker said quite tartly: 'Why was I not told of this?' He grinned. 'Because, dear lady, none of your gossiping old cronies have got round to hearing about it. The police are not telling because it must make them feel a bit silly. Their only trouble is that they can't think how.'

'And did you?'

He shook his head and grinned. 'That would be telling, wouldn't it?'

She looked at him reproachfully. 'I think this is most reprehensible of you, Anthony. I give you my time when I might be much more profitably employed, I tell you everything, and you refuse to answer the most innocent little question.'

'It is not an innocent little question, Lady Meaker, because a few well-chosen words might land me in an innocent little gaol.'

'Of course I do understand, Anthony.' And she added spontaneously: 'But it's so maddening not to know.'

'But I can tell you that Eve is quite safe,' he said.

She nodded sentimentally. 'Take care of her, dear, she is a sweet girl!'

He wouldn't have applied the word 'sweet' to Eve, but that was a personal opinion.

'You knew her father, didn't you, Lady Meaker?'

'Yes, a charming man, but of course quite incapable of taking care of himself.' She added seriously: 'He really should have gone into the Church. The women would have vied with each other in spoiling him. But I must say he was most conscientious about his work.'

'His work?'

'Of course it was not productive work. He was studying the psychology of the gambler and, I understand, writing a book on the subject.'

'Oh, yes, of course. Well that, at least, was harmless enough.' She looked at him reflectively. 'You know, Anthony, if you dig deep enough into any matter it is possible to make astonishing and alarming discoveries.'

He laughed. 'They would have to be astonishing and alarming and also they would have to involve Leonardo Manetti.'

'Leonardo Manetti was certainly interested in his numbers, Anthony.'

He looked puzzled. 'Numbers?'

'Yes, didn't you know? A lot of us used to keep a record of the numbers as they turned up at roulette. Eve's father made himself a sort of headquarters for us. We were all trying to find out if there is such a thing as a numerical cycle.'

He grinned. 'And is there?'

She sighed and said quite seriously: 'I'm afraid if there were it would spoil all the fun. Somebody clever would spot it long before I did and then of course all the Casinos would be bankrupt and I would be completely at a loss. I was pleased to think that Eve's father was much too helpless ever to have brought about a situation like that.'

'But not Leonardo.'

'He, thank goodness, is dead.' She gathered up her black lace gloves and sensible handbag. 'And now I suppose I must go to the Casino.' She added accusingly: 'I am quite sure that I shan't win today, you have disturbed my concentration.'

'Does that matter?'

'Certainly.'

He smiled. 'I shouldn't have thought it mattered what you did at roulette, the chances are the same.'

She looked at him pityingly. 'My poor boy, my poor boy, you must concentrate, as, of course, in everything else, you must concentrate.' She tapped his wrist with a long, thin, slightly withering finger. 'It is utter folly to play roulette unless you can give every bit of your mind to it.'

He smiled. 'Sort of mind over matter idea.'

'Yes, that's it exactly. You must concentrate on the numbers and positively *will* them to come up.'

They stood up and he thanked her for the help she had given him, but she replied absently. Lady Meaker was already composing herself for her afternoon wrestle with fate.

'I'm afraid there was very little I could tell you. Perhaps I should have mentioned that odd business about six at Beaumont.'

He was puzzled. 'Six at Beaumont?'

'Yes, dear, at the Casino. Of course it was much too far away to interest me.' She was looking through her bag, checking her roulette card, her pencil, her purse and her handkerchief. 'Much too far. Eve's father could tell you all about it, no doubt.' She held out her hand and then disappeared through the door, and he guessed that she had dismissed him from her mind.

She hadn't been able to help him very much, but then he had not very much idea of how he wanted to be helped.

He found Picoy leaning against the side of the car smoking one of his drooping, untidy cigarettes.

'Hello,' Anthony said, 'still following me about?'

'I heard you were in Monte Carlo.' He raised his unfriendly eyes. 'Lady Meaker is a friend of Miss Raymond.'

'I'm sure she is.'

'So you are keeping each other informed.'

'I say, you know,' Anthony said mildly, 'I've known Lady Meaker ever since I was a kid. I remember causing a sensation by asking her if she was as old as Noah.'

'Very interesting.'

'Well, you will insist on talking to me, I must say something.'

'It might be worth searching Lady Meaker's villa.'

'Oh, indeed it might. There is a picture of me there in an Eton jacket. It might interest you as an example of English Boys' Wear.'

'I might find other things.'

Anthony laughed. 'Oh yes, you'd probably find Lady Meaker ringing up her Ambassador in Paris. These old ladies have very sturdy ideas of their rights.'

'There are some people along this coast who are far too arrogant.'

'Of course there are. But you see they made the place and you know it and they know it. Personally I am all for modesty.'

The hooded eyes swept over the luxurious car.

'You seem to have ways of making it pay, Mr. Tolworth. Royal immunity can be turned to good account, it seems.'

Anthony protested amiably. 'It's no use grumbling at me about it, old chap. I didn't make your laws.'

'Just the same it might be interesting to see what you really have got on that royal yacht of yours.'

'It isn't mine, you know.'

'No, but I understand that you have a great deal to do with the organisation.'

'I do my best.'

'It would be quite easy for you to take a passenger aboard.'

'Of course. We have a group of passengers aboard now. Interesting people if you like politicians. We picked this lot up off the coast of Yugoslavia. They didn't like the Government so the Government had sentenced them to death. They hated that and so we popped over and picked them up.'

Picoy sneered. 'Very romantic.'

Anthony smiled. 'No, no; it was very profitable. They brought a proportion of the state coffers away with them. They have learned by experience that there is no exiled patriot so unsung as a poor one. As a matter of fact, Picoy, you might be able to help me. I am wondering what would be the best way of going about getting small change for a few bars of gold.'

'So you are sheltering thieves.'

'Nothing of the sort; they have salvaged what they could from the Usurpers. Anyway that's their story and they are sticking to it.'

'It does show that you have some skill at smuggling passengers on to the royal yacht. Miss Raymond, for instance.'

'Ah, we're back to Miss Raymond.'

'Yes, Mr. Tolworth, we are back to Miss Raymond.'

'Very well,' Anthony said. 'Let's put it another way. Would you be prepared to tell your chief, whoever he is, that you took every possible precaution to prevent me from smuggling Miss Raymond on to the yacht?'

'I had you under observation. I am not a fool.'

Anthony said seriously: 'That is the last thing I would call you. Naturally, you kept an eye on me, I was the logical accomplice.'

'You admit that?'

'Of course I do. But unless you are the fool I don't think you are, you were watching the yacht also. In fact I know you were.'

'The nights are dark.'

'Not particularly.'

'I think you know where she is.'

Anthony laughed again softly. 'I know you do, but if you were sure I would be under arrest.'

The turtle-lidded eyes had been probing the interior of Anthony's car. Suddenly a long eager arm was thrust through the window.

'That is funny.'

Anthony looked over his shoulder. 'Yes, it's funny what the girls wear nowadays. That is supposed to be an earring.'

'It belongs to Miss Raymond.'

'I shouldn't be surprised.' It was an ornate thing of plastic. Chanel had been making a feature of them. 'Ridiculous pieces of nonsense, aren't they?'

'Quite unusual.'

'Is it?'

Picoy tossed the trinket up and caught it with eager satisfaction. 'I have reason to believe that Miss Raymond dropped that in the corridor of the Judiciaire the other night. A janitor picked it up and handed it back to her.'

'That was very polite of him.'

'If it was the same one it would prove that you were with Miss Raymond after she escaped.'

Anthony smiled. 'But if it were the other one of the pair it wouldn't prove anything, would it?'

'You think Miss Raymond has the other one of the pair?'

'Presumably, if your janitor gave it back to her.'

'When she walked on she was carrying it in her hand. It would be quite natural for her to lean forward in the car and drop it in the pocket where I found it.'

'Oh, quite natural . . . if I had picked her up in the car. It would be equally normal for her to do the same thing on the way from Beaumont to Nice.' His smile widened. 'You know I'd give up worrying about the wretched trinket if I were you. You can go to your superiors and say: "I can't find Miss Raymond, but the janitor found an ear-ring in the Judiciaire." They might even suspend you and call in the janitor.'

Picoy's yellowing features took on an angry flush.

'You might tell Miss Raymond that the next move I am contemplating in this business is to place you under arrest.'

'The theory being that the moment she heard of that dire threat she would surrender herself to Justice and to Picoy?' He shook his head. 'We would both be in an awful mess if she didn't . . . galling for you and most unflattering for me. Then, of course, there is this assumption of yours that I know where Miss Raymond is.'

'I am satisfied that you know.'

'That is guessing, Picoy. Why don't you advertise in the newspapers?'

'I advise you to tell Miss Raymond what I said.'

'No, it would be too ungallant . . . Anthony Tolworth, the man who permitted a lady to take his place in gaol. Think of the sneers, the scorn.' He laughed. 'If you try me much further, Picoy, I'll confess to the damned murder myself.'

'The threat may not sound so funny to you during the next few days, Monsieur.'

Anthony slipped in behind the driving wheel of the car. 'I'm sure it won't. None of my jokes stand the test of time. Anyway the murder may be solved by then.'

The police official put his hands on the window. 'Perhaps you have some ideas, Mr. Tolworth?'

'My brain is teeming. I am thinking of the word six.'
'Six?' The cold eyes looked at Anthony suspiciously.
'That's it . . . six.'
'Six what?'
Anthony smiled at him and gently let in the clutch.
'Perhaps, M. Picoy, if we knew that we would know all.'

As he drove away he looked in the mirror and saw Picoy looking after him. He twisted the car up on to the Grand Corniche, the lovely clean road on the mountain tops.

CHAPTER 10

ETHELDRA MARTHA TRUMAN gritted her teeth and hauled her evening gown over her corsets. Then in the mirror she made a careful inspection of the seams. They seemed to be standing up to the strain quite well. She thought gratefully of Millie Westbrook, the determined little needlewoman at home. She took her powder puff and struck herself viciously several times on the nose with it. Then she took her ermine wrap and her handbag and went down to meet Anthony. The average age of all her garments was at least twelve years and yet somehow she looked singularly well-dressed.

'Well,' she said, 'Have you finished gallivanting after those young women of yours?'

'The one I saw this afternoon was not exactly young. Lady Meaker; do you remember her?'

'Anne Meaker? Very well. Her husband was killed in the war before the last,' she sighed. 'We have come to reckon women's ages by the war in which they lost their husbands. It's very bitter, isn't it? Anne Meaker was very quiet and very brave about it. Then she went away to grow old by herself.'

'She seems happy enough.'

'Perhaps she is. One learns not to expect too much.' She shook her head. 'And, of course, when you have learned that, it means that you are old.'

'I see. I must remember always to expect too much.'

She snorted. 'From the way you behave I doubt if you'll ever grow up. What did you suppose Anne Meaker could tell you about this affair?'

'I didn't know. But she does know a lot of the people involved; Eve and her father, and even Manetti, so I understand.'

'Did she tell you anything you didn't know before?'

'Not a lot. Manetti seemed to have had some sort of hold over Eve's father.'

'I could have told you that myself, but you were so bemused by that girl Avril that I doubt if you'd have heard me.'

'Of course, you went to see him, didn't you?'

She scoffed. 'Oh yes, I went to see him. I climbed that damned hill with the sweat pouring from me like summer rain.'

He laughed at her. 'You poor old thing. It's your weight, of course. But I'd no idea you were going to discuss the murder with Mr. Raymond. The reason for your mountaineering was to let him know that his daughter was safe.'

She looked at him coldly. 'The man was not in the least concerned about his daughter, as you very well knew. You had told him yourself. What you wanted me to do was to pump him.'

'Pump him! Aunt Etheldra, you pain me.'

She ignored that and sat thinking over her visit.

'You would think, wouldn't you, that a man who had been carrying a load of guilt for more than twenty years would show it.'

'I expect so, yes.'

'He looks younger than he would have done if he had stayed on with his nose in the ledgers of that bank he worked for. It did not suit him.'

'Do you suggest his guilty conscience did?'

'He has not judged himself too harshly, you know, Anthony.'

'That's a bit unkind, isn't it?'

'Not at all. He just isn't capable of it. Francis Raymond is a kind, gentle man. He couldn't deal harshly even with himself. By now the whole thing would very likely have faded from his memory. The trouble was that although his own memory was prepared to be weak, Leonardo Manetti's was very good indeed.

'So Manetti had some sort of hold over him.'

'Very much so.'

'Poor devil.'

'Considering the fantastic mess he got himself into I think he hasn't had much cause to complain. Fortunately for him Manetti seems to have regarded him more or less as a waste of time. It would be a blow to his self-esteem to think so, but I think it's true. That was the situation till just recently. Then there was a change, a crisis in fact.'

'Still if he's just a mild chap, there doesn't seem much that he could have done.'

'I may have given you the impression that he was a wastrel, Tony. That would be wrong. Francis Raymond sees himself as a man of honour. The first crime he committed was part of his attempt to save the woman he loved.' She thought a while and added slowly: 'I doubt if he would consider it a crime to defend the honour of the only other woman in his life.'

Anthony was silent. He was aware of an empty feeling in the pit of his stomach. He knew Eve's father only slightly, he had been half amused at the old-fashioned courtliness with which he treated Eve. He also knew that nothing mattered in Francis Raymond's life but his daughter. She was his world and his life. Perhaps Aunt Ethel had put into words what Eve was afraid to mention.

He heard himself saying his thoughts out loud.

'Lady Meaker said, and I think you said too, that the best thing to do would be to do nothing. You may know what you are looking for, but you can't be nearly so sure what you'll find.'

She interrupted abruptly: 'No use, Anthony; you've started something. You've got to finish it, no matter how much you dislike the mess you've got yourself into.'

'As usual, of course, you're right.' He looked at his watch.

'I think we might be moving. They'll be expecting us.'

'Who are they?'

'Ticker and his mother. We're dining on the yacht.'

'Has he a mother? I'm glad there is somebody responsible on that boat of yours, Anthony.'

He grinned at her ironically. 'If everyone old had a sense of responsibility what a wonderful world it would be.'

She looked shocked. 'She isn't one of those flighty queens, is she?'

This time he really laughed. 'No, I wouldn't describe Queen Charlotte as a flighty queen.'

He waited till the launch was well clear of the jetty and then he said: 'Eve is on board, as well you know.'

'I didn't know, but if you'd asked me to guess I'd have said she was there.'

He laughed. 'If you asked him that would be Picoy's guess too . . . only he can't see how it was possible for her to get there.'

'Are they watching the yacht?'

'Like hawks. There is a rowing boat on each side of the yacht . . . fishing, of course. There was that other chap we passed on the jetty. He was fishing too. I should warn you by the way that he speaks English perfectly. So any idle chatter you indulge in on the way back had better be about the weather.'

Aunt Etheldra sniffed. 'He probably thinks I'm the young woman in disguise.'

Anthony looked at her speculatively. 'No, no, I don't think so. You couldn't look like that and not be natural.'

She nodded resignedly. 'Grim thought, isn't it?'

'Not at all. I find you the best possible type of aunt.' He stood up. 'Here we are.'

The launch slid in alongside the hull of the yacht and his aunt heaved herself unsteadily on to the gangway.

Lights switched on above their heads. Two smart sailors waited to hand Etheldra aboard, which they did with stiff solicitude, and then sprang back to attention. Rudolph himself was waiting with gracious charm to receive her.

'Welcome to Our Realm, Mrs. Truman,' and added boyishly: 'Or rather what's left of it.'

'Hello, Rudolph. You have grown quite good-looking.'

Anthony glanced at the two sailors. They were standing stiffly and their faces were if anything more expressionless than before.

Rudolph was pleased. 'Have I? Do you really mean it?'

He flicked his fingers and the sailors moved smartly away.

'Of course, I mean it. For one thing those wretched pimples have gone. And I'm very glad to see that associating with Anthony has not spoiled your manners.'

'He does his best. You must come and meet my mother. She is waiting in the forward lounge. Tony, come along.' He gave his arm to Etheldra and they went forward.

Queen Charlotte was sitting in her favourite high-backed chair knitting. Count Otto had a lower chair at her side. He was reading aloud from the *Daily Telegraph*. He dropped the paper and sprang to his feet, which to Etheldra's surprise seemed to make him no taller than when he had been seated. But he exuded respectful dignity.

'Mother, may I present Mrs. Truman? She is Anthony's aunt, you know.'

'How nice. Do come and join us.'

Aunt Etheldra steadied herself for a curtsey, achieved it, shook hands with the Queen and looked round grimly to see if Anthony was laughing at her. He was not . . . quite.

'I do hope you won't find it a little too close in here,' the Queen said. 'But you see now that we have Eve with us His Majesty says we must have the blinds drawn. The police are watching us.'

'The effrontery of them,' Count Otto exclaimed. 'Your Majesty, shall I officially protest?'

'No,' said Rudolph.

'It's not too bad,' Etheldra said. 'Anyway I always did like the curtains drawn at night.'

'Oh, but so did we at home,' the Queen said. 'But that, of course, was to prevent tiresome people from shooting at us.'

'Anarchists, of course,' said Otto diplomatically. 'And not our own happy people.'

Rudolph laughed. 'Count Shavia, Mrs. Truman, has dedicated his life to the whitewashing of the Royal House of Badenburg.'

'He must be a busy man.' She added hastily: 'I mean it must be a big house for one man to maintain.'

'Oh, he's busy all right.'

It was at this point that Eve joined them. Anthony thought she looked pale and tired. He introduced her to his aunt.

'I've seen your picture in Anthony's flat,' she said and smiled. 'I prefer the original.'

'That's very kind. I've got a feeling that the next picture will be taken by the police. I don't suppose that will be very good either.'

'You seem to forget, my dear,' the Queen said, 'that we have given you our protection.'

Eve gave a little laugh. 'I am so sorry, Your Majesty, you see I can't get used to the idea.'

'You must,' the Queen said practically, or at least it seemed so to her. She turned to the King. 'I must say, dear, that it does seem unreasonable that the child should appear only at night, Surely . . .'

Rudolph interrupted: 'It's a little more complicated than you think, mother. It's simpler not to be seen.'

Eve said: 'I don't in the least mind going into hiding in the daytime. Anyway the crew have made me a nice little sunbathing shelter on the bridge. It's terribly private and rather fun.'

To Anthony's annoyance Rudolph added: 'Yes, we were up there most of the afternoon.'

'I thought,' he said, 'that you'd be occupied on the garage deck.'

Rudolph laughed pleasantly. 'I was occupied on the bridge. This has been the happiest day of my life.'

The Queen nodded her satisfaction and turned to Mrs. Truman. 'I'm so glad. His Majesty has so few opportunities for enjoyment.'

Count Otto screwed up his monocle into his eye and oozed his satisfaction. He looked at the object of His Majesty's pleasure with as much satisfaction as if he had produced her himself. In fact, Anthony thought sourly, a good time was being had by everyone but himself. He looked at Eve. She was sitting quite demurely, with her hands crossed in her lap. But he thought he detected a nasty little self-satisfied smile in the corners of her lips. But when her eyes met his they were full of innocent inquiry.

'Did you have a nice day too, Anthony?'

'Marvellous,' he said. 'What with interviewing little boys and old ladies and clashing with the police, I have not had a dull moment.'

'The police, oh dear!'

'They suggested that if I didn't appeal to you to return to them, they would arrest me instead.'

'How amusing.'

'Yes, that's what I thought you'd think. The silly fools seemed to imagine that rather than let an innocent man suffer you would give yourself up.'

She looked at him quite seriously. 'And what did you say to that?'

'I laughed in a sneering sort of way that suggested that they didn't know their man, or woman.'

'Do you think they would arrest you, Tony?'

'I think friend Picoy would, except that he dislikes the idea of having me on his hands. He irritates me so much that at times I am tempted to confess to the wretched murder and force him to prove that I couldn't possibly have done it.'

'Anthony,' said Etheldra, 'You are talking like a fool.'

To everybody's surprise Count Otto rose to protest. He really did stand up to speak.

'I see nothing wrong in confessing to this murder. If my King will forgive me, I should say that a confession is overdue.'

Etheldra was quite startled. 'Overdue; but what would be the point in it?'

Otto looked at her almost with pity.

'The Royal House, madam, must not be persistently reminded of this ridiculous corpse.'

Rudolph nodded approval. 'There are more congenial topics certainly.'

Anthony said: 'If I confessed to the murder, Count, it would be solely from a desire to annoy and confuse. Ultimately no doubt the man or woman who did the job will be caught and punished.' He added grimly: 'At the moment they would prefer it to be Eve. Somehow or other we'll have to change their minds for them.'

'Yes,' Eve said, 'but how? Did you see my father, Tony?'

'I saw him,' Etheldra said. 'It was the first time for twenty years.'

'You knew him?' Eve's eyes widened.

'Yes,' Etheldra answered quite gently. 'I knew him, we were neighbours.'

'He never told me . . . he never spoke. I mean . . .' She stopped in confusion.

'My dear, it was all so long ago. Often enough you don't recall the past because you don't want to be reminded of it.'

Eve nodded and almost against her will said: 'Yes, but why? It's that . . .' again she stopped.

'Why? There could be a dozen good reasons. Your mother was very ill.'

'Yes, I remember when she died. I can just remember. We were very . . . very quiet, father and I. Or that's how it seemed to me, very quiet.' She raised her head and looked round the door as if she were surprised to find herself in the room. She added in quick apology, 'I'm so sorry.'

'Poor child.' The Queen's deep voice was husky with emotion, and she added: 'I always wanted a daughter.'

'Good heavens,' Anthony thought. 'She isn't being sorry for Eve, but herself.'

'But, mainly, I wanted to tell you,' Etheldra was saying to Eve, 'your father is perfectly all right.' She chuckled. 'Now that he has recovered from the shock of seeing me. It appears that when he saw me last I was quite good-looking. If that was so I bet I made him feel his age today.'

Eve looked at her gratefully. 'I'm glad you knew him. Did you talk about the past?'

'Of course we did. What else could we talk about? I believe he quite enjoyed it when he got used to the idea. Anyhow I'm sure he preferred me to the police.'

'The police?' Tension jerked her body erect again.

'Oh yes, the police called before I did. The visit apparently was not a success. Your father, it seems, didn't want to talk about the murder and the police did not want to talk about your father's hobby. So presumably they bored each other equally.'

'They came to ask about me, didn't they?' She seemed eager to be assured that this was so.

'I expect so. I think among other things they wanted to know where you were. I gather your father told them not to worry, that you were quite safe in excellent hands, and that he hadn't the slightest idea where.' They laughed as she added: 'I think they have gone away with the impression that your father is the most skilful liar.'

'It was good of him not to tell,' Rudolph said. 'Wise and courageous.' He turned to Eve. 'The sort of father I should expect you to have.'

Eve gave an unhappy little laugh. 'I'm afraid he doesn't know where I am.'

'Oh.' Rudolph was quite hurt. He felt somehow Eve's father had let him down.

'He's really rather helpless, I'm afraid,' Eve went on. 'If he knew he would try so hard not to tell, but he's not awfully good at hiding the truth.'

'All the more reason,' Anthony said reasonably, 'Why he shouldn't know it.'

Rudolph stood up. 'I heard the launch coming alongside. That will be Avril. Come along, let's go out on deck.'

Eve made a movement to go with him and turned back reluctantly. 'I'll wait here, shall I?'

'Of course not.'

'But I can't go on deck. I'd be seen.'

He laughed. 'I've got another surprise for you. We've screened off the boat deck. The only way anyone can see you there will be to grow wings and fly over. Take her up from the inside, Tony, while I go out to the gangway and fetch Avril.'

The Queen looked inquiringly at Mrs. Truman. 'Personally, I think it's far more comfortable here, don't you?'

'I do. I'm old-fashioned about the night air. I don't like it.' She paused to watch the others walk out.

'Handsome children, aren't they?' the Queen said with satisfaction. 'Our Kings have always been renowned for their good looks. Rudolph is the first one without a beard. It is a pity, because a golden beard is most striking. The people would almost certainly have called him Rudolph the Golden and names like that are so important in a monarchy. But Rudolph is quite against a beard. He tells me it is most dangerous when dealing with motors because it might get caught in the wheels.'

Etheldra looked at her suspiciously, but she was quite serious. 'And so hard to keep clean,' the Queen added.

'I had no idea,' Mrs. Truman said, 'that a Royal family had so many things to think of.'

'Oh yes, for although God has called us to our high estate there is much that we must do on our own behalf, particularly when the people are so tiresome about taxes. Fortunately for us the present regime in Althenia is proving much more expensive than we were. The trouble about a people's government is that it is so numerous.'

'And so corrupt,' prompted Count Otto.

'And, of course, corrupt.'

Etheldra discarded these comments as natural in the circumstances but unimportant.

'When my nephew told me,' she said, 'that he was taking service in a Royal Household I confess I was a little disturbed. Of course it was not new in the family. His is a military family and as such has reorganised numberless armies and states, but these naturally have been either in Arabia or in some other countries with close affiliations with our own. Anthony was the first Tolworth to serve a European Household for several hundred years. The last was a Richard Tolworth who was military adviser to Charles the Second of Sweden. Richard regarded him as something of a cad, I believe, but he respected him as a soldier.'

'You are honoured to be associated with the House of Badenburg,' said the Queen in her deep voice.

'We Tolworths are a clannish lot,' Etheldra went on. 'We worry about each other. Frankly I'm worried about the way Anthony is mixing himself up in this murder. He's an odd boy and no matter what it costs I know he's determined that this girl Eve is to be protected.' She snorted angrily. 'I hope for all our sakes she's innocent.'

'Innocent,' Count Otto actually scoffed. 'Don't you realise, madam, that the King has shown the young lady his favour? Naturally she is innocent.'

Etheldra looked at him with interest. Count Otto was something quite new.

'I wish,' she said dryly, 'that all problems were as simple as that.'

'You can take my word for it,' Otto repeated, 'she is quite innocent.'

'But that does not seem to help Anthony find the murderer, does it?'

'And in the meantime,' said the Queen, 'we have the girl. She is very close to Rudolph and I am afraid he is very susceptible. He has fallen a great deal under Western influences during the last few years and I'm afraid he might even think of marrying her.'

'Oh Lord,' said Etheldra, and then added defensively: 'But why shouldn't he marry her? She is a perfectly charming girl.'

Count Otto had turned quite pale. A few minutes ago he had been rejoicing in his master's happiness, but this new suggestion left him gasping.

'But Your Majesty, you can't think, you can't mean it.'

'The trouble with you, Otto, is that you are behind the times. You take it for granted that Rudolph will see his duty as you do. I do not, of course, say that Rudolph would not marry someone of Royal blood if one could be found. But the few available are either not attracted to Althenia, or Rudolph is not attracted to them. It is all a great temptation to him, I'm sure.'

The little man was wringing his hands. 'Marriage,' he cried. 'Marriage! It is unthinkable. She is not even a Countess.' He raised his voice piteously. 'Not even a Countess.'

'We might,' said the Queen doubtfully, 'arrange for a Polish or a Russian title to be conferred on her.'

'No, no, Your Majesty. We could not afford the risk. Why, in a matter of days I am sure we will be going back . . . and now this.'

'There is one slight matter,' Etheldra said dryly. 'The girl herself may not want to marry the King.'

Her audience looked at her as if she had taken leave of her senses.

Count Otto said in a strained voice: 'Not want to marry the King?'

'She may not.' She tried not to be impatient with them. 'I'm quite sure that there are a number of advantages in the position the King has to offer; but on the other hand the girl may be enjoying life as it is. I'm quite sure there are a great many things the wife of a King can do. But you must take the word of a commoner that she misses a lot of fun.' She asked curiously: 'Have you ever tried earning your own living, Your Majesty?'

'Good gracious!' The Queen's voice was a hollow boom.

'I assure you there is a lot to be said for it. There are plenty of disappointments, but also there is now and then a fine sense of owning the world.'

'I'm afraid, Mrs. Truman, I have no wish to own the world. It has always seemed enough that my husband and son should rule a part of it.'

'Yes, I am sure that is quite true.' She gave the Queen a friendly smile. 'But then you were equipped by nature to be a Queen.'

'By divine providence,' amended Count Otto.

'Whatever the method, it was sufficiently effective.'

Etheldra added: 'Not everyone is equally endowed. Also I am sure it required a good deal of training and a considerable degree of irksome self-discipline.'

'I regret, Madam,' the Count said, 'that you choose to treat our problem with levity.'

'Count,' the Queen's deep voice was severe, 'Mrs. Truman is not treating our problem with levity. What she has said is nothing but the truth. But we accept our duties and responsibilities with pride, Mrs. Truman. We are different from other people. We know that and accept it. From what I have seen of this girl, I like and admire her. If Rudolph should decide to marry her nothing will stop him; he is the King.'

Count Otto rose from his chair to dart about the floor. He was so disturbed that he almost blundered into the furniture. This behaviour in so odd a little man should have been funny, but in fact it was pathetic.

'We must save the King.' He repeated it and kept on repeating 'We must save the King!'

The Queen, too, was disturbed. 'Otto, you must not be so upset. There is nothing we can do. The King will make up his own mind and then we will know.'

'No, no. I have been lazy, careless; plotting and scheming and ignoring what was happening under my nose. This girl, this nice girl; no background, no prospects, no money . . . no money.' His voice raised on the reminder of this last straw.

Suddenly, white-faced, he stopped in the middle of the room.

'We must act,' he said. 'Tonight, this very night I will do something. The girl must go.'

'I say,' Etheldra protested at this unsporting suggestion. 'Look here, you can't chuck the girl to the police just because she appeals to the King, you know. You just don't do that sort of thing.'

The Count glared at her. 'Do you think, madam, I am a barbarian?'

'How should I know?' Mrs. Truman was not going to be bullied by anyone.

'I assure you I am not. I am not going to chuck this girl to the police, as you term it.'

'Anyway Anthony wouldn't let you,' Etheldra said as one setting the problem aside.

'I will act in my own way. All this is the filthy hand of the dead man raised against us once more.'

Mrs. Truman's mind sharpened at this reminder.

'You hated him, I understand?'

'Hated him!' The little man actually snarled. 'I hated and despised him, and still he brought us down.'

Count Otto saw that the Queen was about to speak and waited. He stood still, like a small dog waiting with his head on one side for the next command of his mistress. The Queen hesitated for a space and then when she spoke her deep voice was almost hesitant.

'I think this man Leonardo Manetti was the first man for whom I felt a personal hatred. Of course, we as a reigning family have always been taught to hate and to be ruthless with our enemies. But they were enemies as such, not as individuals. We knew when the revolt came that there was someone behind it, someone outside, who had influence outside. We learned later that it was Manetti. We were deposed. We thought of it as a battle that we had lost. But then we learned that we had still to pay Manetti. Manetti had not had enough till he had had everything. Everything we owned was confiscated and sold, our private property, our pictures, our clothes, our little mementoes; sold as souvenirs of our downfall. All that, by arrangement with the new rulers, was Manetti's share for the help he had brought in from the outside. And finally it was he who had my husband murdered.'

Etheldra could almost feel the silence as the heavy deep voice ceased to speak.

'You had good reason for hating him,' she said.

'And for wanting him dead. We do not forgive our enemies.'

Count Otto said shrilly: 'Even in death he seems to pursue us. His rotting body gives us no peace.'

Mrs. Truman was following a line of thought of her own. 'I had no idea that he meddled in such high places,' she said. 'It explains why he left Francis Raymond in relative peace. He must have been too busy to bother with him.'

Count Otto resumed his nervous promenade. 'He was never too busy to interfere in the affairs of Althenia, the monster. When he died it seemed at last we could drop him from our minds. But, oh no! Innocent this girl may be, innocent I am sure she is, but what do we find? We find that she comes direct from Manetti to us, beautiful, helpless, and dangerous, just as he might have planned it himself.'

'Oh, I say, have a heart,' Etheldra said mildly. 'I think the idea of her coming here was something conceived by Anthony and the King.'

He struck his forehead. 'I know, I know . . . But do I? How do I know? Manetti is dead, but the girl who was his associate is here on this yacht, a living threat to our State.'

Etheldra stood up. Even in these Royal surroundings there was a notable dignity about her.

'What you are not saying, but seem to imply, is that my nephew is involved in a rather squalid plot against his friend,' she said.

He protested. 'I told you, madam, I don't know what to think.'

'I, on the other hand, have no doubts whatever.'

He looked at her almost piteously. 'I have to be so careful. I have to think and plan. I have to think of myself as the King's father and his bodyguard. Perhaps I am too humble to be one and too frail to be the other. If I see danger everywhere it is because there is danger somewhere, lurking in the pitfalls.' He sat down and leaned back in his chair looking white and shaken.

'You must forgive him,' the Queen said gently. 'These are difficult days for us.'

Mannishly Etheldra hid her feelings in the exercise of clearing her throat. 'If I can't understand, I can at least sympathize,' she said, and added: 'I think, if you'll forgive me, I'd like to get back to my hotel.'

The Queen protested, but Etheldra thought it possible that she might have been mildly relieved.

'We have bothered you with our private troubles, Mrs. Truman. It is quite unforgivable.'

'I'm always interested in other people's troubles,' Etheldra said. 'Otherwise the tedium and frustration of running a school for little boys would be unbearable.' She looked reflectively at the Count and added: 'I am not suggesting of course that your troubles are childish ones.' Privately she had her doubts.

Count Otto Shavia was holding out her handbag and gloves to her with a hint of haste of which normally he would have been ashamed.

'Perhaps if you would tell my nephew I am ready to leave, he would see me back to the hotel,' she suggested.

But that seemed to throw the Count into a state of nerves again.

'No, no, please, Mrs. Truman. I had been looking forward to that honour myself.'

'Oh, I couldn't possibly bother you.'

'No, no, I assure you it is no bother at all. It would be a great favour to us if your nephew would stay a while longer. You see,' he whispered like an old-fashioned chaperon, 'I don't want to leave them alone together.'

For the first time in the evening Mrs. Truman indulged in the luxury of a hearty laugh.

'One of these days,' she said, 'you will have to face the fact that that fledgling of yours is grown up.' Quickly contrite she turned to the Queen. 'Forgive me, Your Majesty.'

The Queen smiled and shook hands. 'Good night, Mrs. Truman, there is nothing to forgive. I am sure that to you we must seem to speak and act with the utmost foolishness. I suppose that is because we know no more about your world than you do of ours. You will come and see us again?'

Etheldra muttered that she would be honoured and the Queen turned to the Count.

'Take Mrs. Truman home, Otto, and remember not to bother her with our affairs.'

He bowed. 'Your Majesty, with your permission I may be a little late.'

'Of course.' She gave her consent vaguely and stood waiting for them to leave. She looked very regal and to Mrs. Truman a little pathetic.

A servant was waiting for the Count with his top hat, his red-lined cape and his gold-headed cane, all small and all flamboyant. He equipped himself with them and was ready.

Cruising back quietly toward the jetty Etheldra watched the shore lights glinting on the Count. She wondered how much of him was theatrical and how much real. He couldn't possibly be entirely real, because that would be too much. But she guessed that there was something which it would be wise to take seriously. Perhaps it was his loyalty. She was surprised to hear him put his thoughts into words. He was leaning forward with his hands on his stick.

'It is a noble thing,' he said quietly. 'Yes, it is a noble thing to dedicate one's life to a cause. Nothing else matters. All other problems, our own, one's friends, they resolve themselves. Such a thing can inflict unbearable pain but it can repay with great exaltation.' He threw up his head and his white face shone in the light.

'I am exalted now, Mrs. Truman.'

'Oh dear,' Etheldra thought, 'I wish he wouldn't talk like that. It's so damned foreign.'

She said dryly: 'I'm glad to be with you on one of your good nights.'

'I have decided on a course,' he cried.

'I thought a few minutes ago you were in a bit of a fix.'

'Yes, but I have resolved everything.'

He almost leaped from the launch as it touched the jetty. He helped Etheldra and strutted jauntily by her side to the hotel. At the door he bowed low over her hand and then with a swirl of his cape he turned and strode away.

Mrs. Truman turned into the hotel.

'Well I'm damned,' she said.

CHAPTER 11

AS ANTHONY AND EVE walked along the companionway, she put a hand impulsively on his arm.

'Tony, don't let's go up yet.'

He stopped and looked down at her and a half smile tucked into the corner of his mouth.

'What's this; another change of heart, or do we infect him with a spot of jealousy?'

'Please Tony, it isn't funny. I . . . I think I'm scared.'

'So am I,' he said cheerfully. 'What shall we do? Run away and hide?'

He opened a door and stood aside for her to go through. Then he followed her and switched on the light.

'Tony, how attractive. Is this yours?'

'All mine; bedroom through the door facing you, bathroom on the left.'

It was a charming room, escaping as far as possible from the atmosphere of a ship. There was an open book on a small table beside the Knowle settee. A Picasso, blue and freakish, looked down cynically from the wall above. The carpet was silver grey and deep. A bowl of fresh flowers stood on a desk by the opposite wall.

Anthony stood looking down at Eve, half serious, half quizzical.

'Well?'

She went over to the settee and dropped into it as if she were tired.

'I don't know, Tony: things seem to be getting out of hand, don't they?'

'By things do you mean Rudolph?'

'No, not Rudolph. Rudolph is all right.' She smiled. It was a reminiscent, inward smile that he found quite maddening. 'He's such a baby, isn't he, Tony?'

He planted himself in front of her. 'Listen, Eve, do you realise the number of women who have set their first foot on the road to perdition with the nauseatingly syrupy thought that a man was such a baby? Tell me, have you thought of it?'

'I'm no good at statistics, I'm afraid, Tony dear.'

'Then take my word for it, the number is enormous.'

'Yes, Tony, I'm sure you're right. You are so clever about these things. I'm sure it's a gift.'

'And what is more Ticker is not a baby. He is an adult, and he is about as babyish as a Bengal tiger.'

'Yes, dear. You look sweet when you are angry, Tony.'

'I do not look sweet when I am angry and what is more I am not in the least angry. It simply embarrasses me to witness the break-up of a good intellect.'

With a quick gesture of surrender she gave up her pose of flippancy.

'It isn't Rudolph, it isn't anybody, it's just the whole beastly tangle that I've got myself into. I don't imagine anyone could be nicer to me than you've been, Tony. But then, of course, you're the only one of us with any brains.'

'Let's say the only one who uses them.'

'Perhaps that's it. Anyway you are the only one I'd care to depend on.'

He looked down at her. She seemed at that moment almost pathetically vulnerable. This is the moment, he told himself, when the dominant male takes the little thing in his reassuring arms. Instead he laughed.

Eve looked up in surprise. 'Did I say something funny?'

'No, darling. There's a quirk in my nature that spoils things —for myself that is. I wanted to make love to you, that's what made me laugh.'

She straightened. 'Yes, I suppose that would be funny.'

'Not so much funny for its own sake, but so beautifully in character. I see you in distress, a great globule of emotion rises up inside me, I perform the motions known as gathering you in my arms, we exhaust our emotions and when it's over you are still in distress, and the great big protective male is faced with the fact that what is needed is something rather more practical.'

'I'm glad you explained,' she said.

He grinned at her. 'I'm not telling you, darling. I'm telling myself. The trouble is that sitting there as you are looking sort of crumpled up, you are terribly alluring. It's wrong and ridiculous. It's not a bit like you. I imagine you'd like to cry on my shoulder and that isn't a bit like you either. I'd hate to fall in love with the wrong girl.'

She looked up at him and her eyes were bruised with anger.

'Have you finished laughing at me, Tony, or should I be patient till you've had all your fun?'

He walked over and sat beside her. He took her hand and played with the fingers without looking at her. 'Oddly enough I wasn't trying to be funny. You see I meant it, or anyway some of it. I had an honest conviction just now that you actually wanted me to make love to you.'

'I'm sorry I was so obvious.'

'Don't be an ass, Eve. You were feeling desperate and you wanted to escape, that's all.' He put a hand under her chin and lifted it till he looked into her eyes. 'If and when I make love to you, darling, you'll remember it with awe.' He smiled into her eyes, half amused, half arrogant. 'Now powder your nose and get rid of that demeanour of hopeless despair.'

He got up and walked over to the cocktail cabinet and began pouring out two drinks. Stiffened with rage she straightened on the settee and almost automatically powdered her nose.

'Ha,' he turned with a glass in each hand. 'That's better. That's very much better indeed. Apart from a burning spot on either cheekbone you look like the Eve I used to know. The spots I understand indicate indignation.'

Then to her own astonishment Eve heard herself say quite mildly: 'You are impossible, Tony.'

'Yes, aren't I? I poured you a whisky. It's a homely sort of drink, strong and forthright, businesslike as one might say.'

She sipped the drink and said reflectively: 'I suppose I did want you to do all the things you say. Does it make any difference?'

'Not the least. Next time I shall be panting to oblige.'

She said defensively: 'I promise it won't happen again.'

'Let's ignore that and go back to the point where you said I was the one who had the brains.'

'I said I could depend on you,' she laughed shortly. 'It seems I was right.'

'Yes, but it seems to me that Rudolph is the one you have to depend on currently. He isn't being difficult, is he?'

'Rudolph,' Eve smiled. 'Oh, dear no. I'm the light of his life, his dream, his queen . . . his queen; I'm not sure yet whether I'm to take that literally or as a figure of speech.'

'He probably means it.'

She brushed a hand over her forehead. 'I can't go on staying here, Tony. I'm grateful to everyone, but I can't go on.'

'Is that because of Rudolph?' He wondered why he kept on insisting.

'So far his intentions are quite honourable. This morning we discussed the implications of our marriage.'

'You're joking.' He said it quite violently.

'No, but it might have sounded funny if you'd heard it. I said I was only a poor commoner and he brushed that aside with the greatest of ease.'

'I should have said it would take quite a brush.'

'No, he said I could become a princess overnight. It appears that there are countless Althenian nobles who would be only too happy to discover that I was a long-lost kinswoman. Count Otto Shavia I was given to understand is an absolute master at arranging such matters.' She gave an affectionate laugh. 'Father would be pleased!'

'What, at the idea of your marrying Rudolph?'

'No, at the idea of a title; he'd have to have one of course. He would look awfully distinguished in Court robes, Tony.'

'Yes: but I seem to have forgotten to ask how you feel about it; personally I mean?'

She twisted the glass in her hand. 'It's hard to know what you feel when you aren't sure whether you are on the way to a throne or a guillotine.'

There was a pause, and then he said in a dry voice: 'I imagine you would be pretty safe if say tomorrow it was announced that you were engaged to the King of Althenia.'

'And father?'

Something in her voice made him look at her quickly.

'Why do you ask that?'

'It would give him a certain amount of immunity too, wouldn't it, Anthony?'

'Your father; is that what you're frightened of, Eve?'

'Don't be ridiculous.'

He smiled at her quite amiably. 'Why not; aren't we all being just a little that way? You, for instance, are sitting here seriously thinking of marrying a king in order to protect your father whom as far as I can gather the authorities don't even suspect. That has elements of comedy, hasn't it?'

'I have not said I was thinking anything of the sort: because of my father I mean.'

'Good. Rudolph will be pleased to know that you love him for his own sake and not for your father's.' He laughed. 'It does sound funny, doesn't it?'

'It isn't a joke.'

'No,' he said seriously. 'Looked at from another point of view it isn't a joke at all.' He hesitated and added: 'But you see, darling, I don't like looking at it from that point of view.' He crossed over and sat beside her again. 'Eve, what is it makes you so afraid for your father?'

'Nothing. He—he's helpless, that's all.'

He said casually: 'My aunt used to know him a long, long time ago.'

He heard her quickly indrawn breath. 'She knew? What was it . . . what he did . . . She stopped and added: 'It must have been nice for him to meet an old friend.'

There was a pause.

She turned to him. 'Thanks for being so nice about all this, Tony. I might as well tell you the truth. I don't know anything about my father's past. Somehow or other, I don't know how, I've learned not to ask about it. It's always been there like a shadow. It has frightened me ever since I was a kid. I used to think that somehow it would cause me to lose him. I had no one else and it was terrifying. At night . . . you know how it is. But I suppose you don't.'

'It doesn't need a lot of imagination to guess,' he said gently.

'It was that,' she said, 'that helped to make me feel as I do about him. That awful fear of losing him made me want to protect him. I must have developed a sort of precocious sense of responsibility. I can see, of course, that he couldn't have known how I felt and of course he wouldn't tell his small daughter something shameful about himself. And then of course when I grew up that habit of silence was too strong to break.' She laughed shortly. 'Sounds too dramatic, doesn't it?' She looked at him, her straight eyes questioning. 'I think I might be told now, don't you?'

'Maybe,' he said. 'When this is over your father will want to tell you.'

She shook her head. 'It would be too humiliating for him. You see, he wants so much to think that I see him as everything that a father ought to be, wise and tolerant and dependable and all the rest of it. I love him very much, of course, but I don't see him like that.' She turned her eyes away and added: 'I think I'd like to know about the past and then no matter what it was I'd just say to him casually: "I know all about it, father.

Now we'll both forget it, shall we?" Do you know how he'd feel then, Tony?'

'No.' But he did know at that moment how he felt about Eve. 'He would feel like a little boy who had been waiting to be punished for a long long time and then found it wasn't so bad after all.'

Then keeping her voice quite casual she asked: 'Do you know what it was, Tony?'

He hesitated and shook his head. 'My version is very second-hand.' And then when he saw the expression of fear come into her eyes he said quickly. 'I don't think you'll find the story very terrible, Eve. If you hear it from anyone outside I think I'd like you to hear it from my aunt. She knows all the circumstances and all the background. She's rather a remarkable old thing, you know.'

Her voice was not quite steady. 'All right, Tony, anything you say. It wouldn't be that you think the whole thing too squalid to talk about, would it? I don't mind telling you I'd be ready to face up to pretty well anything.'

His voice snapped. 'You must know the kind of thing your father is capable of, say under duress. And you must know what under no circumstances he is capable of. I don't know him well, you do. For Heaven's sake do what I ask and wait till you can hear the whole story once and for all from the only person who can tell you in a detached and commonsense way.'

He hated himself when he saw the tears oozing down under the clenched fists she had pressed into her eyes.

'Eve, I'm sorry. I must say I'm a hell of a one to help a friend. Please don't feel badly about it because honestly it isn't so bad.'

'I know I'm a fool.' She tried to laugh. 'I'm being a fool and liking it, that's all. But this damned thing has been with me all my life and now . . . now at last I feel that it's there waiting to smash up everything.' She threw up her head and looked at him, the tears staining her cheeks. 'Don't you see, Tony, that's why I've got to be there when the smash comes. I've got to be there. He's so helpless when he's left alone. He puts on a manner and looks wonderful, but he just can't cope, that's all. I never should have come away.'

'But Eve, what are you worried about, what particular danger can your father be in? After all it's you these people are after, not your father.'

She shook her head with a kind of desperate weariness.

'The night Leonardo Manetti was killed he was not at home.'

He laughed without feeling particularly like laughing.

'Surely, darling, he's entitled to have a night out if he wants one.'

'Yes, of course, only there was more to it than that.'

'What more was there?'

'I can't explain, Tony. I just know, that's all. He hated Leonardo Manetti.'

'So I gather did a lot of other people; some of them are here on this ship.'

'Perhaps, but you see father and I are such obvious candidates. Why should the police look anywhere else?'

He smiled at her. 'Well, anyway they can't say you aren't giving them a run for their money, can they?'

'Yes, but once we're in the trap that will be the end. We aren't politically important. We haven't any influence. Obviously he had some hold over my father and then there was that timely little threat of mine to kill him. The police will have heard all about that, won't they?'

He nodded. 'I expect so, but if every threat that was made was carried out, there would be a lot more corpses, don't you agree?' There was no lack of conviction in the way he said it.

She passed a hand across her eyes. 'What an exhibition!'

'And so,' he said, 'you think that one way out of the difficulty would be to fall in with Ticker's current whim and marry him?'

'It didn't sound like a current whim as you call it.'

'Do you love him?' He stopped and added: 'All right, don't tell me. Anyway the question was not in the least inspired by thoughts of your welfare.'

'I'll tell you anyway. I don't know.' Her voice was defiant. 'It would get us out of this beastly mess we're in and away from the country and anyway it would be exciting.'

'And also it would be running away.'

'Why not?' she said bitterly. 'Isn't that in the family tradition too?'

He shook his head. 'I don't think so, Eve. As a matter of fact I don't think you'll do it.'

'Were you thinking of stopping me, by any chance?'

'I might.'

There was a knock on the door. Anthony opened it and Rudolph walked in. He looked quickly from one to the other and walked over to Eve.

'You have been crying.' His voice was quite hard.

'Is it as bad as all that?' she smiled at him. 'I must be a messy crier, mustn't I? It must be because I'm not used to it. Normally I'm quite tough.'

'What has Anthony been saying to you?'

'Oh, for him they were quite nice things. It must have been that that caused the breakdown. My trouble is that I'm not used to sympathy.'

He turned and looked pointedly at Anthony. 'I'm glad it was only that. I thought possibly, Anthony, that you might have felt called upon to hand out some advice. By some obscure reasoning he has arrived at the conclusion that a King has fewer opportunities for a full life than a commoner. It occurred to me that he might have been arguing that the same might apply to a Queen.'

'Ticker,' Anthony said thoughtfully, 'you are getting pompous. I have a horrible feeling that when you go back to your hereditary cranny you may become a bore. Then we'll part, of course.'

Rudolph was not in the mood to see the humour of that either. 'It is highly unlikely that there will be a place for you,' he said. 'Are you coming, Eve? Avril's waiting on deck.' Taking it for granted that they would follow him, he went out of the room.

Anthony looked speculatively down at Eve, and his lips twisted in a rather lopsided grin. 'He's jealous,' he said. 'Funny, isn't it? The only snag is that if it takes him really badly he may have me put out of the way.'

She gave an uncertain little laugh. 'Tony, you do talk the most utter rot.'

He looked at her half seriously. 'You think so? I don't think you quite grasp yet what goes into the making of a King of Althenia.' He dropped her fur around her shoulders. 'Come along. We won't risk His Majesty's wrath till we have to.'

Eve tucked her arm through his. 'It would be nice to think you were serious sometimes, Tony. I know you never will be, but just the same it would be nice.'

'I daren't risk it. Look what happens to Rudolph when he goes in for it.'

'Do we have to drag Rudolph into it?'

'Well, he is a sort of current topic, isn't he?'

He could feel her hand tightening on his arm. 'I'm scared tonight. I don't know why particularly tonight, but I am. Tony, you said your aunt would tell me about the past, about Father I mean. Do you think she might do it tonight?'

'But why tonight? Look, Eve, the past has lasted quite a long time. Can't you just let it lie for one more day?'

She turned to him, standing close in the dim narrow corridor. Her eyes were wide and afraid. 'I don't think I can wait another day.'

He put a hand comfortingly round her shoulders and guided her on. 'Very well, then, after a decent interval I'll go and haul the old dragon from the Royal presence and she'll tell you all about it. That is she might tell you all about it. But don't be surprised if she gives you a spanking and puts you to bed instead. My aunt is one of those women who believe there is a time and place for everything. For all I know she may decide that a Royal Yacht at the dead of night is neither the time nor the place.'

'She seemed awfully nice.'

'Did she indeed? She'd be astonished if she heard you say that. Don't tell her for Heaven's sake or she'll think she's losing her grip.'

But when Anthony went down to the state apartments to look for his aunt, Etheldra was hanging her evening frock in the hotel wardrobe and looking at it with affectionate respect. The seams showed not the slightest sign of strain.

CHAPTER 12

COUNT OTTO, tiny and gleaming in the night, made his way with purpose along the palm-shadowed boulevard.

He turned into the Casino entrance and waved his stick at an attendant. It is well known that some could wave at a Casino attendant all night and except for an expression of mild irritation crossing the attendant's face nothing would happen. Count Otto was not one of those people. He waved his stick, turned confidently away and sure enough the attendant was unobtrusively at his side.

'My compliments to M. Baretti. I wish to speak with him in his private room.'

The attendant flashed away. The Count placed his legs apart, one hand on top of the other over his gold-mounted stick, and planted thus, he waited, confidently and with poise.

Presently Jean Baretti, discreetly dignified, was at his side. His manner was quite appropriately adjusted to the request for a private interview. He murmured his appreciation of the honour of the visit and led the way through a side door to his office. It was the same one in which the police officials had waited for Eve. It looked better without the police.

The Count divested himself of his coat and hat and laid aside his stick. He sat in the manager's chair and waved him to a rather less imposing one at the side of the table.

'I understand,' he said, 'that you have close ties with the local police.'

Jean Baretti shrugged cautiously. 'In matters of minor importance, yes, there is amiability between us. I am quite sure that if His Majesty's establishment is involved in some small matter it can be disposed of quietly. Or perhaps you would care to meet the Chief of Police here quite informally? That I should be happy to arrange.'

Count Otto replied coldly: 'The Royal Household does not involve itself in difficulties that require the assistance of the provincial police, Monsieur. His Majesty is quite capable of keeping his own house in order.'

Baretti was silent under the rebuke and the Count waited perceptibly to let it sink in.

He may have made the pause too long; but whatever the cause he seemed to find it difficult to find words for what he was going to say. And, at last, in quite an undignified way he asked: 'Have they found the murderer of Leonardo Manetti yet?' And to his own shocked ears the words were such as you might expect to hear in the servants' hall. To counter the impression he screwed his monocle into his eye and stared with fierce dignity at the manager.

If Jean Baretti was surprised at the question he did not show it.

'There is Miss Raymond,' he said tentatively. 'She has disappeared.' He was careful not to look at his guest.

'Of course, of course, Miss Raymond. So they still think it was Miss Raymond?'

'She ran away.'

'Do you think it was Miss Raymond who killed Manetti?'

Jean Baretti shrugged. 'The police opinion counts for more than mine.'

'No answer.'

'There are dozens of others who must be glad that he is dead. Her father for instance.'

'Why her father?'

'One hears things. Their quarrel arose out of some words Manetti spoke about her father, some threat or the knowledge of something to his discredit: something of that sort.'

Otto sat thinking, his white eyebrows drawn down over his bright eyes, his head on one side like a bird's.

'She would want to protect her father?'

'The bond between them is very close, I understand.'

'And so the police are satisfied that it is one of these two?'

'Why not? There was a suggestion at first that it might be a political affair.' Again his eyes carefully avoided those of the Count. 'That would have been very unpleasant for the Government. Fortunately the police have satisfied themselves that the other more obvious explanation is the right one. That will be a much more satisfactory solution for everyone. She will have a trial and much sympathy and the public will rejoice to think that very soon she will be released.'

The little Count fixed him with a cold stare.

'She did not kill Manetti.'

Baretti jerked upright in his chair. 'But . . . but the police . . .'

'I know she did not kill him.'

'Then you must know who did?'

Otto nodded. 'Certainly.' He drew the manager's writing pad towards him and took up a pen.

'I have come to a difficult decision, Monsieur,' Count Otto said. 'I am going to describe how Manetti was killed.' He tested several pens till he found one that suited him. 'I would be pleased if you would leave me alone for a time. I wish to do some writing. I may be an hour. That side door leads into the passage, I think? Good! I'll let myself out.'

As he went to the door Baretti could hear the sound of a pen scratching busily across the paper. He turned and looked back. The little man was hunched over the desk. His eyeglass was screwed into his right eye, his brows were drawn together in fierce concentration, the light was gleaming on his mane of white hair. The manager went out softly and closed the door.

Eve's father sat looking with a quite unfamiliar distaste at the pile of manuscript on his desk. He should have been taking advantage of all this quiet in the house to get on with it. But somehow he could not concentrate. He had been working on it persistently for years and in any one year he could have finished it. Only during the last few days had it occurred to him to wonder why he had not. Vaguely he realised now that it was a book that was never intended to be finished. It was an escape and an excuse. If he had finished the book he would have had to start something else and there was nothing else. It was his self-justification, his life work. It was his excuse for stretching out the years in exile and finally it was a bid for his daughter's respect. Out of necessity she had to work and here he, too, had his work.

The manuscript on his desk was neat and the writing precise as a bank manager's. The pages that carried statistical tables were a joy to look at, they were so beautifully set out. On a printed page he felt they would lose much of their character.

These pages on his desk were fresh, but in drawers and in cupboards about the room there were other heaps of manuscript as neatly executed as these, but their edges were yellowing with age and the writing had begun to fade.

He sat looking idly through the pages and suddenly with a sense of relief he knew that he was never going to finish the book. It was as dead as his enemy. He felt strangely elated. It was as dead as Leonardo Manetti. 'And now,' he thought, making a little joke to himself, 'I must get rid of the body.' He chuckled and said aloud: 'Ah yes, one must always dispose of the body.'

He was alone and he felt like a little boy with the run of the house. He opened the cupboards and emptied drawers that had not been opened for months and watched a great untidy stack of manuscript growing on the floor. He knew now that it had never been intended as a book, but as a barrier against his past, against Leonardo Manetti and himself. It was a stockade behind which he had lived for all those years. The massive pile grew and he was genuinely impressed. He was a worker. Whatever else might be said about him, there was no denying that. It was a pity in a way to destroy it all. In other circumstances it might be interesting to keep it; a lot of research had gone into it and in its way it might be considered a remarkable document. But it had to go because the memories it would evoke would be too painful, and how could he explain to those who were bound to ask why he had put all those years of labour into it? No, it was dead and he was much too fastidious to harbour a corpse. He looked at it lying at his feet and began to speculate on how he was going to get rid of it. It was all there now, the top of his desk was swept clean for the first time for years. The empty drawers slid in and out lightly and easily. It was very nice, like having the place to yourself again after a guest who had outstayed his welcome.

He went out into the kitchen. It was neat and spotless and something told him he would be unpopular if he started destroying papers in there. He went to the dining room, came back to where he had started and decided in favour of the empty grate.

He lighted the edges of a few pages of his manuscript and dropped them in. They curled rather sullenly and went out. He crumpled them up and began again. They flared up this time and he dropped another pile on top. These at once smothered the flames and sent a puff of smoke out into his eyes.

He began again, this time seeing that the whole thing got a good start, and he added more pages loosely and hastily. This time the blaze roared up the chimney, carrying a few blazing sheets with it. He began to find that destroying so much paper was a trickier business than he had thought, but he came to the conclusion that the main thing was to keep the blaze going at all costs. His eyes were smarting and a good deal of blackened ash was spreading across the hearth and this he further distributed over the polished floor with his feet. A startled neighbour came running in to see if the house was on fire and he had to break off to explain that he was merely burning papers. By the time the usual courtesies had been observed the fire was out and there was a big heap of ash that flew and spread at the slightest touch. But quite undaunted he crumpled up another handful, smothered himself with ash and began again. This time he kept at it till he had a really roasting blaze. The room was filled with heat and ash and smoke. Blazing soot tumbled down the chimney and bombed more ash out into the room. But now he was diminishing the pile at a really satisfactory rate and a little smoke and soot and the slight risk of burning his house down were not going to put him off. The perspiration was beginning to roll through the grime on his cheeks. Almost any other person no doubt could have burned a pile of papers with much less fuss and discomfort, but not Francis Raymond. And besides, he was enjoying himself. He was quite excited. Now he had a feeling that he was taking a rather big part in a battle scene, right in where the fight was hottest, as it were; not modern battle of course, but rather the old style where you got into a good pose and held it. And then a few minutes later he saw the leaping flames as consuming his past. He was ready to begin again, to take up where he had left off so long ago. He was young again and on the threshold of things. He really felt young, hot, sweating and full of vitality. What had he been doing all these years? Lying fallow, nothing more or less than that. Of course he could begin again and do something really useful this time.

His hand slowed and the fire died down. Wouldn't it be wonderful to go back to the old scene again, to walk the suburban street past the comfortable line of his neighbours' homes, to pause and exchange a word about the roses; or to walk on a soft hazy afternoon on the golf course, to feel the comfortable friendly turf under his feet, to watch the swans, Royal swans, deploying with arrogant grace on the lake? And there was an office desk, not a desk in a study at home, but an office desk, which one left in the afternoon and returned to in the morning. He gave no thought to the kind of work he would do, it was simply a picture of himself at work, appropriately busy, yet greatly at his ease.

His fire almost went out and he hastily went back to work, stoking up again with the last remaining papers on the floor.

Once again and for the last time the bonfire whirled up the chimney and the burning soot answered its challenge from above.

'Mr. Raymond!'

He turned and saw Jean Baretti standing breathless in the doorway,

'Hello, Baretti, my dear chap, this is a surprise. Do come in.'

'But, Mr. Raymond, are you all right?'

'Of course I'm all right, been getting rid of a few papers, that's all.'

'I thought the house was on fire, I ran.'

Mr. Raymond laughed. 'I seem to have created a stir,' he said. 'You are the second who's arrived with an offer to help. Most neighbourly I must say.'

'It seemed to me you were dancing about trying to put out a great fire.'

'Oh well, my dear chap, we all make mistakes. If you just let me open the doors and windows and get rid of some of this smoke I'll ask you to join me in a drink. What with you running up that damned hill and me fire-fighting, we deserve one I think.' He flung open the doors and windows and a blast of fresh air scooped up a cargo of blackened embers and swirled them in a mad dance about the room.

'Ah, that's better,' Mr. Raymond said. 'Now if you'll forgive me for a moment I'll wash my hands and we'll settle down to that drink.

He went off to the bathroom and the sight of his blackened face and red-rimmed eyes surprised him. He thought rather proudly that the job he'd completed must have been bigger than he'd thought. And with this thought still in his mind he relaxed presently with his drink as a man does at the end of an arduous but satisfying day.

His guest was not the relaxing type. Any man whose business it is to see to the comfort and ease of others must be endowed with a darting mind. Before Jean Baretti settled with his drink he sipped it, savoured it, and complimented his host. And then instinctively he looked round as if the spirits of his demanding clients were here in the room with him.

'Well, my dear fellow, I must say that it is nice to put one's feet up as it were.'

'You must have been very busy, Mr. Raymond. To make all that ash you must have burned very many papers indeed.'

'Well, there was rather a lot of the stuff to get rid of. It accumulated over the years, you know, and one hardly realises till one is going away how much there is.'

Baretti asked slowly: 'You are going away, Mr. Raymond?'

'Yes, I'm going home.'

'Home? but I thought you'd made your home here.'

'I have lived here for some time, yes, but it isn't quite the same thing, you know.'

With only the slightest hint of irony the little Frenchman said: 'That is a decision you have had ample time to arrive at.'

'Oh, there is never any doubt in one's mind really. They are having a spot of trouble at home and it seems only fair to go back and do what one can. England is England, you know.'

'To a Frenchman there is only France. To an Englishman there is only England,' and he added again with that touch of irony: 'Even if he does spend as much time in France as he can afford.'

Mr. Raymond conceded amiably: 'There is the climate and, of course, the food. However all good things come to an end. I still think there are a few jobs I can do for the old country.' He was quite serious. 'I don't know what it is that tugs one back. A sense of duty, I suppose. And you know we are in rather a tight spot,' he smiled with deprecating confidence. 'However I've no doubt we shall muddle through. We're only at our best when we are really up against it.'

Perhaps Jean Baretti had heard all this before. Most likely he had. He nodded, but obviously he had been only half listening.

'But what makes you take this sudden decision to go back

to England? You have been here so long.'

'Yes,' the older man spoke gently, almost to himself. 'Yes, it has been a long time. Only when one looks back on it does one realise how long. It is like being let out of prison. At first I imagine one will feel a little lost.'

'Leonardo Manetti, Mr. Raymond?' Jean Baretti's voice was quite gentle, but it shocked his host.

'Leonardo Manetti? Good gracious man, what have I been saying that makes you bring his name up? Really, it's most extraordinary I . . . why . . . I don't understand you.'

'He was an evil man, Monsieur.'

'Yes, I've heard rumours about him, ugly ones.' Eve's father was much more wary now. Its owner was dead but the name Leonardo Manetti inhabited the room like a breath of fear. 'I understand that it is a widely held view that the man is better dead.'

'I agree with that view.'

Almost against his will Francis Raymond continued on the subject.

'I didn't know that you knew him.'

'One could not be the manager of a Casino on this coast without knowing him. He was rich and he was a gambler. One had to know him . . . just as your daughter had.' At the mention of Eve there was a little pause and then Baretti asked conversationally: 'But how is your very charming daughter, Mr. Raymond? She came to the Casino only the other night in the King's party. She looked exquisite. Together they were a sensation.' The business man showed through and he added: 'It has been wonderful for business.'

'My daughter is very well indeed, thank you. She is spending a few days with friends.'

Jean Baretti looked at him with bright curious eyes and said with underlined diplomacy: 'One must not be so indiscreet as to ask where.'

Eve's father managed a rather secretive smile and said

nothing. It would never do to let this little man know that he hadn't the least idea where his daughter was and that he had only Anthony Tolworth's word that she was all right. That, of course, was good enough for him, but it might not be good enough for the gossips.

'Yes,' he said, 'I think my daughter will enjoy going back to England as much as I do.' He chuckled. 'Do you know, Baretti, I noticed the other day that she speaks English with a French accent.'

'Perhaps,' the little man said reasonably, 'as she has lived with us most of her life she feels a little French.'

Mr. Raymond looked at him in pained astonishment. 'Good gracious, my dear fellow, we're English.' He spoke the last word as if he saw it in capital letters.

Tactfully Jean Baretti said no more, but his bright darting mind passed in review some of the English people he had known; residents, members of the colony, making France their home and refusing to admit it. Some of them had been here when he was a page boy at the Hotel du Parc and were here still, emphatically English as ever. They bought their clothes in England, banked at the local English bank, subscribed to the English papers and periodicals, and avoided the English tourists. These, they felt, were on the whole a shabby lot, who dressed in the wrong clothes and did the wrong things and generally cluttered up the place. And worst of all they put the prices up. He remembered how after his first week as a page his father asked him what he thought of the English and he had said that they were tall and thin and calm with long teeth. Since then he had seen them fat, short, ruffled and without teeth, but the first impression remained. Today he knew that if he had to pick out a typical Englishman he would select Francis Raymond.

How different they were, he and his host. With a quick little smile he wondered if Mr. Raymond would pick him out as a typical Frenchman. He might; on the other hand he would probably prefer his typical Frenchman to have a beard.

His eyes flickered back to the heap of charred paper on the hearth. He wondered what it was that the Englishman had made such a bonfire of on a hot summer night. Something he must surely have been most anxious to be rid of. There was evidence that he had risked setting fire to his house in his haste. He wondered whether it was in anticipation of departure: or flight. The disarray in the room seemed to make him aware of his own personal neatness. He adjusted the sharp creases in his trousers precisely over his knees.

'I had another very distinguished visitor this evening,' he said. 'The Chancellor to King Rudolph.'

'Oh yes, I think I've seen him; foreign looking little chap, gives you the impression that he wears rather too much of everything. Outlandish name which I can't for the moment recall.'

'Count Otto Shavia.'

'That's it, what extraordinary names they do have.' If Baretti thought of some English names he had encountered, he said nothing, but held the conversation to his visitor.

'He asked to use my private room.'

'Not for the purpose of anything fishy, I hope?'

'For the purpose of writing, I think.'

'Good gracious, why should he borrow your private room for that? Have they run out of paper on the yacht?'

'I wondered also why he should want the room. I could only think that whatever he was doing he wished it to be quite dissociated from the King. That would explain why he came to me.'

'I say, you don't think he's mixed up in one of those Middle European plots against his master, do you?'

Baretti shook his head. 'He is devoted to the King, I'm quite certain of it.'

'Hmm, very mysterious. However, it's no affair of ours, I

take it?'

'I can't help feeling, Mr. Raymond, that it has something to do with the murder of Leonardo Manetti.'

Francis Raymond looked at him quickly and when he spoke his voice was stiff.

'I still don't see, Mr. Baretti, what concern that is of ours.' But the manager persisted.

'He told me, Mr. Raymond, that he knows who committed the murder.'

Francis Raymond was sitting very stiffly in his chair, and he seemed to have difficulty in speaking.

'Well, even so,' his voice was thin and trembled noticeably. 'How can he possibly know? And why should I . . . we concern ourselves?'

He might not have spoken. The little man went on in the same persistent way as before.

'It is quite obvious what he is writing in my room. He is writing what he knows of the murder of Leonardo Manetti. I know he is. His mind is full of it. He is a very determined man and something important to him has brought him to this decision. And now he is writing it all down and nothing will stop him.'

He paused and his bright little eyes were fixed on the man listening. He waited, but Mr. Raymond, sitting before him white-faced and stiff, seemed incapable of speech.

'I have been wondering, Mr. Raymond, what could have caused him to come to this decision. It is something to do with his Royal master or somebody associated with him. You see I know him, and anyone else who knows him will tell you that in his devotion to the King he is a fanatic. What he will do with what he writes I do not know, but either of us can very easily guess.'

There was a long pause and then the other man spoke. His voice was completely normal.

'Why are you telling me this, Mr. Baretti?'

Jean Baretti set aside his glass and stood up.

'For no reason, Mr. Raymond, except perhaps that during your stay here you and your daughter have shown me many little courtesies.' A faint suggestion of a smile touched his lips. 'We Frenchmen here had come to regard you almost as one of us. But there, you have explained to me that you are not.' He held out his hand as his host stood up. 'Good-night, sir. My wife will be waiting for me.' He asked curiously: 'Did you know that I had a wife?'

'Well I, since you mention it, Good Lord old chap I hadn't thought of it.'

The little man shook his head. 'You are quite right after all, after all these years you are still a visitor. And I am still the little man who welcomes you to the Casino.'

'My dear fellow, what nonsense!'

'I will take you into my confidence, Mr. Raymond. I have a wife, who worries about her figure, who occasionally snores, who buys me pyjamas with the most foul stripes and to whom I am completely devoted. I have a son six feet tall in a medical school in Paris, who loves me I am sure, but who regrets my humble background, and I have a beautiful daughter of eight years old. I own the speedboat which you see towing the water skis up and down the bay and I greatly regret that for business reasons I must avoid garlic which I love. I am a citizen of good standing.'

Mr. Raymond replied inadequately: 'I'm sure you are, old chap.'

They stood looking at each other with interest and then Baretti said thoughtfully: 'Life has dealt easily with you, Mr. Raymond. In France the climb is very hard. For me like the rest it has been hard, but I have nearly reached the flat summit of the little cliff I set myself to climb.' With a sudden violent emotion which Mr. Raymond found touching and yet a little embarrassing he cried: 'I am so near that I can feel my fingers clutch the turf that grows in the soft earth above. I must not fall. My family must not fall with me back to the barren misery that I left below.'

'Yes, yes,' Mr. Raymond said gropingly, 'I see what you mean. It's the family that matters, isn't it? I can see that, of course. It's the sort of thing one has to face.'

'Good night, Mr. Raymond.'

'Good night, Mr. Baretti.'

He turned back into the room, his thoughts turning on his guest. Odd little man; emotional . . . well it wasn't that so much as that he didn't mind talking about it; funny thing about chaps in restaurants and such places, somehow you supposed they spent their entire lives bustling about in a tail coat, but, of course, they had troubles of their own. Decent little chap, nice of him to have called . . . And then suddenly, overwhelmingly the news Baretti had brought came back to him. He turned out of the room and walked slowly and mechanically to the railings of his terrace. The night was soft and still. All the familiar lights were glowing steadily down below and glittering flamboyantly in front of the Casino. The sounds of the Casino orchestra floated up to him. And he pictured, in Baretti's private room, a man writing; silently, hurriedly, fatefully.

CHAPTER 13

IT was nearly midnight when Anthony came ashore with Avril Pares. The launch put them ashore and, as usual, slid away back to the ship's side.

'There'll be a taxi at the Casino,' Anthony said.

'Why not walk? Or don't you like walking?'

'Not much; there are exceptional cases, however.'

'Is this one? Or would you feel that you were doing some dirty work for Rudolph?'

'I never do anything I don't want, not even for Ticker.'

'He didn't exactly leap at the chance to see me home though, did he?'

'Should he have done?'

They walked along the breakwater and up on to the road before she spoke. 'I don't know.'

'What don't you know?'

'You asked me about Rudolph?'

'Oh yes, but that was hours ago.'

'Well, I've been giving some thought to the matter.'

'And even after that you still don't know?'

'Perfectly true.'

'Well, he should be gratified that you have given him so much thought.'

'Rudolph is the kind of human being that would make any girl think.'

'He isn't a human being, he's a King.'

'Maybe, but he still makes you think. What's so maddening is that I feel so awfully sorry for him.'

'If he heard you say that he would be the most mystified little King in Europe.'

'Yes, I know; but how would you like to be in his place?'

'I couldn't bear it. Anyway I'm not the type.'

'I think you would make a very nice King.'

'I say, you know, this conversation is getting just a little bit unreal. I never will be a King, so it really doesn't matter whether my ears would go with a crown or not.'

'I still think it's a pity. I might even fall in love with you.'

'I suppose,' he said, 'You wouldn't struggle with your ambitions and love me just a bit for myself?'

'Do you want me to?'

'My angel, who wouldn't?'

'Maybe Rudolph.'

'Ah yes, Rudolph. What makes it all the more maddening is that he's a King?'

She shook her head. 'No, I think I'd love Rudolph more if he were just ordinary, like the rest of us.'

'We aren't ordinary. As a matter of fact we are quite remarkable.'

'Maybe, but we aren't remarkable like Rudolph is.'

'The poor chap can't help it, you know. Think of the way he was brought up.'

'I will if you like, but just now I believe I'd rather think about you. I think I'll tell myself I'm in love.'

'With me?'

'Of course. Are you ready?'

'As always, darling, as always.'

'Right, I've done it.'

'Really, how does it feel?'

'Not as bad as I thought.' She raised her face to his, laughing, but perhaps a little serious. Her lips were parted and her eyes inviting. 'I think it must agree with me. How do I look?'

He stopped and looked down at her.

'This darling, is completely crazy.'

'But it's fun, isn't it?'

'What would happen if I said no?'

'That would depend on why you said it, wouldn't it?'

'Yes.' He bent down and kissed her lips and said softly: 'You adorable child, who on earth could say no?'

For a little while her surrendering body pressed close to him, then with a little gasp she pulled herself away.

He laughed softly. 'Am I boring you?'

She slipped her arm through his and began to walk on slowly. 'I rather forced that on you, didn't I, Anthony.'

He laughed again. 'I don't know, perhaps with a little more time I'd have thought of the idea myself. I think I've known for some time there was something I should do. Don't tell me you didn't like it.'

'Yes, oh yes, I liked it.'

'Well . . .?'

'Well, you see, I don't believe that thinking about being in love with you is a very good idea.'

'Really, I was beginning to think that there was something to be said for it.'

She shook her head emphatically. 'No, it's too dangerous.'

'Well, it was nice having you in love with me, darling. If at any future date you feel like harbouring another set of dangerous thoughts, do let me know, won't you?'

She laughed. 'No, in future I think I'll have them when you aren't there.'

'Selfish, very selfish. Very selfish indeed.'

'Maybe,' she laughed again, but not quite so steadily. 'What I'm trying very hard to do just now is *not* to think of you. And I might even do that better if you weren't here.'

'Do you think it would help if I walked on the other side of the road? Then if you change your mind you can give a shout.'

'No, that would be giving in to my weak nature. No, I'll just hold on to you and hope for the best. We haven't very far to go.'

In fact a few yards further on they turned in to a curving shadowy drive that led to the big white villa that overhung the sea. Anthony had not been to it before; but from the sea it looked one of the most beautiful on the coast. Obviously it had been built for a man who could afford to indulge his good taste.

When they approached the house Avril stopped and held out her hand. 'Good night, Anthony, thank you . . . Oh . . .' She had told herself she would say good night just like that, but now she was in his arms again and idiot that she was, Avril Pares was behaving like a fool and loving it.

Presently she said in a muffled voice: 'Anthony, will you do something for me?'

'Certainly, but what more do you want?'

'Would you please turn me round and give me a nice hard shove towards the door?'

He sighed regretfully, turned her round and gave her a good hard shove.

'All right?'

'Fine, I don't think I could stop now even if I tried. Good night.'

He stood watching till the door slammed behind her and then turned and walked slowly away.

Strange . . . it had been a strange evening; two experiences with two girls that in some ways were oddly alike. Emotional both of them, with the emotion directed to himself, but not entirely inspired by him.

Avril . . . he pulled his thoughts away. Eve . . . Rudolph . . . Everything was somehow distorted. What they were all in at the moment was not even a straightforward mess.

Avril was about to hurry upstairs when she noticed that the light in her father's study was burning and through the half open door she could see him at his desk. This was surprising because it was unlike him to work at night except in a serious emergency. She went on upstairs to get rid of the traces of what she regarded as her maudlin performance in the drive. She examined her face in the mirror and would have liked nothing better than to throw a hairbrush at it. She glowered at herself and went to work on her face as if it belonged to her worst enemy, but the most maddening thing of all was the curious little feeling of rebellious pleasure. It was quite disgusting and disturbing.

She was glad now that she had found her father awake; it would be nice to talk to somebody sane for a change. She ran downstairs hoping that he wouldn't just say good night and push her off to bed again.

Avril put her head round the study door.

'Hello, what causes this?'

He looked up with a start. 'Oh it's you, Avril. I didn't hear you come in.'

'You must have been concentrating, because I came in like a train.'

'I have been busy.' He tossed his pen on to the desk and for a second pressed his hands to his eyes.

John Pares was barely up to average height. He was slim and hard and straight. His thin face was lined and deeply brown. His bright dark eyes seemed to look with sardonic amusement on the world he lived in.

'Do you think I might have a drink? Pierre brought in the tray a couple of hours ago, but I've been too busy to do anything about it.'

She poured a drink and brought it to him; brandy with a little soda. Then she curled up in the big leather chair by the desk. Since she had been a little girl she had curled up in this same chair every time she was allowed in the study. Its enduring leather was as soft as a glove and its sensible strength always brought her a feeling of security. There had been many different studies in many different countries, but the chair was constant.

'I'm keeping you from your work, aren't I?'

'No, I've done all that I intend to.'

'Was it terribly important?'

He smiled briefly. 'To those most concerned it is very important.'

'Secret?'

'Very. It's a report. I'm coding it to the Secretary of State.'

She whistled silently. He sipped his drink and added casually 'As a matter of fact it concerns you.'

Avril sat up. 'Me?'

'Yes, among others.'

'But, daddy, no one told me the Secretary of State was a fan of mine.'

'He isn't, darling, anyway not yet. His interest is in Althenia.'

Avril was silent and her father watching her had the impression that she was half afraid to speak. And he himself was conscious of a sudden feeling of resentment. Why should a few coded words from Washington uproot them both? Duty to the State . . . to what State? One was entitled to suppose that an American citizen had the right to live in his own country; but not John Pares; not Avril Pares; they had engagements elsewhere.

At last she spoke quite casually. 'Is it all too secret to talk about?'

He shook his head. 'No, I imagine it will be in the headlines tomorrow. The uprising has begun.'

'In Althenia?'

He nodded. 'They've had enough of the crowd in power. The reasons are the usual ones. Corruption, tyranny, hunger and hate. Like damn fools they didn't even pay the army.'

She cried passionately: 'But we know them, father, they are such lovable people; why can't they live in peace?'

He shook his head. 'They can't, it seems. Our agents have been warning us for weeks that things were going to blow up.'

'So they'll begin killing each other again?'

'They have begun,' he said.

'Rudolph . . .'

'Rudolph of course is the trump card. He is their King, their shining knight. They want to see his glittering processions in their streets again.'

Her eyes lighted with a sudden memory and then as suddenly clouded again.

'Listen, daddy, do you think that if . . . if there had been no Rudolph waiting to come home that they would have staged this revolt?'

He shook his head. 'It is difficult to know. They are romantic people and the idea of Rudolph appeals to them. But apart from that, Heaven knows they have every justification for kicking out the gang that's in control. Unfortunately for democracy they know of only one way of doing it and that is by using them as decorations for the lamp-posts. When Manetti died so conveniently it was like a portent of things to come. He might not have been in the Government, but he was the boss at the back of it and the only one with the slightest idea of where to go for money.' He looked in his glass as if gazing into a crystal. 'Whoever killed Manetti is sure of a welcome in Althenia.'

'Supposing a woman killed him?' she asked quickly.

'The result would be the same, I should think. I don't think they would even bother to ask why she killed him.'

'And Rudolph, what about him?'

'If Rudolph is going back now he should go quickly. The sooner the better, in fact.'

'And you?'

He smiled at her. 'A few minutes ago, Avril, I was filled with bitter resentment at the fact that an ungrateful Administration was going to toss me back to the lions. Now, well now I'm thinking of the work that was left undone when we came away. It is slow heartbreaking work, but I honestly believe we are the only ones who could take it on. Yes, when the State Department gives the word I'll be off. In fact I've had a bag packed this evening and there's a 'plane standing by.'

'I know what you are going to say next, darling. You are going to say you'll let me know when it's safe to join you.'

He smiled. 'No, not quite that. I'll arrange for you to go on the yacht. And, my dear, you'll stay on it till I tell you you can come ashore.' He paused and added: 'And on the way down you might give Rudolph a few hints on the art of being chivalrous to a fallen foe. I'd be embarrassed if he had too many people shot. It would solve a lot of problems if that young man were to fall in love.'

Avril looked down at her hands.

'He might even do that,' she said.

CHAPTER 14

AS ANTHONY TOLWORTH walked back along the quiet road there was a mood on him that he could not shake off. It was not occasioned by one thing so much as by everything.

He stopped by the sea wall and leaned over, looking down into the softly dark water. Only a couple of days ago he had stopped to look down on the inanimate body of Leonardo Manetti. Yet it seemed that the crime had become a permanent thing in all their lives, unsolved and threatening. His own efforts had been futile and the most industrious of them had only directed him back to his friends.

None of his other efforts had been too bright either. It had seemed a good thing for her when he invited Eve to join the King's party at the Casino. It did not seem quite so good in retrospect. His other bright idea that landed her on the yacht was beginning to look a little tarnished too. And now there was Rudolph, unmanageable and unpredictable.

He wondered why his aunt had left so early and why the Queen had been so disturbed about Otto. She had come to tell them that he had gone ashore with Etheldra and had not returned. He had said he was going to do something about the murder. What was it that he knew? If he were anywhere at this late hour it could only be at the Casino. Anthony pushed himself away from the parapet and went to look for the Count. He was not in any of the gaming rooms. Play had finished and the place was deserted. The croupiers and the cashiers were checking in for the night. He asked them, but they had not seen the Count.

The doors leading on to the terrace were closed. He walked back the way he had come and down the passageway to the beach.

Anthony it seemed was destined to be the finder of bodies. He found the remains of Count Otto Shavia in almost exactly the same spot as he had found Leonardo Manetti. He was attracted by a gleam of white in the darkness. It was the little man's shirt front. Anthony was carrying the torch he used to signal the launch to take him aboard. He shone it now on the Count. He was quite dead, stabbed through the chest; the weapon that had killed him was still in the wound. It was the Count's own swordstick. He had not known that there was a steel blade hidden in the little man's cane. He should have guessed, of course, because it was so characteristic. The empty scabbard lay on the sand beside him.

His coat had fallen open and Anthony saw the top of an envelope protruding from the pocket. He pulled it out cautiously. There was no address on the envelope, just the one word 'Police.' The word itself seemed to tell what the contents would be. The Count had written a confession and had fallen on his sword. Poor pathetic, loyal little man. All his vitality and vanity were gone from him, leaving a crumpled scrap.

He put the envelope in his pocket and hurried away, leaving everything else as it was. It was his intention to tell Rudolph first and then come back and phone the police.

He was halfway to the ship when he heard a voice hailing him softly from the darkness.

'Hoi.'

He shut off the engine and curved round in the direction of the sound.

'Who is it?' He could barely make out the shape swimming easily in the water.

'Me . . . Eve.'

'Eve, what on earth are you up to? You must be stark, staring, raving mad.'

She laughed softly in the dark. 'If you shout at me I'll scream.' A brown hand caught the gunwale. 'Where have you been? I've been swimming round here for hours waiting for you.'

'You have no right to be swimming round for hours waiting for me.'

'Well, how was I to know it would take you so long to see Avril home? Don't tell me what you were doing because it will only make me jealous and I have enough on my mind already.'

'You'll have a damn sight more on your mind, my beautiful mermaid, if those fellows in the fishing boats see you.'

'Oh, but, darling, I wouldn't dream of letting them do that. I'm not even going to get into the launch.'

'You're not? Then why the forlorn cry for help.'

'Well, you see, I've got to get up the gangway, and I can't go up while the lights are on.'

'You came down it presumably.'

'Oh no. I crept aft and dived over the stern.' Again she laughed softly in the darkness. 'It was only when I was in mid air that I realised that I couldn't just dive up again.'

'When did this take place; the dive over I mean?'

'The minute you left. I had a sudden urge, it was an inspiration really.'

'Do you mean to tell me that you've been swimming about here for more than an hour?'

'No, of course not. I've been home.'

There was a long pause and then he said with a kind of deadly patience. 'I see. So you've been running about the streets of this beautiful and populous resort in the small hours of the morning dressed appropriately in practically nothing.'

'Of course not. I crept up to our bathing cabin. I keep a shirt and slacks there the same as everyone else does. I slipped them on and dashed home.'

'I see, and just how many residents not including the gendarmerie saw you dashing home?'

'Not a soul. Honestly, Tony, nobody saw me.'

She was holding the launch-side and they were moving slowly towards the yacht. 'Once I got across the sea road I took the little empty back lane that runs right up behind the villa. Hardly anyone ever uses it and there aren't any lights.' She added in a different tone: 'I wanted to see my father. I felt I had to. It was a funny sort of urge. I couldn't resist it.'

He hardened his heart. 'And there you sat, you and your father, having a nice homely chat.'

Her voice was flat. 'He wasn't there. I left him a note.'

There was a long pause in which the only sounds were from the quietly turning engine and the whispering ripples from the stealthily moving boat.

'You aren't exactly chatty this evening, Tony. Are you cross with me or are your romantic thoughts with Avril?'

'I was thinking,' he said, 'that your father must keep late hours.'

'Oh, but he doesn't as a rule. I was sure I'd have to wake him up.'

Uneasily he thought of the little tragic body lying on the beach. He wondered again where the Count had gone to make his call. The Casino had seemed the most likely place, but presumably he had not been there. It could be that he had gone to see Eve's father . . . There was no time to speculate. The lights from the gangway were picking up the launch. He leaned over to warn Eve to keep out of sight and turned in alongside the platform. He told the boatboy to wait and ran up the steps. On deck he strolled over casually and switched off the lights. Then he waited while Eve came clambering up in the darkness.

She stood for a moment and shivered.

'Brr, it's cold, and how wet!'

'You won't get dry standing there in the dark. If you take my advice you'll have a hot bath and get into bed.'

'I think I will. I'm sorry you think I've been a fool.'

'I'll get over it. Good night, Eve.'

'Good night.'

Anthony went along to his own rooms. The light was on in his sitting-room and Rudolph was stretched out on the settee, reading and smoking a cigarette.

'Oh, hello there, Anthony. I've been waiting for you a hell of a time.'

Anthony said ironically: 'I seem to be running late everywhere.'

Rudolph got up and strolled to the drinks cabinet. 'I'll have a nightcap if you don't mind. How about you?'

'Thanks. I could do with a big one.'

Rudolph looked at him with quick concern. 'As a matter of fact you do look a bit queer. Something gone wrong?'

Anthony took his glass and drank before he spoke.

'Yes, Ticker, something has gone wrong. It will be a shock for you I'm afraid. It's the Count.'

Rudolph put his glass aside. 'Otto? What's he been up to? I knew he'd gone ashore, but I supposed he'd come back. What's happened to him, Tony?'

'He's dead.'

The King's face went white. 'Dead, dead . . . but where? Where is he?'

'He's lying on the beach.'

The King threw back his head. His eyes blazed. 'He's lying on the beach! You left him there?'

'I had to.'

Without a word Rudolph walked stiffly from the room. Uneasily Anthony followed him, along the corridor out on to the deck and down to the waiting launch.

Anthony said nothing as they drove back to the shore. It would have been useless. Rudolph was standing in the bows facing the shore. He was standing as still as if he were a piece of statuary.

He jumped on to the landing stage and called over his shoulder: 'Which way?'

Anthony pointed along the beach and Rudolph turned to the boat-hand. 'Follow us along the shore and come in as close as you can.' The boy saluted and the launch slid away.

The men walked along the beach and when they came in sight of the body Anthony halted instinctively and Rudolph went forward alone. Anthony saw him drop to his knees, and turned away.

After a while Anthony walked over and put a hand gently on the King's shoulder.

'If you don't mind waiting here a little while alone, Rudolph, I'll go and find a phone and get in touch with the police.'

Rudolph looked up and Anthony saw that he had been crying. Now he looked surprised. 'The police?'

'Yes, they'll have to be told. In a case like this there'll have to be an inquiry.'

'You mean they will claim his body?'

Anthony nodded. 'Yes, for the time being they will claim it.' Rudolph stood up. 'I am a King,' he said, 'and this is one of my people.'

'Yes, I know, but this happens to be French soil.'

To Rudolph the objection was merely trivial. 'I will take my loyal servant to the place where he belongs,' he said and Anthony saw that it would be futile to try to reason with him. He was bending over the body and gently withdrawing the weapon from the wound. He slid the sword back into its scabbard and dropped it on the sand. Then he gathered the body up in his arms and walked to the waiting boat. Without hesitating and seemingly unaware of it, he walked into the water and lifted his burden lightly over the launch's side. Anthony picked up the discarded sword-stick and followed Rudolph into the launch.

The same silent procession was repeated at the foot of the gangway. Rudolph carried his Chancellor's body to his own sitting-room and put it to rest on the couch.

Anthony hesitated in the doorway. 'Is there anything I can do?'

'Nothing, thank you. I'll take care of him.'

Anthony turned away. Tomorrow he knew there would be a bier covered with flowers with a sailor at each corner, head bowed and silent. He sighed; well, the little man was dead, and he was being dealt with more tenderly here than he would be with the police.

He walked back to his room and found that he was still carrying the cane. He wrapped it carefully and put it away in the corner of his wardrobe. Then he refilled his glass and took out the envelope that had been destined for the police. Now he had to decide what to do with it.

It seemed to Anthony as he read that some of the life that had departed from the little body clung to these pages in his hand. The loops, the twirls, the underlinings and exclamation marks seemed alive with florid vitality.

'I, Otto Shavia, depart, but in this hour before I depart I speak! Manetti, the treacherous dog is dead. None mourn, but many rejoice! Surely it would have been more fitting to have left his worthless carcase to rot in its own unsavoury way, but that it seems is not to be. Instead of gratitude we have a hunt as if for a criminal! The innocent are threatened with arrest! How laughable and how strange!

'Manetti is dead, therefore his executioner must be brought to view and all must be told; how and when and where and why!

'Why? I will tell you why. Three years ago in a hot and dusty prison yard in Althenia, I gave the signal to a firing squad and they shot my only and beloved son . . . a traitor. He died and I who gave the signal shared his death.

'Also in that second I condemned Manetti to death! Oh yes, Manetti was behind it all. In the last hours we were together, I heard the story from my son. It was of course an old story, the older man steadily and relentlessly corrupting the young and so on to the final climax; the staggering debts and the shameful story of how they were acquired. And at the last moment he is shown the one way of escape. My son must become the agent of Manetti inside my house. I began to suspect the most trusted members of my staff. I laid traps and I was horrified at what I caught. I it was who demanded that he should be shot. My son told me the whole sordid story, not in the hope of saving himself, but in the hope that my own memories of him should be less black. He died bravely with his eyes steadfast and his head held high.

'I hunted for Manetti, but he was out of the country now, working behind the scenes. From beginning to end his only motive was greed.

'The revolution came and we were driven out. In some ways the area of my search was widened and in others it was prescribed. We travelled in many countries. Many times I heard of him, but never till that fateful day did he cross my path. He did not cross it then. I rejoice to say I left him lying in it.

'Where and when? That is well known, and so it remains only to tell how.

'It was late dusk. I barely recognised him as he came down to the beach for a swim. But as he passed quite close I knew that it was he. As I waited it grew quite dark; he was in no hurry it seemed to come out and I, of course, was quite content to wait.

'The beach was quite deserted and I could barely see him as he came towards me shaking the water from his hands and hair.

'Within several feet he saw me and stopped and I spoke to him "You are Leonardo Manetti," I said, "and I am Count Otto Shavia. We have an appointment I think?" Then quite deliberately I drew the sword from my stick and drove it into his heart. I regret that it was too dark to see his face. I tidied his body neatly and left him to decay in tomorrow's sun. I cleaned my blade in the sea and sand and went on to hail the launch.

'That is the story which I faintly regret I shall not be there to tell. But a higher duty forbids it. A purely personal matter has been settled and my honour has been satisfied.

'And so I go! That I shall no more see the beautiful land of France is a wound in my heart. It consoles me that I have rid her of her vilest guest!'

And underneath was the signature, a regular flurry of curves.

For a long time after he had finished reading Anthony sat staring reflectively into space. He was not thinking of the recent crime, but picturing the scene in the far-off prison yard. With a sudden resolve to get away from it he went out on deck. A few yards away from him were Rudolph and Eve. She had changed into a pair of slacks and a pullover. His arm was round her shoulder and her head leaned back against him. With the path of the rising moon on the sea in front of them they looked like one of those highly romantic conceptions of a young couple bravely facing the dawn. But Anthony had had enough of such emotions for one night. He was merely angry.

'Eve,' he said, 'you may or may not give a damn, but I would like to remind you that four men at least are out there trying to discover whether you are on this ship or not.'

She turned quickly. 'Oh Tony, Rudolph has just told me what happened.'

'I see, and so the only thing left for you to do was to come out in the moonlight and express your public sympathy.'

'That isn't very funny, I think,' and without looking at him she walked across the deck and disappeared.

Anthony shook his head. 'No, that wasn't very funny. It must be that I'm not in a very funny mood.'

'You might at least try to have some manners,' Rudolph's voice was unfriendly.

'Possibly you're right. But I think it should have occurred to both of you that she might have been seen from those police boats.'

'What does it matter?'

'It may not matter.' He came to the rail and leaned over. 'In fact I don't think it will matter if you're prepared to let some police formalities be gone through.'

'Formalities?' Again there was that stubbornly contemptuous note in the King's voice.

Anthony was not in the mood for diplomacy. His reply was wearily patient. 'Yes, Rudolph, formalities. The Count has left a letter. I think you should read it.'

'Why?'

'Because it is a confession. He says that he murdered Manetti.'

'Of course, he had every reason to murder the unsavoury brute.'

'Well, don't you see that when the police know the circumstances they'll call off this ridiculous hunt for Eve?'

'I am quite able to take care of my problems without the help of the police. I have told Eve there is no need to worry now.'

'I see. But, unfortunately, somebody has to tell the police.'

'Why?'

'Look here, Ticker, it's too late at night to be academic about these things. You know as well as I do why.'

'Eve is coming away on the yacht.'

Anthony hesitated and then asked: 'Did she say so?'

'Of course she did,' Rudolph turned to face him. 'Is there any reason why she shouldn't?'

Anthony took the Count's letter from his pocket. 'Would you like to read this before you make up your mind?'

'No thanks. I mean yes, later I'd like to read it. But I know what is in it, you told me.'

'He completely exonerates your House.'

Rudolph said: 'Of course he does. Did you think he would say that he was acting on my instructions? You might just as well reconcile yourself to this at once . . . As far as we are concerned this matter of Manetti is closed. I've told Eve and she agrees with me. If she were in danger of arrest now it would be different. She isn't in danger. As for Otto, I am going to take him home to lie in the soil of his fatherland. Have you any objections to that?' His voice took on a different note, he raised his head. 'I am going to see that he is buried with all the honours of the first hero of my country.'

Anthony opened his mouth to speak and decided that it would be quite futile.

'I suppose that is what he would have wanted,' he said and added: 'But that presupposes that you can take him home.'

'I can.' The King's voice was ringing. 'I can, Anthony; it's only a question now of hours.' He put an arm round his friend's shoulder. 'The time is measured by the clock's ticking, one minute, two minutes and then . . . Look, I know I haven't been behaving naturally. I'm just as much your friend as ever I've been, but now I'm something else, I'm King of Althenia, Tony, and I'm King by divine right. Let me tell you something else, a King in exile is one thing but a King behind the palace guard is quite another!' He leaned against the rail and looked at Anthony. 'I say, I honestly hope you're going to like it, old chap.'

Anthony's uneven grin widened reluctantly on his face. 'But it doesn't matter a damn whether I like it or not, does it, Ticker?'

Rudolph threw back his head and laughed. 'Not a damn. And by the way, you realise, don't you, that you are calling me Ticker for the last time?'

'Like hell I am. Ticker you are and Ticker you stay. Good night.'

He turned and left Rudolph to the realization of his destiny. Above his head he could hear the ship's wireless working busily. No, the Rudolph of a few days ago was not the same Rudolph of this evening. To Anthony this ship had always been in the nature of an old-fashioned trading schooner. It had offered him a way of life that suited his nature and Rudolph had always been a wayward but a good companion. Now it looked as if he would have to perform that loathsome evolution that is known as settling down.

CHAPTER 15

ANTHONY TOLWORTH slept till eight o'clock. He would probably have slept longer but the commotion overhead woke him. The ship was alive. A winch was at work on deck and below in the engine room a dynamo was sending its vibrations throughout the hull. There was an urgency in the hurrying footsteps. He knew without being told that preparations were being made to put to sea. He dressed quickly and went on deck.

Away up on the fore deck of the ship he could see Rudolph. He was alone, standing very erect and looking out to sea. The morning sun was glinting on his blond hair. Anthony strolled along and stood by his side.

'Is this splendid isolation deliberate or can anyone join in?'

Rudolph turned. His face was strangely set. He seemed much older.

'Isolation . . . yes, it's funny you should use that word. Isolation, it can have a special meaning, can't it?'

Anthony was looking at him in surprise. 'I say, Rudolph, there isn't anything wrong I hope?'

'Do you notice a change, Tony?'

'Well, no; but the manner is a little formal if one may say so.'

'You notice that also?'

'Of course. I'm curious to know what brings it on.'

Rudolph took a paper from his pocket and handed it to Anthony. It was an ordinary ship's radio form, but after the first few lines Anthony began to have the impression that he was reading from a scroll.

'To His most Gracious Majesty Rudolph the Third by the Grace of God King of Althenia. Sire: Through the power of Your Majesty's Army and the loyalty of your citizens we have this day unfurled the standard of your Royal House above the Palace of our King. In your absence, but with your wishes close to my heart, I have placed myself as your servant at the head of the State and have ordered the rout and destruction of all your enemies. Those who have asked for mercy I have told that mercy is the prerogative of their King whom they drove from his domain and that it must await his return. My only and humble duty is to avenge the wrong that has been done our King. Today their blood is staining the soil that they have shamed and the people of Althenia are singing as the traitors die.

'On this glorious day Your Majesty's subjects look to one more glorious: to that day when you set foot once more on Althenian soil. The spirits of your people are high with hope and your Army is frenzied with success. The few who were disloyal are dead. May it please Your Majesty to name the day and hour of your return. Althenia is hungry for its King. Your Gracious Majesty, in humble duty I subscribe myself—Frias Amantos, General.'

Without speaking Anthony folded up the message and handed it back.

Rudolph was watching him. 'Well?'

Anthony looked at him and a sardonic grin twisted the corners of his mouth. 'It would be slightly out of place to call you Ticker, wouldn't it?'

'Is that all?'

Anthony walked to the ship's side. 'What I am really wondering,' he said quite seriously, 'is whether to congratulate you or not.'

'Would you refuse to go back?'

'I would, but you, of course, can't. I suspect, Rudolph, that you are realising for the first time that the people of Althenia not only belong to you, but that you belong to them.'

'Perhaps I am. That's what I meant about isolation, Anthony.'

'None the less you've got to go back.'

'Yes, naturally, they're my people. But I'll be alone. The only one I knew and trusted is dead. But you'll be there.'

Anthony shook his head. 'No; you know as well as I do that I won't be there.' He laughed suddenly. 'I think I'll wait till they chuck you out again.'

The King's face changed. He raised his head with an odd gesture of arrogance. 'That they will not do,' he said.

'You know,' Anthony said seriously, 'I don't think they will.'

'Why don't you change your mind and come with me? I need your help.'

Anthony was watching a big white launch racing across the water to the yacht. He could see Avril and her father sitting in the stern.

'I think there's someone coming now,' he said, 'who can be very much more help to you than I can.'

Rudolph looked over the rail. 'John Pares, of course!' His face lighted with pleasure. Impulsively he started down the deck. Then he stopped. 'No, a King must wait.'

Anthony laughed and walked on. 'This is where I have the advantage over a King,' he said.

Avril came running up the gangway. She stopped and looked with quick speculation at Anthony as if re-appraising him in the cold light of day. He smiled back at her, blandly impersonal. She wrinkled up her nose at him and her eyes danced mischievously. Then she turned to Rudolph. He had changed his mind and had walked slowly down the deck. Quite seriously she dropped a little curtsey. 'Congratulations, Your Majesty.'

'Thank you. I. . . I mean thank you very much, Avril.' He seemed oddly shy. 'But please don't be too formal, I mean not now. We're still friends, aren't we?'

'Oh, yes.'

John Pares was a diplomat and his first greeting was a formal one. He bowed gravely to Rudolph.

'The Secretary of State has instructed me to present my Government's compliments, sir.'

Rudolph took his hand eagerly. 'Does that mean you are coming back with me?'

'Not with you exactly. If it's agreeable to you I'll fly over this morning.'

'Of course. I'm glad you're going to be there,' he hesitated. 'I thought I was going to be very much alone.'

'Yes, there are difficulties in being a King.' His bright shrewd eyes looked at Rudolph in swift speculation. 'It is more difficult still to be both, a man and a King.'

Rudolph drew himself up. 'I am not afraid,' he said.

'I know. I was not thinking about courage.' He smiled and Anthony thought how oddly like Avril he looked, 'I took that for granted. I was wondering if you realised what a tremendous job you are taking on.'

'I know the responsibilities of a King, Mr. Pares.'

His visitor nodded. 'Your people have had a taste of governing themselves. They will expect to continue.'

Rudolph looked astonished. 'But the Government has been overthrown.'

'Because it was a bad one.' Again he smiled. 'I'm afraid you are going to find your responsibilities far more complicated than those of your ancestors. You may even find that the overthrow of that other gang was not entirely due to the People of Althenia.'

Rudolph was looking at him thoughtfully. 'I see. Mr. Pares, how did you know about my recall? I heard it myself only a few hours ago.'

John Pares laughed. 'I belong to a very inquisitive race, Sir. We like to know what is going on . . . in your part of the world particularly. When we are making an effort to buy world peace we like to be sure that we aren't throwing our money away. We know by the way that Althenia is broke again.'

Rudolph laughed. 'The first thing I learned about the history of Althenia was that it is always broke.'

John Pares smiled. 'That is something you and I will have to work together on. In the meantime, Sir, I am leaving Avril in your care. I don't want her running risks.'

'I promise I'll take care of her,' Rudolph said. 'She will land in Althenia when I say so and not a minute before.' He treated Avril to a royal glance which made her want to laugh.

Avril's father patted her shoulder affectionately and turned back to Rudolph. 'I'm full of fatherly advice this morning and now I've one piece more. On the journey down it might be a good idea to talk to Avril and young Tolworth here on the functions and responsibilities of a limited monarchy.'

Rudolph threw back his head and laughed. Standing erect in the morning sunlight, he looked very self-assured. 'They can tell me all they know about limited monarchies,' he said. 'But nobody can teach me how to be King of Althenia.'

For no reason at all Anthony thought of the little Chancellor, lying in state in his flower-decked coffin below, and he wondered if Rudolph was right and if indeed there was nothing they could teach him about being King of Althenia. There might be cases where one royal gesture was worth a year of honest legislation.

They watched Avril's baggage being transferred from the white launch to the yacht. John Pares said goodbye and hurried down the gangway. Rudolph and Avril stood watching him leave. Anthony went below to look for Eve. She was in her cabin restlessly turning the pages of a magazine.

He leaned against the door watching her with irritating amusement. But when she dropped the magazine and turned to face him he saw that there were tears in her eyes. He walked over and took her hands.

'Tell me if you want me to clear out,' he said, 'and I'll apologise and go.'

'No, I just keep on being an ass, that's all. There's no need for anyone else to worry.'

'You mustn't let things get on your nerves.'

'I can't help it, Tony. It's like being caught in a trap.'

'Yes, I know how you feel, darling. But I can tell you quite definitely that it is better than being in a French gaol. They are not exactly cruel, mark you, but they are awfully careless of a person's well-being.'

She answered quickly; 'No, no, I wasn't talking about myself. If it were just myself I wouldn't mind a bit. In fact I think this would be rather fun.'

'Would you care to tell me what it is then?'

'It's father. Ever since I went there last night and he wasn't there, I've been worrying. Then Rudolph told me how he had brought the Count's body in from the beach. Of course I know my father had nothing to do with it; but the poor little man died on the beach in just the same way that Leonardo Manetti did. It seems that we all have places in some horrible design. All night I've been imagining all sorts of things. Suppose my father were next. He is up there alone, last night he was out, probably wandering about the deserted streets. The other two were stabbed in the dark,' she shuddered.

Anthony put a protecting arm about her shoulders.

'Eve, I want you to come along to my room. There is something I want to show you.' He stepped aside and waited for her to lead the way.

He explained how he had found the Count's body and the Count's own swordstick. Then he unlocked a drawer in his desk and produced the letter. She read it slowly. Then she sat for a long time holding it on her knees. Her head was bowed and he could see that her hands were shaking.

He went and sat beside her and took the letter gently from her fingers.

'So you see, don't you, it's all right now.'

She nodded. 'It's terrible, isn't it, to be made to feel happy by someone else's tragedy?'

'Perhaps,' he said. 'But his real tragedy was enacted years ago in the prison yard in Althenia. I think you know that that really was when he died.'

She brushed a hand across her forehead, sweeping aside her golden hair. For the first time since he had met her at the Casino, her eyes were level and serene.

'I can tell you now how afraid I've been. I've been terrified, Tony, ever since the day we met. And now . . . think of it . . . all that has gone.' She laughed unsteadily. 'I can go home.' She caught his hands impulsively. 'Tony, let's go on deck and look at the town.'

He laughed and put his hands on her shoulders and quietly but emphatically he pushed her back on to the settee.

'Listen, my little impulsive sweetheart. Your spirit may be as tranquil and as free as the air, but that shapely body of yours is going to stay just exactly where it is.'

Her eyes widened. 'But Anthony, why?'

'Because of Rudolph's impulsive little act of last night. If the police had found the body with the confession in its pocket you could have gone home to your daddy. But the police did not find it, and they don't even know about it.'

'But I can't stay here for ever.'

'There always is a snag in these impulsive gallantries of Rudolph's. Someone else has to come along and clean up after him. In this case I'm afraid it will have to be me. But then as far as your staying down below for ever is at issue, I doubt very much if you will be here more than an hour or so.'

'But you said I couldn't leave the ship.'

'True, but the yacht can leave its anchorage, and if you had any experience of these things you would know by the noise that it is preparing to do so now.'

Eve's jaw dropped. 'You mean we're going to sail?'

'Yes, darling.'

'But, Anthony, I can't. I mean, what about my father?'

'I've thought of that too. I think the best thing to do would be to have my dear old auntie Etheldra Truman make another call on your father. She can tell him that you are well and happy and have gone to see them crown the King of Althenia.'

It seemed to Eve that everything had happened while her back was turned. 'Is Rudolph really getting his throne back?' It seemed impossible to believe.

He nodded. 'As from today's date. John Pares has called, bowed and given him a few broad hints on what is expected of him and has left Avril on the yacht as a Westernising influence. But Rudolph has a sort of faraway look in his eye that tells me he is thinking of the rolling heads of his enemies.'

'It's rather frightening, isn't it, Tony?' She shivered. 'Do you think Rudolph has that sort of cruel streak in him?'

'I think, darling, that Rudolph can be as gentle as a lamb . . . if everybody behaves as Rudolph thinks they should.'

'You'll have to keep him under control, Tony, I mean help him to see things as we do.'

He shook his head. 'My partnership with Rudolph will end when he steps ashore. He asked me to go with him and I refused. You see I like him too much to quarrel with him.'

'But why should you?'

'Because I'm more than half civilized.' He appeared to hesitate and then said: 'I do think somebody might have some influence with him, but I'm quite sure it wouldn't be me.'

Eve turned away quickly and spoke with her back to him. 'Am I to take that as a hint?' Her voice was casual, but her body looked tense as she waited for him to reply.

'It was an observation and not a hint. It's based on my own estimate of Rudolph's character.'

The silence that fell between them was antagonistic. It was an appropriately dramatic moment for Rudolph to appear.

He came through the open door and stood looking from one to the other curiously. A little smile touched the corners of his mouth.

'Backs turned, heads up; something tells me I'm in the way.' But he didn't sound as if that worried him in the least.

Eve turned quickly. 'No, of course you're not. Anthony just told me your news. Isn't it marvellous?'

He laughed. 'Is it? I thought you were looking rather angry about it. I expect Anthony told it badly. He has a jealous nature. I'm sorry, too, because I wanted to tell you myself. Eve, you are going to see my country.' He spoke as if he were laying it at her feet.

She glanced hesitatingly at Anthony, but he was leaning back on the settee watching with what seemed a kind of detached curiosity.

'I thought,' she said, 'that after all that has happened it might be better if I didn't stay on the yacht. There isn't any real need, you know.'

He was looking at her in astonishment. 'But, Eve, there is a need. I need you. What sort of a triumph is it going to be if there is no one to share it with me?'

'There will be Avril, of course,' Eve said with what Anthony considered quite brazen invitation.

'Of course there'll be Avril, but I want you too. I want everybody with me. It is going to be glorious. There will be the bonfires and the torchlight processions, the banners and the dancing in the streets, the parades. We'll stand on the balcony and look down at the crowds in the palace yard.' He squared his shoulders and threw back his head. Already he was living his triumph. 'Somebody may even have a shot at me. I might be wounded and have to carry out my engagements with my arm in a sling.'

Anthony laughed in spite of himself. 'Rudolph, you are so incredibly theatrical that I wouldn't put it past you to have yourself wounded in the arm.'

Rudolph turned on him indignantly. 'I see nothing theatrical in the return of a King to his subjects.'

Anthony stood up and patted him on the shoulder. 'The curse of my life, Rudolph, is that I can't take the serious things seriously; not even you. Instead of laughing at a time like this we should be all holding our thumbs. By the way, while you are toying with that little idea of a bullet in the arm has it occurred to you that it might equally be in the heart?'

Eve said quickly: 'Please don't, Anthony.'

But Rudolph laughed. 'Yes, I have thought of that too. It's a challenge to fate.'

Anthony shook his head, resigning to Rudolph the stage. 'In the meantime,' he said, 'I am going to do something quite normal, just to see what it feels like. I am going to call on my Aunt Etheldra and say goodbye.'

'Tony, you will ask her to explain to my father, won't you? I wish I could do it myself but I don't suppose . . .'

He interrupted her firmly. 'I don't either. Have you any other requests before I go?'

'Yes, in the excitement I nearly forgot. When I went home last night I packed a dressing case with some personal things. I put it in our bathing hut on the beach.' She slipped a hand into her pocket. 'Here's the key. It's number ninety-three in the group below the Casino.'

'Very well. I don't a bit mind if the police ask me what I'm doing with a lady's dressing case.'

'It's only a small case. I thought if you took one of your own ashore you could put mine inside.'

'I stand rebuked. Any other instructions?'

'No . . . yes. If the Casino is open go in and put a chip on number six for me just for luck, will you?'

'Number six? Why number six?'

'No reason, it's just my number, that's all.'

CHAPTER 16

ANTHONY found Etheldra asleep in a deck-chair under a coloured umbrella. Her face was covered with a sensible-looking scarf. He spoke to her and she growled at him:

'Go away. Go away. It must be obvious to the meanest intellect that I am trying to sleep.'

'You are asleep.'

'I know I am, go away.'

'You look undignified.'

'I don't care a damn how undignified I look, go away.'

'You look pathetic, like a very big rag doll of the lowest price.'

'Go away.'

'The passers-by are nodding at you and sniggering.'

'They aren't; they're all unconscious.'

'I am ashamed to be seen in your company.'

'Good, go away.'

'I'm going. I came to say goodbye.'

Etheldra snatched the scarf from her face and sat up. She glared at him. 'What did you say?'

'I'm going away, leaving.'

'I see, so you are going away leaving me with an unsolved murder on my hands?'

'No I'm not. The murder is solved.'

She looked positively crestfallen. 'I say, Anthony, that does rather mess up one's holiday. Now what does one do in this foreign outpost?'

'Go home, presumably.' He pulled a chair up beside her and gave an outline of what had happened during the night. When he finished she shook her head. 'That poor little man. The awful thing is that I found him quite ridiculous.' His unpredictable Aunt took up the scarf from her knees and unashamedly began to cry into it.

'Poor, brave, tragic little man.'

He waited without speaking, astonished at her outburst and at the same time moved by it. It was unlike his aunt and yet so like her. Presently she sat up and fixed him with a cold eye. 'It's the heat,' she said. 'I think I must have got a touch of the sun. The only mercy is that that performance of mine was not witnessed by Bassett and Carpenter.'

'The point is,' Anthony said, 'as far as the police are concerned the situation is as before.'

'Aren't you going to tell them?'

'Not till I get out of their way,' he said. 'There are some things better told in a letter. This is one of them.'

'I suppose that means that they are still looking for the girl?'

'It means also that she'll have to come with us to Althenia.' She shook her head. 'I have an idea that that is what the Count was trying to prevent.'

Anthony's answer was more violent than he knew. 'Why on earth shouldn't she go?'

'Don't ask me, Anthony, and furthermore don't shout. You always did shout when you got yourself into a mess.'

'Very well, you dear but ancient aunt, I will repeat with all the patience at my command, why shouldn't she go?'

She looked at him with sardonic affection. 'Any discussion on the point at this late hour would be purely academic. Have you told her father yet?'

'No, that's a job for you.'

'What, that frightful hill again? I do wish these activities could take place either in flatter country or in winter time. Why is it that people insist on living on hills?'

'You can wait till it's cool.'

'No, no, the wretched man will see the yacht go out and be sure to start worrying.'

'I don't think he knows that Eve is on the yacht.'

'Perhaps not, but I think perhaps I'd better get the business off my mind.' She struggled to her feet. 'In view of his last encounter with me I shouldn't be surprised if the poor man sees me coming and locks the door.'

'In that case you'll have to shout at him through the keyhole. While you are changing I have to get something from Eve's bathing hut. Then I'll walk with you as far as the Casino.'

He left his aunt and walked along to the hut. He opened it and stood staring inside. Eve's dressing case was on the seat. On the floor, lying close to the wall, was a long thin-bladed knife. Eight inches of the blade were stained brown. In the middle of the floor there was lying an ordinary piece of blackened driftwood about two feet long and two inches square, but clinging to it and shining in the shadowy little hut was a single white hair. It was at this that Anthony found himself staring with fascinated horror.

When Anthony got back to his aunt she was waiting in by no means an amiable mood.

'Where have you been?'

He looked surprised. 'Been? Why, I told you, to collect something for Eve.'

'You've been so long I can only think you must have been collecting a suitcase full of green fleas.'

'No.' He said it so grimly that she looked at him in astonishment. 'No, it was something quite different.'

'As a matter of fact, my boy, you look as if you'd had a shock.'

'I have. I'm not so sure that I should be going away.'

'I'm not so sure that any of you should be going away,' she said grimly. 'You don't clear up a mess by leaving it behind.'

'It is cleared up,' he answered doggedly.

'Do you honestly believe that that little man committed suicide?'

'Why shouldn't I?'

'Personally, I don't think you do. I certainly don't think so. I saw him last night and talked to him. There was something he was determined to do. But his mood was aggressive, Anthony, not resigned, as it would have been.'

He stopped and turned to face her. 'Listen, Aunt Ethel, as

far as you and I are concerned the Manetti case is solved and finished with. I want you to forget the whole thing and in particular don't interfere with anyone or anything connected with it. For one thing it is much too dangerous.'

'Poppycock.' But she relented when she saw how much in earnest he was. 'Oh, very well, if I must be coddled in my old age I suppose I must. I promise.'

'Anyway it was suicide.' He said it angrily, as if arguing with himself. 'It has to be.'

They dropped the subject and over a drink in the terrace they talked about their own affairs. They were interrupted by a long blast on the yacht's siren.

Tony smiled. 'That will be Rudolph. He's quite capable of going without me if I don't get a move on.'

His aunt stood and presented a weather-beaten cheek to be kissed. 'Goodbye, my boy, and do please try to keep some sort of order on that ship.'

He grinned. 'Aren't you forgetting the Queen?'

'No, but I was thinking more of the King.' She patted his shoulder. 'Well, now for the Alps. I perspire at the very thought of that climb.' He stood and watched her march off the terrace.

Anthony was about to go down to the beach again when he remembered Eve's other commission. He turned and strode quickly into the Casino. Only a few people were at the roulette tables and these were playing listlessly. Anthony tossed a five hundred franc note to the croupier and asked for one plaque.

'Hello, Mr. Tolworth, you are an early gambler today.' He turned and smiled as he saw Jean Baretti at his side.

'Once and once only,' he said.

'A hunch perhaps.'

'No, an instruction.'

'And the number?'

Anthony tossed the plaque on to the table. 'Six.'

There was a little silence, and then Baretti spoke again and there was an odd note in his voice. 'Six; why six, Mr. Tolworth?'

'Don't ask me.'

'Six is not a usual number.'

'Isn't it? Oh, well, there's no accounting for tastes, is there?'

'I was wondering if the commission had been given to you by Mr. Raymond.'

Anthony looked round at him. 'Why should it have been?'

'No reason. I just wondered, but if it was not . . .'

The wheel began to spin, and Anthony saw that the little man was watching with curious intensity.

'Six,' Jean Baretti spoke the word like a sigh. 'That is a lucky number for Mr. Raymond and unlucky for his enemies.' He spoke very softly, and then without another word he turned and walked quickly out of the room. As he gathered up his winnings Anthony heard the siren again hooting imperatively.

Anthony collected the suitcase from the bathing hut and went back to the ship. The gangway was raised almost as soon as he set foot on deck. The launch was hauled out of the water and secured in its place on the boat deck. The anchor winch had begun to groan at the chains as he went below. He opened his suitcase and took out the knife and the length of timber that he had found in the hut and laid them on the desk. Then he took the swordstick from his wardrobe and laid it beside the others. A swordstick, a knife, and what might be called a blunt instrument; weapons that between them had almost certainly been the cause of two violent deaths. For a long time he stood looking down at them. Then almost reluctantly he left his room, locked the door and made his way to the little room where Count Otto Shavia was lying in state. He found there what he had been afraid to look for. It was a bruise on the back of the dead man's head.

Anthony went back to his cabin; wrapped his exhibits carefully and locked them away. It had been as much as he could do to resist opening the porthole and dropping them into the sea.

The ship's engines had settled now to a tireless rhythm and he could feel the motion as the yacht responded to the undulations of a lazy sea.

Anthony carried the dressing case to Eve's room. She was still there, waiting rebelliously.

'You don't have to sit here if you don't want to,' he said. 'Or is it that you prefer to be alone?'

She glowered at him. 'You told me to stay here.'

'How touchingly obedient. But you know, darling, we're away out at sea.'

Without speaking she dashed out and he followed her up on deck. She leaned against the rail looking over to the coastline of France. Her head was thrown back and her lips were parted. The fingers of the breeze were playing in her hair.

When she spoke it was softly, as if she were saying the words to herself.

'I can hardly believe we are going away.'

'Sorry, Eve?'

'Sorry: it's like sailing away from a nightmare. Tony, I feel as if nothing can touch me; I'm free from everything. . . at last.' She turned to him and laughed. 'That sounded melodramatic even to me. But melodrama gets pretty near the truth sometimes, doesn't it?'

He laughed. 'I suppose when one has lived in the shadow of the guillotine there is a certain element of melodrama in one's life. . . particularly when one is rescued by a King.'

She laughed and again there was the note of excitement. 'This is where I start living happily ever afterwards, isn't it?'

'No. There's generally a last minute hitch. You get out of the dark wood only to find yourself in the kingdom of the human newts who nibble their victims with their front teeth like women eating olives at parties.'

'No, I'm not going to be eaten now, not even by a human newt.'

'All right, but there's still the dark dungeon under the castle keep. Speaking of dark, it must have been pretty dark when you were changing last night in that bathing hut of yours. It was dim even by daylight.'

'It was as black as the pit.' She laughed. 'I know because I tripped over a log of wood or something, and banged my head against the wall.'

'How do you suppose a log of wood got into your hut?'

'Goodness knows.' Eve was definitely not interested. 'I suppose some kids shoved it under the door, or over the top. There is a gap of a couple of inches top and bottom you know.'

'I noticed it when I went there today, the wood I mean. There was a knife too.'

'Oh dear. . . well, I didn't put my foot on that, thank goodness. I say, I do hope father doesn't go blundering in there and tread on it.'

'He won't do that,' Anthony said. 'I removed them both.'

'That was very nice of you, Tony. What a treasure you must be in the house.'

'You think so?'

'Positive.' She turned to look at him and repeated: 'Positive. I've known it for some time.'

They stood facing each other in the bright sunlight, without speaking. It was Eve who broke the silence. 'But you aren't interested in houses, are you, Tony?'

He shook his head, still looking into her eyes. 'Not in the least.' He heard himself speak almost with astonishment. What he heard was not in the least what he had wanted to say. Eve turned quickly back to the rail. He stood beside her for a while and then stole away, angry with himself, with Eve and with the whole muddled set-up: but mostly angry with himself.

CHAPTER 17

AFTER the flurry of putting to sea the Yacht steamed slowly and sedately. The business of preparing a royal welcome, it seemed, took time. And the loyal subjects were determined to make a memorable job of it. It would never do for the royal master to arrive home while they all had their aprons on. So the yacht was accommodating its pace to their needs. Rudolph was so frustrated at the delay that it was all they could do to prevent him from going to the engine room and personally opening things up.

The wireless operator was the busiest man on the ship. If he slept at all it was with his head on his desk. Hour after hour, day and night, his senders and receivers were sparkling and chattering. On the second day into this stream of communications to and from the King there was injected one for Anthony. It was from his aunt, brief, matter of fact and devastating.

Francis Raymond arrested charged with murder of Leonardo Manetti. Tried to see him, told to mind my own business. If you contemplate doing anything about it, you had better get a move on. Await your further instructions. Signed Etheldra Truman.

Anthony thrust the message into his pocket and went to the wireless room. He wrote out a message for his aunt.

Dear Aunt Etheldra: My further instructions same as those of the police, mind your own business. I'm coming back, much love and thanks. Signed Anthony.

Then while he was there he wired for reservations on the morning 'plane from Naples. He went to find the King.

Rudolph was with his valet, trying on uniforms. Anthony paused in the doorway in astonishment. Clothes may make the man, but it requires a uniform to make a King. And there stood a King. Anthony realised with surprise that till this moment he had never taken Rudolph quite seriously. There was no doubt about it now. He stood half smiling at Anthony's surprise, quite satisfied that he knew the reason for it. He motioned the valet away and strolled across the room, tall, straight and fantastically handsome.

'For the military parade,' he said. 'The uniform of the Commander-in-Chief. Like it?'

'Who wouldn't?' And for once Anthony meant exactly what he said. There would be fluttering hearts in Althenia very soon. . . perhaps before Althenia.

Rudolph said: 'I must wear these things on the ship to get used to them again.' And he added boyishly: 'In uniform again; it's marvellous.' He strolled to the mirror and practised a salute. 'Nice of you to come in to see how I looked, Anthony.'

'As a matter of fact I didn't.' Anthony walked across to him. 'Listen, Rudolph, I want you to call in at Naples and put me ashore.'

Rudolph swung round in surprise. 'At Naples? Whatever for?'

'I've got to get back to France.'

The King said coldly: 'This is a very odd time to make up your mind.'

Anthony said patiently: 'It has been made up for me, I'm afraid.' He took Etheldra's wire from his pocket and handed it to the King. Rudolph read it, frowned and handed it back. 'At a time like this you can hardly expect me to be interested in these people's affairs.'

'Whether you like it or not, you've got to be interested.'

'May I ask why?'

'Because, my royal little pal, they happen to be your affairs as well.'

'Don't be an ass. I've never met the man in my life.'

'True, but his daughter is your guest on this ship and she is going back with you.'

'I am quite capable of taking care of Eve. She knows that.'

'Yes, and every newspaper in the world will have your blasted name associated with a murder story. Not good, old boy. For a royal beginner distinctly bad.'

Rudolph dropped into the nearest chair. He looked morosely at his friend. 'God, what a mess. Suppose you do go back, what can you do about it?'

'There's only one thing I can do. I'll take the Count's letter and hand it over to the police.'

Rudolph shook his head. 'That would mean a bigger scandal than ever.'

'Not a scandal, only a sensation. The people will know that you are bringing home the body of a hero. . . the man who rid their country of its most dangerous enemy.'

The King jumped to his feet. 'You're right. Anthony, you're always right. When do you want to be put ashore?'

'I want to get a 'plane first thing in the morning.' He turned back from the door. 'I wonder if you'd mind not mentioning this to Eve? Tell her you've sent me on a special mission.'

'Certainly. You don't think I want to cause her unnecessary distress, do you?'

Anthony grinned. 'No, but I find it pays to tell you what not to do before you do it. The idea of taking her on the top deck and sympathising with her and telling her what you had done in her interests might appeal to you.'

Rudolph smiled reflectively. 'It might.'

Anthony went away with the uncomfortable feeling that he had said too much.

But it was Anthony who talked on the top deck. He had packed his bag and put the Count's letter in his wallet and the swordstick on the dressing table. The other pieces of evidence, the knife and its companion piece, he had left locked away in his desk. Then he had gone to the upper deck to think of a coherent story to tell the French police. It was not easy. He knew too much and too little.

The night was still and warm. Away out ahead of him he could see a vague reflection in the night sky and he knew that under it was the lovely, clamouring, brazen, endearing city of Naples, laughing, singing and suffering.

He should have been thinking of his story. Instead he found himself thinking of a chapter in his life that was coming to an end, of the few crazy years during which he and a deposed King had gone swashbuckling about a crazy world. But the crazy world was settling down, Rudolph was going back to the place where he belonged, and as for himself. . . he refused to look forward.

Better to look back and think what wild fun it had been: gentlemen of fortune with a private yacht and a king's name as their stock in trade. Running expenses had been high, but the profits had been higher. Even if Rudolph had not been recalled their game would have had to come to an end. It was still easy to get new motor cars on a King's priority, but customers were no longer clamouring for them at ten times their market price. There were still a few deposed heads of states who wanted to put the sea between themselves and their opponents, but there were not so many, and even these were inclined to bargain.

He thought of his haphazard, happy-go-lucky days with Eve, meeting after six months, treating the absence as if it had been since dinner the night before. Automatically as soon as he arrived in the South of France he looked her up and just as automatically she put off whatever else she had on hand and they swam, sailed, danced, gambled or simply lay side by side, baking in the sun. Then just as casually they parted and went their own ways again.

'Hello.'

He turned in surprise and saw Avril leaning against the rail by his side. 'You must have floated,' he said.

'I wondered how much longer I was going to be ignored.'

'I didn't even catch a whiff of your elusive perfume and some seventh sense didn't warn me that I was not alone. I must be losing my grip.'

She laughed. 'Or maybe the wind is blowing the wrong way. Or maybe it was just that you had something else on your mind.'

'Perhaps, but I haven't now.'

'It's Rudolph, isn't it?'

'What makes you think that?'

'Well, you have to admit he's pretty much the dominant male just now.'

'You can't blame him for that. If there is such a thing as what is called a big moment, this must be his.'

She nodded thoughtfully. 'Yes; this is what he's been taught to think and live for all his life. He looks proud and arrogant, but you see that's how they want him to look.' A tender little smile touched her lips. 'He's just a kid.'

Anthony laughed. 'He's three years older than you, isn't he?'

'What difference does that make?'

'Well, it makes it sound a bit odd when you talk about him like a fond mother.'

'He's going to need someone to take care of him, if that's what you mean.'

'It's no use reminding you that he has a mother of his own.'

'No, because as far as she is concerned every little thing that Rudolph does is perfect, and that isn't much use. She worships him.'

'And you don't?'

She was silent for a while, and then she said: 'Maybe I do, but it isn't blind worship. He's going to meet people like you and me,' and she added after the slightest hesitation: 'and Eve.'

He turned to look at the glow ahead. 'I'm afraid I won't be there.'

She turned to him swiftly, almost alarmed. 'Anthony, why, what's happened?'

'Nothing serious, I hope. But I'm leaving the yacht tomorrow morning at Naples.'

'But why? Does Rudolph know?'

'Yes, he knows.'

Her voice was so grim that he was reminded of his Aunt Etheldra. 'Anthony, have you and Rudolph been quarrelling?'

'Good Lord, no.'

'Then what's he getting rid of you for?'

'My beautiful child, nobody could get rid of me if I didn't want to go. . . not even Rudolph. I'm going because I have some private business to attend to.'

'Anthony Tolworth, you're not running out on us by any chance?'

He laughed. 'No, if I had my choice I'd be in at the death. Unfortunately, I have to be in at another one.'

'Another one?'

'Another death.'

'Please don't joke like that, Anthony.'

'I'm not joking. I've got to go back to Beaumont-sur-Mer.'

She touched his hand in quick concern. 'What happened? Why must you go back?'

He looked down at her hesitating, and then he said: 'I'll tell you, Avril. Eve's father has been arrested for the murder of Leonardo Manetti.'

'Oh. . .' She was too shocked to say anything else.

'So, you see, I have to go back and see what I can do to help.'

'Is there anything you can do, Anthony?'

'I hope there is.'

'Anthony, he didn't do it, did he?'

He was silent for a long time then he said almost against his will: 'I don't know. Honestly, I don't know.'

'Does Eve know? Know that he's been arrested I mean?'

He said quickly: 'She doesn't know. I don't want her to know, not yet.' He looked down at her. 'Can I ask you to take care of her, Avril?'

She nodded and said softly: 'You love her pretty much, don't you, Anthony?'

'Why do you think that?'

She laughed. 'My vanity tells me.'

'Your vanity?'

'That's it. My vanity tells me that if you hadn't fallen for someone else already you'd have fallen for me. I would be less than honest, Mr. Tolworth, if I did not admit that I consider myself a very worthwhile piece of material.'

'You're adorable.'

'Yes, but that isn't the same thing as saying you love me.'

'I thought I gave a pretty convincing performance the other evening, you know.'

'Technically it was impeccable, but thinking it over I decided that it was art without depth. I'm awfully cunning for a girl of my age.'

'You're awfully sweet.'

'That suits me, Anthony. In other days and other climes two nice people like you and me might have. . .' She had been speaking lightly, but now she turned away with an odd little gesture of unhappiness. 'Now, I imagine we're both swimming for our lives. It's funny, isn't it, wishing the man you do love was more like the one you don't love?'

He took her by the shoulders. 'I'll remember you as the lovely elusive little creature I might have loved but lost in the moonlight.'

'The trouble with us,' she said, 'is that we've got to have someone to protect. And the trouble with you is that you don't need anyone to protect you.'

'No,' he said. 'But I may need consoling.'

'That should be nice work for any girl.' She put her hand briefly over his. 'Good night, Anthony, and good luck.'

She turned away and he watched her small figure till it was absorbed into the night. She had gone and left him with a painful sense of finality.

CHAPTER 18

FRANCIS RAYMOND was not surprised when the police arrived. He was frankly interested in the workmanlike way they set about searching the villa. What did make him faintly irritated was that they messed up his clothes. He was very fastidious about these and they seemed to treat them with a complete lack of respect. Picoy directed the search and at the same time fired questions at his victim.

'How do you live?'

'As you see, quietly with my daughter.'

'I know that. Where does your money come from?'

'I have sufficient for my needs. I refer you to my bank. Barclays in the Boulevard des Anglais at Nice. If you wish I will instruct them to let you inspect my account. But I can assure you that there is nothing to learn from it.'

'You hated this man Manetti.'

'Yes, I think you may put it as strongly as that.'

'He had you absolutely in his power.'

'I have no doubt that he thought he did.'

'So quite naturally you would want him out of the way.'

'Certainly. I often thought that his death would be a source of satisfaction to me.'

'And was it?'

Mr. Raymond smiled faintly. 'I had not anticipated of course that I would be suspected of his murder.'

'You thought you were too clever. Or did you think you were too stupid?'

'That, my dear sir, is a question to which I am too well-mannered to reply.'

'None the less to be on the safe side you were about to run away.'

'I. . . run away? Run away where?'

'To England.'

'My dear fellow, England is my home.'

Picoy's lips drew back from his yellow teeth in a sneer. 'Home, eh? The records show that you have not been outside France for at least fifteen years.'

'Time does slip away, doesn't it?'

'And what about all those papers you were burning?'

'Oh dear, my little bonfire seems to have made me quite famous.'

'When Jean Baretti arrived and found you burning papers you were in a great state of excitement, weren't you?'

'Yes indeed, I was like a kid at a bonfire.'

'How innocent. What were you burning?'

'The manuscript of a book.'

'Well, well I didn't know you were an author.'

'I discovered that I was not. That is why I burned the manuscript.'

One of the searchers turned away from the desk and handed a sheet of paper to his chief. Obviously he was excited. Picoy held the page close to his heavy eyes, reading it slowly and carefully. Then he held it towards Francis Raymond. His voice was very soft.

'I think you forgot to burn this. Do you recognise the writing?'

'Yes, of course. It is Leonardo Manetti's writing.'

'Well, well. Then you know of course what he has written.'

'Not without reading it, my dear chap. He wrote me on more than one occasion. In fact he had a habit of making use of me. May I see it?' He reached out his hand for the letter, but Picoy snatched it out of his way.

'No, I'll read it. Just listen quietly. The first page is obviously missing, but this is enough.' He bent over the letter and began to read.

I will expect you therefore at my suite on Sunday evening when we can discuss this matter quietly. I am sure you will be able to give me excellent reasons why I should not go directly to the police. Naturally in view of what I know they will have to be powerful reasons. Two things I will find unforgivable: one is that you should not keep the appointment and the other is that you should bore me by throwing yourself on my mercy, because, as you know, I have none whatever.'

Picoy finished reading and added: 'It is signed, of course, Leonardo Manetti.'

Francis was shaking his head helplessly. 'I have no memory of that letter. I can't understand it.'

'No memory of it?' Picoy's voice purred sceptically. 'I should have thought it was the kind of letter one would remember for a long time. Don't you remember? You had to provide a good reason for his not going to the police. I congratulate you. You couldn't have found a better one. You killed him.'

'I know nothing about that letter.'

'Nothing about it even after seeing one of my men find it in your house?' The taunting voice went on: 'But that would leave me with the only other alternative, wouldn't it? That the letter was addressed not to yourself, but to your daughter Eve.'

Eve's father remained quite calm. 'That, of course, is quite absurd.'

'Perhaps. Perhaps, too, you can convince me why I should look for the murderer outside this villa. You may, but I doubt it.'

Francis Raymond sighed. 'I doubt it also, M. Picoy. Are there any other questions you wish to ask?'

'My questions have not even begun. But I think we can go somewhere where we are not in the way of my searchers. Are you ready?'

'Ready. . . oh, I see, are you arresting me? Perhaps I should pack a few things.'

Picoy laughed without mirth. 'No, don't bother to pack a few things, they would only be taken away from you when we arrived. Later something can be arranged, if you have friends.'

They took him to the Gendarmerie d'Antibes in the Boulevard Dugommier, but the questions they asked him there were mainly routine. They took his fingerprints and photographs and filled in a long formal questionnaire, but he had the impression that several young policemen were merely practising on him. The real case was being prepared somewhere else. He spent the night with a down-at-heel little pickpocket and an elegant young woman with red fingernails and painted lips, who cried a great deal.

Next morning he was moved to the Police Judiciaire in the Rue Gioffredo in Nice. This he knew was going to be the real thing. His companions were no less squalid than those of the night before. They were obviously quite familiar with their surroundings and were trying to cringe or bluff their way out.

He should have been experiencing shame and despair. But he felt neither. A curious serenity had taken hold of him. Now at last his fate had overtaken him. It was right and proper that he should be where he was.

When he came before the Procureur de la République he was the least disturbed man in the room. It was as if this man under attack were someone else whose fate was immaterial. They flew at him from darting angles like carrion crows on a body, pecking and tearing. But he was eager to help them, disconcertingly eager to go so far with them and calmly stubborn when they tried to go farther. Their respect for him grew. They thought him subtle and dangerous, whereas he was merely doing his best to get the whole thing straight. He was quite patient with their accusations and boyishly eager to applaud when they were on the right track.

It went on for hours. In the end they knew all about his life and nothing about the murder of Leonardo Manetti.

When it was all over he smiled at them and told them how sorry he was that he couldn't have been more helpful. The Procureur nodded to him with a kind of desperate respect as he was led away. And when he had gone they looked at each other warily to see who was laughing at whom.

In a hot little room in the Police Judiciaire Anthony Tolworth sat facing Picoy. Between them on the desk lay the Count's swordstick and the Count's confession. Picoy had finished reading it and had dropped it in front of him. For a while neither of them spoke. Then Anthony broke the silence with a cheerfulness that he wished he felt.

'Well, there you are. That seems to be that, doesn't it?'

Picoy raised his eyes in cold surprise. 'Seems to be what, Mr. Tolworth?'

'The end of your case.'

The detective shook his head and treated Anthony to one of his unfriendly smiles. 'The case, oh, yes, we have completed the case. The murderer is in our hands. We are quite satisfied. We even managed without your help.'

Anthony said patiently: 'Really, you know, we all make mistakes. Why not admit you made one this time?'

Again the headshake and the smile. Picoy was enjoying himself.

'We have made no mistake,' he tapped the letter. 'This, of course, is nonsense.'

'You mean it doesn't fit in with the case you've made against your prisoner?'

'No, I mean nonsense.' His heavy lids lifted and he looked at Anthony with cold patience. 'All that part about the little man and his son. . . that is quite true. We knew that and we knew that he had very good reasons for killing Manetti. But as for killing him. . .' he shrugged. 'He imagined himself doing that. I suppose he had seen himself performing some such dramatic act many times. He was a very dramatic little man. But in actual fact somebody else did it for him.'

'You do seem positive.'

'Quite positive. You see, Mr. Tolworth, at the time the Count tells us he was murdering Leonardo Manetti, he was, in fact, dining with a discreet lady in Nice, in a private room in a hotel on the Boulevard des Anglais,' He snarled. 'Do you think we are such utter fools as not to have checked up on him?'

'In that case he must have mistaken the time.'

'Must he? But look how vividly he describes the fading light.'

Anthony said violently: 'I suppose you are asking me to believe that he wrote his confession and then rushed out and committed suicide just to make it look genuine.'

Picoy shook his head. 'No, I think he met Leonardo Manetti's murderer.'

'That of course would be Mr. Raymond?'

'Naturally, who else?'

'Brilliant. Perhaps you can tell me why he should kill the man who had just confessed to the murder of Manetti.'

'There is no reason why I should tell you anything,' Picoy snapped. 'But I will do so because it amuses me. He did not know what the Count had been writing was a confession. No, far from it. The Count came to the Casino, told Jean Baretti that he knew the name of Manetti's murderer and asked for a private room so that he could write a full report for the police.'

It seemed to Anthony that the little room was darkening and turning cold. The voice went on:

'Baretti showed him to the room and showed him also the little side door that led on to the passage down to the beach, so that when he finished he could leave unobtrusively.'

Anthony interrupted sarcastically: 'And your prisoner of course knew all this?'

Picoy's smile was almost genuine. 'Then Baretti left the Casino to go home. On the way up the hill he saw so much smoke and flame coming from the Raymonds' villa that he ran in to see if he could help. Raymond was burning papers in such a hurry that several neighbours were afraid he would burn the house.

'Baretti helped him to straighten the room and was invited to a drink. It was then, Mr. Tolworth, that Baretti told my prisoner that the Count was in a private room at the Casino writing to the police.

'Baretti went home, and shortly after he had gone the neighbours whom Raymond's fire had disturbed saw him leave the villa and make his way down the hill.' The cold eyes looked up with an affected innocence. 'Is there anything else you wish to know?'

Anthony stood up. 'I would like to know who murdered Leonardo Manetti.' And as he turned to walk out of the room Picoy's laugh was following him triumphantly. 'Oh, Mr. Tolworth?'

Reluctantly he turned back. Picoy was thumbing through a file. Now he picked out a sheet of paper and handed it across the desk.

'Just in case you think we are being hasty or unfair, perhaps you should read that. It was found in Raymond's desk. He himself was witness to that. He can offer no explanation.'

Anthony read the sinister note from Manetti and without speaking passed it back.

'Still not satisfied?'

He didn't bother to reply. He walked thoughtfully down the echoing uncarpeted stairs and out into the street.

They had their case. There was no doubt in his mind, knowing Eve's father, and knowing the police, that if there was a trial there would be a conviction. The people of France have no sympathy for those who settle their quarrels on French soil.

CHAPTER 19

ETHELDRA TRUMAN looked at her glass of French beer without enthusiasm and said: 'I don't so much mind being dragged down here against my better judgment, but I resent intensely having to acknowledge that I'm licked.'

Anthony shrugged. 'I thought I was quite clever a few days ago. Now I'm beginning to have my doubts.'

'Dispel them,' Etheldra answered. 'You aren't in the least clever.'

'No.'

'Francis Raymond did not commit two murders.'

'No.'

'Don't keep on saying no.'

'I can't think of anything else.'

They sat looking depressed. It was one of those too-hot mornings. The orchestra was working away loudly and dutifully as if they were being paid by the note. The old waiters were looking their age. The patrons were limp under the umbrellas. It was too hot. Jean Baretti alone seemed to be standing up to the wear and tear. He darted about like a firefly, and if he could not inspire his staff, at least he would keep them on the move.

If Jean Baretti had had time to notice he might have been unnerved by the undivided attention that was being given to him by Roger Bassett and John Carpenter. Leaning forward with their chins almost touching their ice-creams they followed him relentlessly with their eyes.

'Mrs. Truman,' Bassett spoke without taking his eyes off their victim.

'Don't interrupt.'

'I'm sorry, Mrs. Truman, I didn't know you were speaking.'

'I wasn't.'

'Then I was not really interrupting, was I, Mrs. Truman?'

'You were interrupting my thoughts.'

'But I couldn't hear your thoughts, could I, Mrs. Truman? Please will you tell me when you have finished thinking, Mrs. Truman?'

Anthony said wearily: 'Something tells me that will be just about now.'

Etheldra glared at the two boys and demanded: 'Well?'

Carpenter got in first and said: 'That man tells lies.'

'Which man? Don't shout and don't point.'

'The busy one,' said Bassett. 'That little busy one,' he added as Jean Baretti flew to welcome a client.

'Nonsense. Get on with your ice-cream.'

'He does, Miss Truman. He told lies to us.'

'Rubbish, you don't even know the man.'

'Yes, we do. We asked him to take us out in his speed-boat and he told us he didn't go out in a speed-boat. We said we'd seen him.'

'And my goodness, he was angry,' Carpenter added.

'Perhaps he stole it,' Bassett said, 'and that's why he told lies.'

Anthony explained: 'As a matter of fact he owns the speed-boat you often see out off the beach to wing people on water skis. But he pays someone else to handle the boat and give the skiing lessons, a chap named Alberte. I've been out with him lots of times myself. I imagine that's who you two kids saw in the speed-boat. Baretti and this other chap are rather alike, they're cousins I think.'

They were too polite to argue about it, but clearly they were quite unshaken. They continued to watch Jean Baretti.

So did Anthony, reflectively at first and then with a tightening of his chest that made him feel rather sick. Then without a word or look at Etheldra he got up and walked quickly off the terrace and along the beach. His aunt was left staring after him in astonishment.

The speed-boat was tied up to the little jetty, resting inert on the flat sea. François Alberte was sitting in the stern mending a broken mooring rope. Looking down at him

Anthony confirmed the likeness to his cousin Jean. François looked a little heavier and a little more rugged, but almost certainly it was François whom the boys had seen. He looked up now and pushed the white covered yachting cap to the back of his head.

'Hello, Mr. Tolworth, I thought you'd gone away with the yacht.'

'I did, François, but I came back. Had some business to finish.'

'Are you coming out?'

'Not just now.' He jumped down and made himself comfortable. 'How's business?'

'Oh, fine. Always is at this time of year. So many want to learn while they are on holiday and they fall off such a lot that I hardly use any petrol at all.'

Anthony laughed. 'An honest man would charge them half price.'

'If I did they'd think I was no good. But I don't mind wasting petrol on you; when do you think you can come out?'

'As a matter of fact, François, I'm not sure. You see the reason I came back was that a friend of mine, Mr. Raymond, has been arrested for the murder of Manetti. He didn't do it, of course, but. . .'

François shrugged. 'They have to get hold of someone. I am lucky it wasn't me.'

'Why on earth should it have been you?'

'Well, I had an appointment to take him out the night he was murdered.'

Anthony looked surprised. 'To take him out at night?'

'Yes, he often did that, you know. Water skiing at night is a lot more exciting than in the daytime. You feel that you are being towed through space. But even among the experts there are not many who can do it. Manetti was one of them.'

Anthony said casually: 'But that night you didn't take him out?'

'No, I heard from my young brother that he was passing through Toulon on his way to North Africa. He's in the army, you know, and it was the only chance I'd have of seeing him. I told Jean and he said he'd ring up Manetti and put him off. I told Jean he'd make a fuss but Jean said he'd smooth him down. He is very good at that sort of thing.'

Anthony nodded slowly. 'Very good.'

François got up and went to the helm. 'Well, I'm afraid I must go. I have an appointment in a few minutes at Antibes.'

Anthony jumped up on to the pier and stood watching the boat curve out from the jetty and lift her bows from the water as she gathered speed in the long straight run.

He walked back to the beach and looked about till he found Carpenter and Bassett. They were playing with sticks in a rather squalid little stream that ran out from under the promenade.

'Your Aunt is cross with you,' Bassett said as if that meant something definitely sinister.

'Really, why is that?'

'You went away and left her to pay the bill. She was very cross and counted the money three times.'

'I see. Well, she was cross with you, too, for accusing people of telling lies.'

'Oh, but we didn't tell lies and we did see him.'

Anthony looked sceptical. 'What day?'

'The day before we saw the dead man,' Carpenter said promptly.

'What time?'

'Just before it got dark.'

'Just before it got dark, eh? I suppose you'll say next that you can tell me what he was wearing?'

'Yes,' Carpenter said. 'He had on a white cap and a sweater like a sailor's and short trousers.' His lip trembled. 'We did see him, Mr. Tolworth. I don't care what you say, didn't we, Bassett?'

Bassett looked as unhappy as Carpenter, but he stoutly supported him. 'Yes, we did, we did. We can't help it if you're cross with us.'

Anthony ruffled the little boy's untidy hair. 'I'm not cross with you, Bassett, just cross with myself, that's all.' He handed him a hundred franc note. 'Here, go and buy yourselves the biggest ice-cream in the world.' He turned away choking back a desire to be sick.

CHAPTER 20

ANTHONY TOLWORTH walked into Jean Baretti's room without knocking. The little man was sitting at his desk. He looked up, and was about to spring forward with professional courtesy. Anthony shook his head.

'Please don't move, there's nothing social about this. I'll sit down if you don't mind.' He moved to a chair and slumped in it.

The little man said quickly: 'Mr. Tolworth, you look ill.'

Anthony said flatly: 'I went into Nice this afternoon to tell Picoy how you murdered Leonardo Manetti.'

Jean Baretti started to his feet and then slowly shrank back into his chair. His lips worked, but he was unable to speak. He lifted one hand gropingly to his face. Anthony looked at him once and then quickly looked away again.

'You saw how it could be done as soon as your cousin François told you that he wanted to meet his young brother in Toulon. You told him that you would ring up and cancel Manetti's appointment, but, of course, you didn't. Picoy tells me that he can prove that there were no incoming calls for Manetti that day.

'No, you kept the appointment with Manetti. It was dark by the time you picked him up in the speed-boat and you were wearing the same sort of white topped cap and dark sweater that François wears. You were seen going to the boat in them. You let him get on the water skis and you towed him off on that last ride in the dark. It must have been as exciting for you as it was for him. I suppose you went further out to sea than usual just in case he made a noise. Then you stopped the boat and waited and as Leonardo Manetti tried to haul himself aboard you let him have it with the knife.' He glanced again at the shrinking little man in the chair. 'That's right, isn't it?'

There was still no reply from Baretti, and Anthony went on.

'Then you sat out there in the dark watching the lights ashore and waiting for them to go out. You had decided that it would be safer for the body to be found on the beach than picked up from the sea. There on the beach anybody could have killed him, but only a few would have the means of taking him out to sea. So you waited with the body. I don't suppose you used the engine coming back. It's more likely you rowed. Then you left the launch, floated the body ashore and dragged it onto the beach and arranged it on the sand.

'From then onwards you were on the spot to see what turns investigations took, and everything was satisfactory till the other night when the Count told you with terrifying confidence that he knew who the murderer was and that he was going to write out a long statement for the police. It must have seemed to you that he was deliberately giving you the chance to try a getaway.

'But instead, of course, you decided to kill him. You saw that the best way for you to get away with it would be to implicate someone else. So you went to call on Mr. Raymond. You didn't go there because of the fire, you were going there anyhow. You were careful to tell him that the Count was at the Casino and that he was naming the murderer. You made it seem that you were giving him a friendly warning, and then, of course, you had to leave that page of the letter.' He half smiled. 'Not even anyone as woolly-headed as Mr. Raymond would leave an incriminating letter like that after he had burned everything else.' Anthony shook his head. 'No, that page was not from a letter written to Francis Raymond, but to you.'

The little man shrivelled speechlessly in his chair.

'You stayed in the villa as long as you dared and then, instead of going home, you ran back and waited in the dark on the beach. You knew about the swordstick and you knew how you were going to use it, but you wanted a supplementary weapon. You found a solid piece of driftwood. When he came along the beach you knocked him out with that and then to make it look like suicide you finished him off with his own weapon.

'All you had to do then was to take the letter and get away.

You remembered of course to push your bludgeon under the door of the Raymonds' bathing hut.

'You had the letter and the temptation to read it must have been too much for you. You could easily have slipped into your room here without being seen. Anyway, when you did read it the shock must have been overwhelming. You pulled yourself together and went back to leave the letter where you had found it. You left the little man as I found him and went home to your wife.'

Anthony finished speaking and leaned back in his chair. He felt too weary to move.

Then Jean Baretti spoke.

'I would consider it a favour if you would ask Mr. Raymond to forgive me.'

Anthony nodded and the little man spoke again.

'It happened just as you say. I killed Manetti because he would have ruined me. Do you remember the other day in the Casino when you came and stood beside me and put the money on number six? I knew then that you were warning me that you knew.'

Anthony sat forward in his chair in surprise. 'Warning you?'

'Of course, about number six.'

'I don't understand.'

'I might as well tell you the whole story, Mr. Tolworth. It doesn't matter now and you may even think a little better of me. It began a long time ago when the Italians were in occupation here. A lot of us in the Casino were working for the Underground and someone had the idea that if we could fix a crooked roulette wheel it might be very useful to us. Well, at that time we had a very clever electrician and he and several others did design one magnetically controlled that could turn up number six or one of its immediate neighbours almost when we liked. We installed it and used to cheat the Italians. Of course when they backed six we let the wheel run naturally and six took its chance with the other numbers. But if they were backing the other numbers we could always have our little six on our side. We got more than one of them into our clutches that way.

'When the war was over we quietly removed the wheel and put back the fair one. I thought ours had been broken up, but it hadn't been, and two years ago when things were very bad for a lot of us in France one of the men in the know came and whispered to me that if there were enough of us who would trust each other we could put the old dodge to work again.

'Well, I was just looking about for the staff for the opening of the new wing. So I could engage the men I was looking for. We were very discreet and we were careful to put a limit to the amount we would win.

'Of course it was Mr. Raymond with his endless tables who showed that there was a persistent bias in favour of six. One evening he told me quite proudly what he had found out. He thought it proved some theory or other that he held. You can imagine how I felt. I would have felt very much worse if I had known that he was passing his records on to Manetti.

'Of course we stopped our operations at once, intending to let a decent interval elapse before we began again.' His face twisted as if with pain. 'There is always someone you can buy, Mr. Tolworth. Manetti found one of us and my world fell to pieces two weeks ago when he told me what he knew. He was coming in and he was going to smash the Casino. And of course in the end I would be found out and ruined.

'That letter we talked about. . . yes, it was for me. . . meant that I was to go to Manetti for my final instructions.' He finished speaking and glanced up at the clock. 'The police are late,' he said.

Anthony stood up. 'I suggested to Picoy that it would be time enough if he arrived at seven o'clock.' He took up his hat and walked out, taking with him a picture of a crumpled broken little man huddled in a chair that was too big for him.

Anthony climbed slowly up the hill to the villa. He felt sick and exhausted. The front of the house was closed but he could hear sounds coming from Antoinette's kitchen at the side.

He rang the bell and after an interval she came to the door and peered out, angrily suspicious. Her eyes were red and he guessed that she had been crying. She saw who it was and her manner changed.

'Oh, Mr. Tolworth; but I thought it was the police, the beasts, the brutes; prying, poking into everything, questioning, bullying.' She seemed on the verge of tears again.

Anthony patted her shoulder. 'Don't worry, Antoinette.'

'Don't worry: but how can I help worrying?'

He smiled down at her. 'Because there is nothing whatever to worry about.'

'But Mr. Raymond, poor Mr. Raymond.'

That's what I came to tell you about. Mr. Raymond is coming home. I don't quite know when, but it would be terrible, wouldn't it, if he did come home and there was nothing ready for him to eat?'

'Oh.' Her hands flew to her face in dismay. 'But, Mr. Tolworth, this is impossible, why was I not told? I am not ready, I am not prepared.'

Anthony grinned. 'You will be. In her own kitchen, Antoinette, no Frenchwoman has ever owned defeat. By the way, do you think I might have a drink?'

She almost danced across to the cabinet, unpocketing a bunch of keys that she had chained to her waist. 'The police,' she said. 'You may be sure I kept them away from here.' She flung open the cabinet and waved to the contents. 'I will bring the ice.' She brought it and darted back into the kitchen, where Anthony could hear her crying and singing and cursing, all, it seemed, in the same breath. He mixed a drink, carried it out on to the silent terrace and sat down. Drowsily and unobtrusively the sounds were coming up from the plage below. The bay was dotted with the white sails of the little pleasure boats making their way sedately home. The small breeze that came in from the sea had picked up the scents of the terrace gardens on the hill. He should have been lulled into a sense of peace, but he was not. He was waiting, and what he was waiting for he hardly dared to think about.

Then after a long interval it came, emphatic and distinct, the sound of a revolver shot.

Anthony sat on for a long time without moving. The drink beside him was untouched.

'Well.'

He started up at the sound of her voice. Eve was standing a few feet from him, and there was nothing in the least friendly in her attitude.

'Eve, what on earth are you doing here?'

'Is it so very surprising that I have come back?'

'No, I suppose it isn't, but. . .'

'But you thought that it would be nice for me to stay away and have a nice time while my father. . .' She broke off with a little sob. 'I went there this afternoon, they wouldn't let me see him. They wouldn't even tell me where he was. Why did you leave me like that. . . why did you?'

'Because,' he said, 'there was nothing you could have done, and even being here would have made things more difficult.'

'You mean I might have had to risk my own skin to save my father? That would be far too much to ask of a fastidious little thing like me, wouldn't it? Why did you interfere? Why do you keep on interfering?' She turned away quickly. 'No, I didn't mean that, Anthony. Honestly, I'm so desperate I don't know what I'm saying, or doing, or anything. To think of him helpless, shut up like that. He. . . he's so incapable of looking after himself.'

He walked over and took her by the shoulders and turned her round to face him.

'Now listen to me. After that appalling exhibition it would serve you right if I didn't tell you that your father has muddled through this without your interference. Your father is coming home. And what is more, my darling, from now on he is going to live his own life in his own way. I have decided that it is time he grew up.'

She was looking up at him with wide eyes and parted lips. Her voice had a note of wonder in it. 'He's coming home?'

'Certainly.'

'Anthony, this is your doing, isn't it?'

'No, it is the doing of two of the most atrocious little boys you ever saw in your life.'

She shook her head. 'You mean he is safe. . . that we're all safe? You mean that it's all over, Tony?'

He nodded. 'Yes, darling, it's all over.' He could feel her shoulders relax under his hands. Her body began to shake.

'Tony,' she gasped. 'I warn you, I'm going to cry again. I don't want to, yes I do, I want to.'

He stood aside. 'That,' he said, 'is a matter which only you can decide. You have my permission to cry, but not on my chest. It leaves marks. You can go and cry under that tree. I'm going to make us a drink.' He kissed her bent head and walked into the house. He told himself grimly that next time he took a girl in his arms it would be because she wanted to be kissed and not because she wanted to be comforted.

He mixed the drinks and looked out on the terrace. Eve was not there, and he guessed rightly that she had gone to her room. He poured a drink for himself and switched on the radio. To his surprise he heard an American commentator broadcasting from Althenia. Then he remembered that this for Rudolph was the day of days.

'And so,' the voice was saying, 'this day of wild rejoicing is drawing to a close. The People of Althenia have welcomed their King and have taken him to their hearts. I have seen many celebrations in many countries, but never have I seen anything to equal this. Down below me there in the streets they are still at it, dancing and singing and cheering their King. You'd imagine that nothing would ever persuade them to stop.' He paused and there was a murmur of voices, and then he spoke into the microphone again. 'Well, well, well; now here is the crowning surprise of this crowded day. It has just been announced from the Palace that the King has conferred on Miss Avril Pares, the young and beautiful American girl whom he has known since childhood, the title of Princess of the Forest. Shall I tell you what it means? Once upon a time many centuries ago a King of Althenia was hunting in the Royal Forests and he came upon a beautiful girl with whom he immediately fell in love and decided to marry. When his followers pointed out to him that she was not of royal blood he conferred upon her the title Princess of the Forest. Ever since that day when a King of Althenia chooses the girl who is to be his bride this title is conferred upon her. And you may be sure of this, none will rejoice more than the people of Althenia, who all know the debt their country owes to John Pares, the father of this lovely girl. And so as one day of rejoicing comes to a close another romantic day is only a little way ahead.'

Anthony snapped off the radio and turned to see Eve smiling at him from the doorway.

'Did you know about this?'

'Of course, it was obvious to the meanest intellect.'

'It wasn't obvious to me. As a matter of fact I thought it might have been you.'

'Of course not. I was just another damsel in distress. And anyway. . .'

He walked over to her. 'Anyway what?'

'Anyway, I wasn't in love with Rudolph.'

'I see.'

'Do you, Anthony?' Her lips trembled and he looked at her suspiciously.

'Are you going to cry again?'

'No, at least I don't think I am.'

'Are you completely carefree and altogether untroubled?'

'Yes, Anthony.'

He was still suspicious. 'If I kiss you, for instance, it won't be because you feel the need of comfort, protection or in any way getting something off your chest?'

'No, it will be just because I want you to kiss me.'

'And do you?'

'Yes, always; every time I look at you.'

'But you're not looking at me.'

'Tony, I think I'm going to cry again.'

'Why not? Who cares about my suit anyway?'

There was a footstep on the terrace and a discreet cough at the door. They swung apart and saw Francis Raymond smiling at them gently, He was unshaven and his suit was considerably crushed, but he carried himself with an air that overrode such things.

'Well, well. This is a pleasant surprise.'

Eve ran across to him. 'You poor darling, what have they done to you? I never should have gone and left you alone.'

He patted her shoulder with tolerant affection. 'My dear child, I am quite capable of taking care of myself. When I had made it quite clear to the police that it was not I who killed the wretched man they let me go. Well, Anthony, I thought you were in Althenia.'

Anthony smiled. 'No, there was a little business I had to attend to here.'

'Successful, I hope?'

He looked at Eve. 'Oh, very.'

'Good. Then we can all have a little celebration. You must excuse me while I bath and change, and then, Eve my dear, I'll make one of my special cocktails.'

'That will be marvellous.'

'Good,' he smiled at them. 'French prisons are not without interest, but I must say it is nice to be in one's own home. See that Anthony has everything he wants, won't you, my dear?'

'But I have,' Anthony said. 'Everything.'